RUSTIC HOSPITALITY

"We're both younger sons." Dirk included Gar in a gesture. "Our Lord has no place for us, so we must perforce seek other positions. We're bound for the King's Town. We thought to seek places in the King's Army."

"Sir, your pardon," said the sergeant suddenly, "but wasn't there word that wandering Gentlemen were goading the churls into joining the rebels?"

Dirk decided on Righteous Indignation. "Sir! We are Gentlemen, and loyal to the King!"

"You will come with us, Gentlemen," the Squire said grimly, turning to the sergeant and jerking his head toward Gar and Dirk.

The sergeant nodded, and nudged his mount forward, bringing up a cocked crossbow . . .

A WIZARD IN BEDLAM

Christopher Stasheff

A TOM DOHERTY ASSOCIATES BOOK
NEW YORK

A WIZARD IN BEDLAM

Copyright © 1979 by Christopher Stasheff

Cover art by Ratler DeWelks

A Tor Book
Published by Tom Doherty Associates, Inc.
175 Fifth Avenue
New York, NY 10010

Tor® is a registered trademark of Tom Doherty Associates, Inc.

ISBN: 0-812-53647-9

First Tor edition: March 1995

Printed in the United States of America

0 9 8 7 6 5 4 3 2 1

CHAPTER 1

Engines bellowed, and the stubby cargo boat wallowed up out of the blastpit. It hesitated for a moment, feeling for balance, then shot up into the sky, roaring like an angry aurochs.

It cleared atmosphere and slewed into orbit, chasing the great globe of the mother ship down the ellipse.

In the control blister, the pilot slapped his board to automatic and looked up at Domigny. "Secure for coasting, Captain—reeling down the umbilicus. About half an hour till we head back into the womb."

Domigny winced. "I've heard of extended metaphors, Lieutenant, but you stretched that one so far that it snapped back."

"Really, sir?" The navigator looked up in

feigned surprise. "I was about to compliment him on his knack for colorful language." He was black-haired and lean, with a look of wiry strength to him—almost the pilot's double. Not as close as twins, closer than brothers—but they weren't related. Not technically, anyway.

"That *is* a polite way of saying it," Domigny agreed, "though I could wish he didn't take the term 'mother ship' quite so literally." He loosened his shock webbing, stood up, and stretched. "Well, to business. Call the Seed of Insurrection, will you?"

The pilot winced as he thumbed the key. "I thought we were done with that metaphor. . . . Lieutenant Dulain to control, please."

The captain grinned wickedly and flexed an arm, kneading his pineapple biceps with the other hand. He was broad in the shoulder and beefy everywhere else, lard-faced and grizzle-haired, with eyes that seemed a little too small but saw much.

The navigator frowned thoughtfully. "I'm not sure that was apt, Captain; the insurrection in Melange scarcely needs seeding. From what Lords Port and Core were saying, I'd guess it's about ready to blossom."

The captain glanced up in irritation. "I was under the naïve impression that conference was private, Charts."

"No, sir." The pilot grinned. "At least, not when you ordered Dirk to listen in on the conference-room bug. Certainly you couldn't expect me to resist a temptation like that."

"I'd expect you to resist many things, Lieutenant, but temptation isn't one of them," the captain groused, settling himself back into his couch.

The hatch opened, and a young man in waist coat, knee pants, white hose, and buckled shoes climbed in. He looked enough like the pilot and navigator to make a man wonder about their mothers. But such a man would wrong those virtuous women—the fault was in their ancestors.

Captain Domigny raised an eyebrow in the newcomer's direction. "You heard, Dirk?"

Dirk made an elaborate bow. "Your wish is my command, O Captain."

Domigny turned to the pilot. "Turn on the blower, will you, Lieutenant? It's getting a little thick in here."

"Not as thick as it was in there." Dirk straightened, massaging his knuckles. "Little out of line, wasn't it? For Lord Core to be there with Lord Port?"

"Ah, you noticed!" Domigny said brightly.

"Do I detect a note of sarcasm there? . . . But it looks a little strange, no? I mean, Lord Core has moved up in the world since I was an overworked brat on his estate—Lord Privy Councillor to His Majesty, and all that—but, personally interviewing a freighter captain? Now, really!"

"Perceptive, perceptive." Domigny nodded over steepled fingertips. "Well, you're supposed to be the dirtside operative—what do you make of it?"

Dirk sat down and leaned forward, hands clasped on his knees. "Offhand, I'd say things are getting tense. I know our spies said there was rebellion in the air—but they didn't say it was the air around the throne."

"Well, it might not be." Domigny shifted in his chair. "Anything having to do with the throne—who knows? Nobody's seen His Majesty since his coronation."

"Yeah, and as I remember, he looked pretty scared then, poor kid." Dirk scratched behind his ear. "But then, who wouldn't be, with Core as his regent? . . . Either way, rumor speaks loudly enough for Core to hear, so here he is, to make very, very sure we don't help out, if anything does flare up."

"Not bad." Domigny nodded. "A little superficial, perhaps, but still, not bad. Now—what does this mean, in terms of your assignment?"

"They'll be watching us like hawks," Dirk said immediately. "Each Lord will keep his radar screen manned, for a change. When you drop me in the gig, alarms'll scream for a hundred miles around."

"Well, not a *hundred* miles," Domigny said judiciously. "Ten would be more like it. But it is to our advantage the Lords allow only one spaceport. That's where they'll be watching with basilisk eyes—so, if we drop you a hundred miles away, there's still a chance you might get by unnoticed."

Dirk shook his head. "This is where the action's going to be—in the capital, near the King. It'd take me too long to leg it in a hundred miles. Don't worry—I can lose any search party they send out."

The captain sighed and shook his head. "Your

choice, I'm afraid. Personally, I'd opt for a hundred miles away."

"I doubt it," Dirk said dryly.

The captain glared at him; but he couldn't hold it, and his face broke into a grin. "Well, maybe you're right. Lord knows I wish it was *my* assignment—but age does have certain disadvantages. . . . What did you think of the 'no tourists' policy?"

"Pretty insistent, weren't they?" Dirk smiled grimly. "No more 'accidental' reconnaissance flights—isn't that what he said? And that line about knowing your crew must get curious about a planet they trade with so much, but never get to set foot on. . . . Think he suspects something?"

Domigny shrugged. "You know him better than I do. What would he suspect?"

"Anything," Dirk said promptly. "Up to and including our landing secret agents to foment rebellion."

"But there've been 'accidental' gig flights as long as we've been trading with them—nearly five hundred years." Domigny watched Dirk keenly. "Wouldn't that lull his suspicions?"

Dirk shook his head. "His predecessors', maybe. Not his. This time, if he spots the gig coming in, he'll call you and cancel the franchise."

Domigny smiled sourly. "Not effective immediately. It'll take them a little time to line up a new freight company. They want their nice little 'best of all possible worlds' to stay safe from outside influence, so they deal with only one company, us—but now their safety snaps back at them, and the bars they put up to keep everybody else out will be keeping them in. Besides"—he spread his hands—"what do we care? Let them cancel us. Will that make us go away?" He jabbed a finger toward the viewscreen, filled with a huge golden sphere. "We'll be sitting right there, behind the near moon in the radar shadow, waiting for your call—and when you send it, we'll break out every boat and drop down on them like a nest of mad hornets."

"What if it's another flash in the pan?" Dirk said softly. "DeCade didn't succeed five centuries ago. What if the rebellion fails?"

"It won't," Domigny said grimly. "We've waited five hundred years for this. The Wizard escaped off-planet under cover of the chaos DeCade created, starved and scrimped till he could start a freight line, took a huge loss underbidding the first company so he could get the franchise, and died happy only because he knew he'd set us on the path to this day."

Dirk listened closely, knowing the words by heart, letting them sink in to stoke the fire of his purpose into flame.

"Ten generations of us have escaped from our masters to these ships," Domigny went on. "Escaped off-planet, crammed knowledge into our heads till they ached, and worked our backs raw to keep this line running, trading with the planet of our birth so we could sneak in information, arms—waiting for The Day."

He fell silent a moment, glaring at Dirk. "It won't fail, Lieutenant."

Dirk took a deep breath and stood, slowly. "No. It won't."

"Not if you do your job, you mean." Domigny stood slowly, never taking his eyes from Dirk's. "If we drop down before the peasants rise, and the rebellion fails because of it, you'll be sitting in the blastpit when the ship lifts off."

Dirk looked into Domigny's grim eyes and knew he meant it.

"Find the rebel leader," Domigny went on. "Make contact with him. Find out what he wants us to do. If he doesn't want us to do anything and the rebellion breaks out, figure out what we should do. But when you call, you'd better be right."

"Don't worry," Dirk said evenly. "When I call, I'll be sure."

Domigny held his eyes a moment longer, then smiled and clasped Dirk's hand and forearm tightly. "Good luck," he said. "And when you drop from that gig, drop running."

The gig swooped down out of the night and slammed to a stop as its hatch boomed open and Dirk shot out. He landed rolling, swung up to his feet, and lit out for the trees at the edge of the meadow. He glanced back over his shoulder—once—to see the gig a hundred feet up and rising; then he turned back to serious business, like running.

He sprinted through meadow grass, feeling as though a hundred snipers had their sights locked on him every foot of the way, and were just waiting for him to slow down a little so they could see if there was a brandmark on his back, to make sure he was a churl before they shot him down.

Then Dirk was in among the trees, and he had to slow down to a rapid walk. He knew the forests well; they'd been his first refuge when he escaped from serfdom twenty years ago, and he'd run seven missions since—all involving the forests now and then, usually for the same reason. He picked his way through the underbrush, striking for the trail and finding it, listening intently to the normal sounds of a night forest—wind in the branches, scurrying of small animals, bat squeaks. There was nothing out of the ordinary yet. He almost wished there were; the waiting was screwing him tight as a piano string.

He swung on down the trail at a long, fast walk, staff slung over his shoulder, moving through patches of starlight. He was a tall, lean, wiry man, dressed like an eighteenth-century gentleman. The broad brim of his hat shadowed the deep-set gray eyes, leaving the blade of a nose, prominent cheekbones, hollow cheeks, and square jaw to the moonlight. It was a lean and hungry face, and the man behind it tried not to think too much.

He stopped suddenly, listening; then he slipped off the trail, silent as a drifting cloud of poison gas, found the tree trunk in the deepest shadow, and did a passable imitation of bark.

He waited, and the night waited with him.

Then, faint but growing fast, came the drum of horses' hooves.

The drum roll swelled to an avalanche, and they swept past him single-file—hard-faced men with iron derbies and chainmail waistcoats. Somewhere in the middle of the string, Dirk noticed the local Lord, in plum-colored tailcoat and white satin, powdered wig uncovered to the night breeze. Then he was gone, and the iron file was grinding by again.

Dirk leaned back against the trunk with folded arms, staff resting on his shoulder, admiring the sight. He'd always loved a parade.

Too bad he didn't have a gun. Not even a crossbow. It was definitely out of character for a gentleman who wasn't in the military—but not as out-of-character as it would have been for a churl. A dead churl, possibly . . .

Then the last horseman whipped on by, and the starlight filtered steadily down. Dirk lifted his head, turned toward the sound of fading hooves. That was all; he stayed still as a crystal till the last hoofbeat had faded. Even then, he waited till he was sure the night was quiet; then he moved out— but not onto the trail. At a rough guess, the local Lord was manning his radar screen and had detected the gig's landing—though it was possible, Dirk supposed, that he was just on his way to a late party, or a tryst with a churl's daughter. Still, the Lords didn't usually bring more than a dozen bodyguards for a social occasion. No, the hunt was on. They'd find the meadow empty, of course, and would turn around and beat the brush till daybreak. But not too deep into the brush; there were dangerous animals in the woods, mostly with two legs and a nasty bite. They could leave a steel barb embedded in a soldier's neck. No, they'd stay close to the trails—and therefore it behooved Dirk to do the reverse.

So he struck out through the underbrush, humming softly to himself, and looking brightly about him. It was a wonderful time to be alive. . . .

He came out of the woods a couple of hours later and stopped in the shadow of an oak to get his bearings. The land rolled away before him, wild meadow rising to a ridge a mile away, dim and lustrous in the starlight.

Maybe an hour till moonrise—not time enough to make it to the nearest village. Dirk looked for cover.

There it was, off to the left and halfway to the ridge—a rocky outcrop. Where there are large rocks, there are, if not caves, at least niches to hide in. Dirk turned toward the little hill.

As he came hiking up to it, the giant attacked.

He burst out of a crevice at the foot of the rockheap and came bounding down the slope toward Dirk, roaring and waving his arms—seven feet, three hundred pounds of maddened, muscled mendicant.

Dirk fell back, his quarterstaff snapping up to guard position, while his stomach hit bottom. He cowered behind his staff in abject terror; then he remembered he was a trained killer, supposedly skilled with the quarterstaff.

He set his feet, grounded the butt of the staff, and aimed its tip at the giant's solar plexus.

The giant scrabbled to a halt and scowled down at him, puzzled.

Dirk snapped the staff back up to guard.

"Rrowr-r-r-r!" The giant threw his arms up, hands curved like talons.

Dirk's mouth tucked into a smile. The roar had a distinctly tentative ring.

"Rrowrrr?" He sounded wary this time. " 'Fraid! ... 'Fraid?"

"Sorry, no." Dirk shook his head, smiling. He pursed his lips thoughtfully, then suddenly stamped the ground, yelling, "Boo!"

The giant started and leap back five feet. There he hesitated, watching Dirk nervously, hands half-raised. He was seven feet tall, and at least two and a half feet wide from shoulder to shoulder, muscled like an ox. That was easy to see because he was naked, except for a filthy rag of a loin-cloth. His whole body was crusted with dirt, and the black hair hanging down to his shoulders was matted and greasy. His forehead sloped forward, jutting out over large, widely spaced eyes. His nose had been broken a long time ago. His face was wide across the cheekbones, but tapered sharply to a square chin. His mouth was thin-lipped, wide, and, at the moment, quivering, as he eyed Dirk warily—in fact, fearfully.

Dirk decided to press the advantage while he had it. He swung his staff up, bellowing, "For God, Harry, and Saint George!"

The giant bleated, leaped up, executing an about-face in midair, and landed running.

Dirk ran after him, bellowing happily and brandishing his quarterstaff. The giant neighed in terror and ran for his life, head flung back, elbows pumping.

Dirk chased him up the path for a good hundred yards, where the giant turned aside and leaped into the rocks. He was out of sight in five seconds, but pebbles rattled under his feet, and Dirk followed the crunching with absolutely no trouble. "Hurry, Watson! The game is afoot!"

He skidded to a halt at the end of the giant's trail, an abrupt cul-de-sac where two miniature cliffs met in a corner. The giant was scrabbling at the rockface, trying to get a handhold. He threw an agonized look back over his shoulder, saw Dirk five feet away, and whipped about, pressing his back against the stone, mewing deep in his throat.

Dirk leaned his head against his staff, contemplating the giant.

Then he leaped forward, yelling, "Havoc!"

The giant jumped, too, then shrank down onto his heels against the base of the rock, arms flung over his head, sobbing like a baby.

Dirk planted the butt of his staff and leaned on it, hand on his hip, head cocked to the side. What—in the names of all the saints—was he to make of this?

He frowned down at the giant, brooding. The starlight darkened the hollows of his cheeks, and exaggerated his gauntness, giving him a battered, world-weary look, bringing out the sadness that always dominated his face. The giant seemed to be a little on the slow-witted side—maybe an idiot. He wasn't exactly a rarity—there were a lot of half-wits running around the countryside. Giants weren't quite as common, but this one wasn't anywhere nearly as big as some Dirk had seen. There were dwarves, too, and geniuses, mostly neurotic—and short-lived, the Lords saw to that. Not to mention large helpings of mental illness and physical deformities—in fact, everything one could expect from six hundred years of inbreeding.

This giant was a case in point, and not really an extreme one. The recessive genes that had given him his size had taken away a large part of his mind, by way of compensation.

What was Dirk supposed to do with him?

He sighed, and eased his hat back on his head. Go off and leave the big fellow, he supposed. He couldn't be encumbered—not on *this* mission.

But it didn't seem right. . . .

The giant dared a peek upward. Dirk's sadness must have reassured him because he lifted his head and, slowly, cautiously, rose to his knees.

Dirk nodded, with a wry smile. "That's right, fella—you've got it figured. I won't hurt you."

The giant's mouth stretched into a loose-lipped, lopsided grin. He crawled forward to tug at Dirk's clothing. "Poor Gar's a-hungered!"

Dirk pursed his lips. "Oh. You can talk."

Gar nodded eagerly and folded his hands together, looking up at Dirk with pathetic eagerness.

Dirk sighed and fumbled in his purse, bringing out a silver coin. "Money—that's all I can do for you. At least maybe you won't go trying to rob travelers for a while. . . . That was the idea, wasn't it?"

Gar's eager grin slipped and faded.

"Jump out roaring," Dirk pressed, "and scare me so badly I'd count myself lucky if all you did was snatch my purse? That's how you live, isn't it?"

Gar nodded reluctantly, eyes downcast like a whipped puppy.

Dirk nodded, too. "I thought so."

He flipped the coin, spinning through the air. The giant clapped at it, missed, and scrabbled after it in the dust. He came up with it wrapped tightly in a fist the size of a beef joint and an ear-to-ear grin.

Dirk smiled bleakly and turned away. He'd have to find another hiding place; an uneasy conscience made uneasy sleep. He knew Gar wasn't his fault, but he still felt guilty for not being able to help him.

Whenever he was on this planet, he spent a lot of time feeling guilty.

He set out for the ridge again, his guilt churning in with the satisfied glow of philanthropy and the self-disgust of feeling like a sucker.

Dirk came out of his morass of self-flagellation when he realized he heard footsteps behind him.

He looked back over his shoulder. The giant was trailing about fifty feet behind him, still grinning.

Dirk turned and leaned on his staff, frowning.

Gar stopped too, but he kept on grinning.

"Why are you following me?" Dirk said carefully.

"Nice man," Gar said hopefully. "Nice to Gar."

A red light flashed in Dirk's mind: SUCKER. He'd been through this before, with a puppy that had followed him home. It had grown into a small horse and eaten up most of his salary. To top it off, the darned thing couldn't be trained. He'd been through it with girls, too, with much the same results.

The grin faded into a lost, mournful look. "No friend?"

"Look," he said desperately, "I don't need a sidekick. I can't be tied down with responsibility right now. Especially right now. You can't follow me now. Maybe later. Not now."

The big man's face seemed to crumple, his lower lip turning under. Tears squeezed out of his eyes.

And a warning blared in Dirk's mind.

Up till then, he'd've bought it—attack, remorse, fear, the whole bit. But—tears? They wouldn't have come naturally; they'd have to be a deliberate play on Dirk's sympathy.

And anyone with enough brains and control to stage deliberate tears couldn't be all that much of an idiot.

And, come to think of it, roadside beggars didn't try to latch onto their patrons. They'd had too many kicks from their masters before they ran away.

Dirk straightened, cupping his hands on the tip of his staff, ready to snap it to guard in the blink of an eye. "You just overplayed it, friend," he said quietly. "You're no more an idiot than I am."

Gar stared.

Then he frowned; his jaw firmed; he squared his

shoulders; and, somehow, he seemed much more intelligent.

Also dangerous.

Dirk swallowed and slid one hand down the staff, ready to snap it up to guard.

Gar's mouth thinned in disgust. He shrugged. "All right, the game's up. I won't try to run a bad joke into the ground."

"Joke?" Dirk said softly. "Game?"

Gar shrugged again, impatiently. "A figure of speech."

"Oh yes, I'm sure." Dirk nodded. "What game?"

Gar started to answer, then caught himself and grimaced in chagrin. "Twice in a row; it's a bad night. Okay, I'll admit it—I was trying to latch onto you for a guide."

Dirk stood very still. Then he said, "Natives don't need guides. Also, a native would have a definite place—he'd be a lord, a gentleman, or a churl. In any event, he wouldn't be wandering around loose—unless he were an outlaw. But then he'd be hiding in the forest with the rest of his band."

"Very astute," Gar growled. "Yes, I'm from off-planet. If I didn't want you to know it, I wouldn't've said 'guide.' "

Very true, Dirk thought; but, by the same token, if Gar was willing to admit he wanted Dirk for a guide, he had another purpose that he *didn't* want Dirk to know about. Second Corollary of Finagle's Law of Reversal: If a man says something *is* true, then it isn't.

"If you did want me to know it," Dirk said slowly, "why'd you pose as a poortom?"

"Poortom?" Gar frowned. "Oh, you mean an idiot. . . . Sure, I'd've rather you would have thought I was a native, just tagging along. But you found me out, so I had to come clean."

Dirk wondered if the man knew how poorly he lied. But he nodded slowly, letting Gar think he believed him. Why not? It was a harmless delusion and might give Dirk an advantage. "How'd you get in? If you'd come on the freighters, I'd have known about it."

Gar shrugged, irritated. "I've got my own boat."

Dirk held himself stiff, trying to keep his face empty of emotion while he absorbed the information. A private yacht bespoke money—*real* money.

But why would a millionaire come to Melange?

"So you just dropped in for a visit," he mused aloud. "Don't you know Melange is off-limits to tourists?"

"Off-limits to just about everyone, from what I hear." Gar smiled contemptuously. "That kind of thing is liable to give a man a bothersome itch in the curiosity bump."

For a moment, Dirk had to fight down boiling rage. Not bad enough he and his kind had to be treated like animals—now they had to be a sideshow, too.

He forced the tension to ease off. "So you just dropped in, managed to shake the search party, and went looking for a guide. Sounds a little thin, friend."

Gar scowled. "No doubt. But it's not quite that simple—I've been here for a month already."

"Oh? Like what you saw?"

Gar's mouth twisted; he turned his head and spat. "It makes me sick to see a bunch of rulers, ostensibly educated and cultured men, so decayed as to treat their people like toys, whose sole purpose for existence is to satisfy their lords' drives and whims." He turned back to Dirk, glaring. "Why do you take it? Isn't there any manhood left in you? Why don't you just rise up and throw them out?"

Dirk pursed his lips thoughtfully, surprised to realize he was suddenly thinking of Gar as a kid. But that's what he was—a spoiled brat with a conscience, a rich man's son with nothing to do and a need for a purpose, a reason for living. He couldn't find one in his own life, so he was looking at someone else's—probably rodding from planet to planet, hoping to find a cause he could believe in.

And, at a guess, he'd just found it.

Which in turn meant . . .

"You could've ambushed a traveler weeks ago, if you wanted to con yourself a guide," Dirk pointed out. "But you didn't; you tried to put the touch on me—tonight—when there aren't many travelers abroad. None, in fact—or at least, no one legal. Why me?"

Gar turned away, disgusted. "All right, all right! I needed someone from off-planet, and when I saw the search party riding out at night, I knew they weren't just out after an escaped serf! Whole thing looked very familiar, in fact—almost exactly like the party that came hunting me when I touched down! Therefore: wherever they were going, there'd be someone coming from, and that someone'd be from off-planet. So I figured out which way you'd come walking, and I laid an ambush! Good enough?"

Dirk nodded slowly. It was fine—except that Gar left out the part about rebels. On an interdicted planet, an illegal visitor was either a spy or a rebel, possibly both. So Gar was trying to latch onto a contact with the rebel forces.

Which meant he might not be from off-planet at all—just a spy for the Lords.

Dirk shook his head. He wasn't a spy—you could see it in his face. This was one planet where you could tell which side a man was on just by looking at him. Inbreeding will do that.

So Gar was trying to contact the rebels, with an eye toward joining up; but of course he didn't want them to know that he knew.

Yes. A kid.

"Well, how about it?" Gar demanded. "Can you hack a tag-along? Or do I keep wandering on my own?"

Dirk was very tempted to refuse; if there was one thing he didn't need at this point, it was an enthusiastic amateur. So he would've told Gar to go on his own, or go to hell, whichever he chose, if it weren't for one nagging possibility:

The revolution might fail.

And if it did, the churls were going to need high-powered help from off-planet: influence—to push an investigation of the local government. And where there is money, there is influence.

The kid had enough money for a private space-yacht. . . .

Dirk shrugged, turning away. "It's okay by me, as long as you try to stay out of the way. But I warn you; it won't be a pleasant tour."

He turned his back and swung off toward the ridge.

After a moment, he heard footsteps behind him.

CHAPTER 2

They came to the village just before sunrise.
Dirk stopped, the life draining out of his
face, looking about him with bleak, starved
eyes.

Gar frowned down at him. "What's the matter?"

"It always hits me like this," Dirk muttered,
"coming into one of these villages after I've been
away a year. It's almost *déjà vu*, it's so much like
the place I grew up. As though I've been here before and it's home—but it's not, it can't ever be. I
don't belong here anymore. . . ."

He caught himself, realized he'd been spilling
his guts to a total stranger, and one he didn't particularly trust. "Come on, let's get moving," he
snarled. "We've got to get undercover fast."

Gar frowned after him, then shrugged and strode

fast to catch up. After putting on his clothes, he was dressed in the same fashion as Dirk. It was gentleman's clothing—their only possible cover—for only gentlemen could travel from village to village at will. Only gentlemen, or Lords—but they all knew each other and would be quick to spot a ringer.

They ambled down the village street, Gar trying to keep from staring at the villagers—the broad, squat men with broad, round faces, brown eyes, snub noses, and ball chins; and the women, almost as broad, with ample bosoms and hips, their faces similar to the men's but a little finer-boned. They were all dressed alike; the men in red or green jerkins and ocher hose, the women in blue or yellow homespun with red aprons. Occasionally a taller man walked by, with huge, muscular shoulders and arms, long-fingered hands, and a square face with a broad forehead and high cheekbones; but they were few.

The houses were like their owners—low, broad, and round, with thatched roofs and mud-and-wattle walls, painted in pinks, pale blues, mint-greens.

"They still look so much alike," Gar muttered.

"Huh?" Dirk came out of a brown study, frowning. "What do you mean, 'still'?"

"Well, I've been here a month. By now I should be seeing individual differences."

Dirk smiled bleakly. "Not really."

Gar turned to him, frowning. "Why? How long will it take?"

"Your whole life," Dirt said sourly, "and even then you'd make mistakes. It's not just a matter of their all looking alike to you simply because you're from off-planet."

Gar scowled. "What else could it be?"

"That they *do* all look alike," Dirk said sweetly. "I told you about the inbreeding, didn't I?"

Gar stopped and stood, glowering down. "No, as a matter of fact, you didn't. Don't you have any taboos against incest?"

"Yes, a very elaborate set. But they don't help much if you've all got the same genes to begin with."

"That's impossible," Gar said flatly.

Dirk shook his head. "Not if you have a small enough gene-pool."

"That small a gene-pool couldn't survive. Not just genetically—the original colony on this planet wouldn't've had enough people to build a self-sustaining society."

"Nevertheless, it happened." Dirk turned to look around the village. "Look it up in the official records—that's what we had to do, those of us who escaped off-planet. You see, we didn't know our own history—the Lords were very careful about that."

Gar cocked his head to the side. "All right, I'll give you the straight line—what did the records say?"

"The original ship . . ."

"Ship?" Gar was restrained—only a little skepticism. "One ship, for a whole colony?"

"Only one," Dirk confirmed. "You see, our lords and masters, in their infinite wisdom, decided not to take along any spare baggage, such as people who might not agree with them; so that one ship was limited to a very exclusive set of people who were sick and tired of not being able to have things their own way. About two thousand of them—at least, the record said six hundred families. Plus, of course, enough sperm and ova on ice to guard against *too* much inbreeding."

"Of course," Gar murmured. "And the churls? Two thousand is a full shipload—or was, a few centuries ago. Figure a hundred farmers to support each Lord—"

"Two hundred," Dirk interrupted sweetly. "You forget such essentials as butlers, cooks, maids, hostlers, and barbers."

Gar nodded. "About half a million."

Dirk shook his head. "Twelve."

Gar held still, staring at him.

Dirk turned away, looking out at the villagers. "Have you seen what these people bear on their backs, under their clothes? Have you ever seen one of them whipped?"

"I've seen it," Gar grunted. "The capital letter 'C.' "

Dirk nodded. "The brand of slavery. They're branded with it when they reach puberty—you might call it our rite of passage, not that we chose it . . ." He broke off, brooding. "Of course, I don't have it. I escaped before then . . ."

He shook off the mood, looked up at Gar. "Do you know what the 'C' stands for?"

"Well . . ." Gar scowled. " 'Churl,' I suppose. That's the local term for the peasants, isn't it?"

Dirk nodded. "It could stand for 'churl.' But it stands for something else, too—'clone.'"

Gar stared down at him, appalled.

"Yes," Dirk said softly, "that's what they did. They brought twelve servants along, only twelve—how they conned them into it, heaven knows. As soon as they landed, they took bits of flesh from each of them, and made clones, then cloned the clones—hundreds of them, hundreds of thousands, until each Lord had as many servants and subjects as he wanted." He stopped, took a long breath. "And that's how my people came into being."

Gar turned slowly, looking at the villagers. "No wonder you all look alike."

"Yes, no wonder. Very efficient, isn't it? You can tell a man's place in life just by looking at him. The broad, stout ones are Farmers, like most of them here. The occasional tall one, with the muscles? He's a Tradesman, a blacksmith or carpenter. They just drafted one man with a mechanical aptitude, and stamped out copies until they had enough to go around. Then there're the Butler family, the Merchants, the Hostlers, the Soldiers, the Woodsmen, the Fishers—oh, and let's not forget the ladies: the Cooks, the Maids, and the Housewives—and that's it." He gave Gar a saccharine smile. "Pretty, isn't it?"

"Inhuman," Gar growled.

Dirk nodded. "That, too." He turned away, his eyes roaming the street. He stiffened. "Well, well, you get to meet another family—the Soldiers. Along with a genuine Gentleman, represented by the local Squire."

Gar looked up.

Five men were trotting toward them on tall horses, four in steel caps and chain-mail jackets behind a short, slender man with wavy golden hair, dressed in pale-blue hose and a purple doublet.

"You might call him a hybrid," Dirk said softly. "You might, if you wanted to be polite . . . You see, the Lords brought along all the best aspects of the Terran aristocratic culture—best for them, that is. Including the *droit de seigneur*, and the right to grab any churl woman and seduce her, or rape her if she's not seduceable. Anytime they want. And the bastard offspring they call 'Gentlemen,' and make them knights and squires, to govern the villages."

Gar nodded. "What do they call the bastards from a churl man and a lord's woman?"

"Dead," Dirk said, too brightly. "Her, too, usually."

The Squire came up, and drew rein. His Soldiers did, too, but managed to let their horses wander a little, nicely surrounding the travelers.

Dirk watched them nonchalantly. Then he turned to the Squire. "Good day, Squire."

"Good day," the Squire replied pleasantly. "You seem wearied, Gentlemen. Has your journey been long?"

"Very." Dirk wondered what the Squire would say if he knew just how long, then sobered as he realized the man might. "And wearying—we found no shelter this last night, and perforce kept walking till dawn."

"A hard tale," the Squire commiserated. "May I

ask your profession, good sirs? What business is it brings ye abroad, on foot, in such unsettled times?"

Dirk noted the "unsettled times," though he saw no sign of it in the quiet, well-ordered village. "We're both younger sons." He included Gar in a gesture. "Our Lord had no place for us, so we must perforce seek other positions. We're bound for the King's Town."

He saw the Soldiers stiffen. What was happening at Albemarle?

"You have no employment, then?" The Squire hid his reaction much better than his Soldiers; he merely seemed wary.

"No," Dirk said slowly. "We thought to seek places in the King's Army." He saw the Squire relax a little—but only a little.

The young man nodded. "Then of course, you'd be bound for the King's Town . . ."

"Sir, your pardon," said the sergeant suddenly, "but wasn't there word that wandering Gentlemen were goading the churls into joining the rebels?"

"I have heard such talk . . ." The Squire gave Dirk a calculating look.

Dirk felt Gar tense beside him.

"Two out-of-place Gentlemen, wandering toward Albemarle," the sergeant mused. "Could be they's carrying word from one nest of outlaws to another."

The Squire nodded, eyes on Dirk.

Dirk decided on Righteous Indignation. "Sir! We are Gentlemen, and loyal to the King!"

"So am I," said the Squire softly. "Yet, when all

is said, each man is most loyal to his own interests. And, to say truth, we seek a spy, known to be near this parish, who would probably go disguised as a Gentleman."

"One," Dirk pointed out, suddenly grateful for Gar's presence. "Not two."

The Squire shrugged impatiently. "Two spies instead of one is to our credit."

"There's this, too," the sergeant pointed out. "Milord Cochon needs more foot soldiers."

Dirk fought down a surge of panic and hauled out his best smile. "Squire, surely you jest. Who would a spy be from? There is only the King."

"And the outlaws," the Squire reminded him. "Have you heard no talk of rebellion?"

Dirk nodded slowly, frowning. "Aye, I've heard—but scarce could credit it; I see no sign."

"But I do," The Squire said grimly. "You will come with us, Gentlemen. If you are not rebels, you will have my apologies, and places with Lord Cochon. But if you are . . ." He let the sentence hang, smiling grimly, and turned to the sergeant, jerking his head toward Gar and Dirk.

The sergeant nodded, and nudged his mount forward, bringing up a cocked crossbow.

Dirk's hands slipped down on the wood, and the quarterstaff leaped end-over-end to crack down on the Soldier's hand. The sergeant yelped; the crossbow clattered to the ground.

Gar's staff lashed out over Dirk's head, parrying a sword cut from the Squire. Out of the corner of his eye, Dirk saw another Soldier forcing his horse off the street into the space between two huts,

winding his crossbow; but he had no time to
worry, for a third Soldier was pressing in from the
left, sword swinging up. Dirk snapped the quarterstaff around, caught the base of the blade near the
hilt; the Soldier howled, and the sword flipped
end-over-end into an alley.

Dirk heard a cry behind him, whirled to see the
fourth Soldier slipping from his saddle, and Gar
spinning back toward him, staff rebounding back
to guard.

Dirk nodded, grinning, and swung back to the
Squire, who had transferred his sword to his un-
damaged left hand and was chopping down. Dirk
brought up his staff just in time; but the force of
the blow slapped the staff back against his forehead. The world darkened, star-shot, as he fell to
his knees; he could barely make out the Squire,
swinging the sword up for another cut; then a huge
body blocked his vision, he heard a CHUNK! and
a shrill cry from the Squire, blessed Gar, and
turned to see the sergeant on the ground, cranking
furiously at his crossbow, bracing it against his
knee with his forearm; but just to his left, the third
Soldier picked up his sword and swung about,
blade chopping down.

Dirk shook his head to clear the mists and drove
upward from a crouch, catching him under the
chin with the tip of his staff. The Soldier flew
backward, hit the ground sprawling.

Dirk shot to his feet, staff back to guard . . .

. . . to find himself facing two leveled crossbows. The sergeant aimed at him from his left; the

trooper between the huts had him covered from the right.

He didn't stay to look; he fell to the ground and rolled, noting in passing that Gar seemed to have disappeared. A bolt hissed where his head had been; another grazed his leg. As he started to roll to his feet, he saw a long arm shoot out from behind the trooper between the huts, wrapping itself around the man's throat. Then he was completing the roll, coming up between sergeant and Squire, waiting for the blade in the back, but bound to bring the smug Squire down with him. His body uncoiled like a spring in a straight line with his staff and caught the Squire in the belly as the sword swung down. The Squire shot backward over the rump of his horse, the blade sliced air a foot from Dirk's face and went spinning, and Dirk whirled to face the sergeant.

Who wasn't there.

He was running toward Gar, bellowing and swinging his crossbow like a club.

Gar's staff shot out like an extended stiff arm. The crossbow clattered uselessly on its shaft; the tip caught the sergeant in the collarbone. He shot backward and landed sprawling, out cold.

Silence settled down over the village street.

Dirk glanced around him and noticed the villagers were conspicuous by their absence. Wise.

He looked around him, at the five unconscious bodies, then up at Gar, who stood, feet wide apart, staff in his hands, a slight, ironic smile on his face.

Dirk limped over to him, panting. "You're a better man than I thought," he gasped. "Where'd you learn to handle a quarterstaff—rich kid?"

Gar's smile twitched. "My own home planet is still a little on the—shall we say—primitive side." He nodded toward the unconscious troop. "Offhand, I'd say our cover is blown."

Dirk turned slowly, looking around him. "You might say so, yes."

"Well, you're the local expert," Gar grunted. "What do we do now?"

A door flew open beside them, and a woman stepped out. "In here, quickly! Before they awaken!"

Dirk stared.

She was tall and dark, with small, full breasts straining against a tight-laced bodice. The flowing skirt followed the gently rounded curve of her hip. This much was like any other Maid—but the heart-shaped face, the small, straight nose, the full lips and large green eyes with long fluttering lashes, and the wealth of darkly gleaming hair, made up a face more beautiful than he had ever seen. *How did the Lords miss this one?*

"Quickly!" she hissed, pointing angrily to the interior of the hut. "You must be gone from sight before they waken!"

Dirk stepped in slowly, feeling numbed; Gar followed closely behind, watching his "guide" warily. The girl whirled in after them and latched the door.

The slam jolted Dirk out of his stupefaction. He looked around him, eyes narrowing. Dirt floor, central firepit, rough-hewn furniture, a little light escaping through small parchment windows—nothing unusual; a peasant hut like any other. The same applied to the peasant woman and her girls, and the two young boys, scarcely more than toddlers. The women were all Housewives built on the wide and generous scale; and the boys were small blocks of beef, undoubtedly like their father. Typical Farmer family, even down to the apprehension in their faces; the churls were never free of it, though admittedly it was a little worse right now. Quite a bit worse—two fugitives in their house.

Dirk glanced at their brunette captor again—make that three. Maybe. Certainly she wasn't a Housewife, equally certainly not related. What was she doing here?

She grabbed his arm and yanked him toward the ladder in the wall impatiently. "Quickly, up to the loft! Men look upward last, when they're searching; 'tis your best chance." She whirled to the wife and children. "Go about your daily round; forget we are here, as much as you can. They'll be gone soon enough; you have only to hold the masquerade an hour at most."

The apprehension vanished from the wife's face, to be replaced by grim, set purpose. She nodded once with decision and turned to crackle commands at her brood. By the time Dirk and Gar were stretched out on the nine-by-nine square of planking that served as a sleeping loft, the whole family were going about their daily tasks, seeming calm and unhurried, with only the faintest trace of anxiety about them.

Gar stared down over the edge of the planking, fascinated. Dirk glanced at him irritably; what could be so fascinating about scraping dishes?

Then he forgot Gar as cloth rustled beside him, and a warm, firm body stretched out next to him. He looked up, saw her tearing a square of home-spun into strips.

"You're wounded, in case you hadn't noticed," she said with a tinge of sarcasm. "Not that I care; but the blood might drip through the cracks in the boards and give us away."

Dirk felt a stir of irritation. "If you don't care, why're you taking the risk of hiding us?"

"Use your imagination," she snapped. "Do I look like a villager?"

Dirk nodded slowly. "So. You're a rebel."

"A courier for the outlaws. You're from our 'friends' in the sky?"

Dirk felt the chill of wariness flow through him from the way she said "friends"—almost as though it were an insult. "How do you figure that?" he said slowly.

She shrugged. "When Lord Cochon and his troops ride out like the Wild Hunt in the middle of the night, it's something more than an escaped churl. If it were an outlaw raid, I'd know of it; and what else could it be but one of your dropping in? So I paced you from house to house as soon as you entered the village; and, when I heard the talking in the street, I knew who you were."

Dirk lay staring at her, feeling the hot flush of desire spread outward through his whole body. Not just beauty—brains, too.

He didn't know how to handle the wave of emotion; it scared him. Simple lust he'd had a hundred times, and knew how to cope with—but this was something different; a fascination, the roots of an obsession. Warning bells clanged in his mind. He lay still, hoping the wave would flow through him, crest, and subside.

The girl pushed herself up to her knees and yanked down his stocking, baring the calf. "This won't hold for long, but it'll soak up the blood till you're out of here. You're lucky—it's only a flesh wound." She picked up his foot and started wrapping the cloth.

Dirk lay very still, trying to ignore the current her touch seemed to generate. "I take it we lie doggo till they've waked and gone away."

"Yes, and an hour after that. Less, and they might still be scouring the village; more, and they'll have the Lord's Sniffer out after you."

Gar's head snapped up. " 'Sniffer'? What's that?"

"A low-grade telepath," Dirk explained, "usually also an idiot; the two qualities seem to go together more often than not. They'll walk him around everywhere they think we might be. If he hears any thoughts out of the ordinary, he'll point us out."

Gar stared at him. "You talk as though a telepath were an everyday occurrence."

The girl stopped bandaging, frowned down at him. "Why shouldn't it be?"

"An excellent question, here." Dirk smiled

wryly. "One of the effects of massive inbreeding, Gar."

Gar turned away, eyes wide, seeming almost numb as he watched the family below.

The girl noticed it, and smiled, almost contemptuously. "I thought all you sky-men claimed to be churls."

Dirk felt his stomach sink. He turned and looked over his shoulder. "We are. This one escaped early—before he was two, in his mother's arms."

Gar looked up, startled. The girl looked skeptical; but, after a moment, she turned back to her bandaging.

Dirk decided it was time to distract her. "What's your name, beautiful?"

The girl's head snapped up, fury flaring in her eyes. "I'm Madelon—not that it'll do you any good, churl! Scrub your mind, if you want my help!"

Dirk stared at her. He could almost feel his eyes bugging out. That wasn't his only physiological reaction, but it was the only one he cared to think about at the moment.

He needed a distraction, himself. He turned back to Gar—and frowned, seeing the big man's total absorption in the domestic scene below. "May I ask what the hell you find so unusual?"

"Nothing—and that's just it," Gar muttered.

Dirk grimaced impatiently. "What's the matter? Never seen a churl family before?"

"Oh, yes," Gar said softly, "and that's just the problem." He gestured at the people below. "Every time I've seen one of your families, I've seen exactly the same thing—*exactly*. They perform exactly the same tasks."

Dirk smiled sourly. "What's strange about that? If people are hungry, you make dinner."

"Yes." Gar's eyes burned into his. "But do you use exactly the same movements? Down to the slightest, tiniest mannerism? Sprinkle the salt in just so, reach for a pot at exactly the same time and with precisely the same tilt of body and bend of elbow?"

Dirk gazed at him for a long moment.

Then he smiled, almost gently. "Why wouldn't that be, Gar? What determines behavior?"

"Why, environment and heredity, of course; but—" Gar broke off, eyes glazing as he understood.

"Yes." Dirk nodded. "When the inbreeding gets this bad, everyone's got the same genes. And, when the Lords make you live in the same kinds of houses—almost identical, in fact—and give you identical cloth for your clothes, and identical utensils . . ." He shrugged. "Sure, the home environments start out different from one another; but, as the centuries pass, the people become more and more alike, homogenized; so the homes start becoming alike, too. Environmental differences tend to be ironed out. By this time, they've disappeared. Everyone of any given type is raised in exactly the same type of home. Exactly." He shrugged. "Okay, so we're low on individualism. We didn't want it that way, I assure you."

"But," Gar said thickly, "if everyone of a given

type is raised in exactly the same type of home, and has exactly the same genes—"

"You get identical behavior. Down to the slightest mannerism."

Gar seemed almost angry. "How deep does the identity go?"

Dirk frowned. "If you mean, do we think alike? The answer is yes . . . Except men like me, of course." He turned away, looking down at the family. "I was raised in a different environment, after I was ten. Makes for some differences. Oh, not the basic ones—but enough. If you ask me what those boys are thinking right now, I can give you a good guess—but I don't *know*. . . ."

His voice trailed off as the feeling of alienation, isolation enfolded him.

Dirk looked up slowly, saw Gar's eyes, saw the pity in them, and shook himself with a growl. He looked back at Madelon, who was gazing at Gar; Dirk saw the watchful, calculating look in her eyes.

And something else—less than fascination, more than interest—and felt his heart sink.

There was a sudden commotion in the street, the Squire's voice bawling orders in a sort of seasick groan, then more groans and the clanking of armor, a few oaths. Then the sound of hooves, fading.

"They've gone." Madelon gave Dirk's bandage a last tug and dropped down beside him. "Now begins the waiting. Think of something, anything—a peasant girl, naked. Make it lascivious, so it holds all your attention; anything to keep your mind off where you come from or the kinds of thoughts men have there." She folded her arms, pillowed her head on them, and became completely still.

Gar looked up at Dirk, in a silent question. Dirk nodded and pushed himself back from the edge of the platform. Gar followed suit, and they both lay down, curled up on their sides, and made an excellent try at becoming inanimate.

A feather seemed to touch Dirk's brain, a shadow of foreboding, then lifted away, gone as quickly as it had come; but apprehension remained.

He rose to his knees. "I think we'd better go."

"Be still!" Madelon hissed. "We've yet half of an hour before the search is away from the village."

Dirk shook his head doggedly. "I may have a touch of psi myself; I don't know. One way or another, when something tells me to get gone, I move. And so far it has always paid off." He started down the ladder.

"You'll have us all killed! Do ye *want* the torture?"

"No." Dirk touched ground. "That's why I'm going." He looked up. "Coming, Gar?"

The big man looked from Madelon to Dirk, frowning dubiously. Then he started down the ladder.

"Go to your dooms, then! I've done all I can, and I'm well rid of you!" But there was a despairing note in her voice.

Dirk paused in the doorway to nod to the

Housewife. "I thank you for your hospitality, madam. May all go well with you."

She nodded, nervously, then turned back to her baking.

Gar closed the door behind him. "Where to now?"

Dirk pointed down along the village street. "Down there—into the forest." He followed his own hand, striding long and quickly; Gar lounged along beside him.

As they came into the shadows of the leaves, Gar mused, "We owe them. You know that."

Dirk nodded curtly and kept walking.

But Gar stopped. "If your hunch means anything, the Sniffer's already onto us. He'll know we stopped at that house."

Dirk whirled about. "We can't help that. We've got to get out of here!"

Gar smiled sourly. "Why? They won't start the revolution without us?"

Dirk snarled and turned away.

Gar waited.

"Look," Dirk growled, "I've got to manage liaison between the rebels and the spacers. Without that, the rebellion might fail."

"What will the Lords do to that family?"

"A lot of peasants will die in this rebellion!" Dirk snapped. "They all think it's worth their lives—and so does that family!"

Gar leaned on his staff, waiting.

With a despairing snarl, Dirk turned back to join him.

They found a thicket, insinuated themselves,

and lay down on their bellies, peering through the screen of leaves, watching the village street.

A bee buzzed by, looking for nectar. He took one sniff and hurried away.

"If the local Lord has a Sniffer, he must have had one with that search party last night," Gar murmured. "Why didn't he spot us?"

"For myself, I was carefully thinking of the lewdest pornography I knew." Dirk turned to him. "But as far as *you* go—it *is* a good question, isn't it?"

Gar said nothing; he gazed through the leaves, the ghost of a smile on his lips.

Dirk's eyes narrowed.

Gar stiffened. "There they are!"

Dirk snapped back to the village street. A party of Soldiers walked their horses between the houses toward them, the Squire at their head. In front of him wandered a skinny, slack-jawed churl with a matted thatch of hair and a shambling walk.

He stopped in front of the house they'd hidden in, pointing vaguely. From their post fifty yards away, Dirk could hear the Squire's shout, saw him wave his arm at the troopers, just barely heard the mutter that ran through the ranks as four Soldiers dismounted and stalked up to the cottage door. One of them pounded on the door with a fist; without waiting, another put his shoulder to the door and slammed it open. The whole search party dove in.

They came back out a moment later, dragging the Housewife, wailing protests, herding the silent children.

The Squire swung down from his horse and strode toward them, fists on his hips.

"Bastards!" Dirk rose to his knees, tensing.

Gar put a hand on his arm. "Not yet."

Dirk's head snapped around; he stared at Gar, unbelieving.

He heard the crack of a slap, turned back toward the village. The wife staggered back against the house, hand to her cheek; the Squire stood before her, rubbing his hands.

The last Soldier dragged Madelon out the door.

The Squire turned toward her and stopped, staring.

Madelon shook the Soldier's hands off and straightened, glaring at the Squire.

The Squire came toward her swaggering, rubbing his hands again. He nodded toward one of the Soldiers; the man uncoiled a whip from his waist as the Squire reached out to cup Madelon's chin.

For a moment, it was a frozen tableau.

Then the Squire's hand flashed to her neckline and ripped. The Soldier behind her spun her around and slammed her face into the wall, ripping the blouse down, baring her back, the whip handler stepped up, shaking out his lash, and Dirk snapped out, "Move!"

He broke from the thicket, running quick and lightly. He heard a drumming behind him; then Gar flashed past him, giant legs devouring lengths of ground.

The Soldier's whip cracked, the children screamed, and the Housewife started wailing. The

Soldiers didn't hear Gar till he crashed into them, staff whirling in a windmill of havoc.

The end of the staff cracked into the whipman's neck at the base of the throat; he went down like a poleaxed steer, and the staff rebounded to crack alongside the head of the Soldier who held Madelon. He slumped as Gar whirled, staff snapped up to block a sword blow, then crashing down on the Soldier's head, leaping back to catch another Soldier in the belly with its butt, while the Housewife all but threw Madelon into the hut, shooed her children in, and followed, slamming the door.

Then the last three mounted Soldiers were in, charging. Gar heard them coming, and spun around, but not quite quickly enough; a horse knocked him back against the wall of the hut, and a sword ripped his shoulder.

He rebounded off the wall, lifting the staff in his good hand . . .

. . . to see an ugly stub of a pistol in the Squire's hand, pointing at his belly.

Gar stood, frozen.

The Squire lifted the pistol, sighting along the barrel at Gar's eyes.

Dirk slammed into the Squire's back. The pistol hissed a shaft of blue light as he fell; it licked the roof of the hut, which exploded into flames. Then the Squire hit dirt with Dirk on top. He tried to roll, but Dirk rose to one knee and chopped down with the blade of his hand. The Squire went limp.

The horsemen were galloping back for a second try, and two of the footmen were staggering to their feet. Gar leaped aside as the horsemen charged past; but the last horseman slewed around, tracking him, sword swinging down. Gar swung his staff, and the sword spun away, ringing; but a footman stepped up behind Gar, swinging a dagger.

The door of the hut flew open, slammed into the Soldier's face. Madelon stepped out, the rags of her blouse tied around her neck and a cleaver in her hand.

The horseman with the bruised hand swung his mount toward her. The other two went for Gar, closing in from opposite sides.

Dirk took a running leap, pole-vaulting on his staff, feet aimed for the rider who was cornering Madelon.

The last foot soldier swung his sword, chopped Dirk's staff out from under him.

The ground leaped up and slammed Dirk flat on his back. Agony screamed through him; he couldn't breathe. A body came between him and the sun; a club barreled toward him, swelling to fill the world. Then pain exploded, and blackness, and there wasn't much to remember after that.

CHAPTER 3

He was drifting through infinite blackness. Somewhere far away, there were stars—he knew that—just because he couldn't see them didn't mean they weren't there.

A tiny pinpoint of light . . . There! He'd known he had eyes! And the pinpoint grew, swelling, no, it was rushing closer, it was a head, or a face, anyway, framed with white, floating hair, and it had eyes—great, luminous blue eyes, or turquoise, anyway; what matter if the rest of the face was too blurred to see, it was a good face, he knew it, he had to have faith . . .

"Little out of your depth, aren't you?" it asked. It had a voice like a brazen gong; only it wasn't sound, really . . .

"Dunno," Dirk said astutely. "How deep is it here?"

"Up to your clavicles," the face answered, "and it's rising. Don't you think you ought to back off and just float with the tide?"

That jarred, somehow; comfortable though it was here, there was the feeling of seduction, of somebody trying to get him to do something pleasant that he knew was wrong, that he didn't want to do . . .

Dirk shook his metaphorical head. "No, I mean, you're a great guy, and all that, but . . . Well, how do I know it'll flow? I mean, somebody's got to make the tide move."

"Let somebody else do it," the face suggested.

Dirk considered that. It was tempting . . . Tempting! That jarred. No, if it was tempting, it had to be wrong. He shook his head stubbornly. "No thanks. I'll stand pat."

The face shrugged somehow. "Your choice. You should remember the option, though." The eyes frowned, peering. "But I see you're almost back. Well, remember." And it turned away.

"Hey, wait a minute!" Dirk felt suddenly clear-headed.

The face turned back patiently. "Yes?"

"Who are you?"

"The Wizard of the Far Tower," the face said. "Didn't anyone tell you?"

It turned away and shrank, going fast, and winked out.

And Dirk felt himself sinking, felt the blackness closing in over him. He fought it, fighting to rise, to move upward, pushing against the weight of it, the weight of his eyelids, they were heavy, all his strength did no good, he couldn't direct it, couldn't channel it to the eyelids, couldn't release it, he needed the valve, just turn it to release strength, the valve-word—any word—but his tongue and lips were swollen, heavy with a ton of inertia, he couldn't release strength to them, either. He fought, straining, to part his lips just enough to release breath, to move the slug-tongue, no matter how little . . .

He felt it; he'd managed it, and it moved easier now, strength flooded through, "Puhleeeze . . ."

And he felt his body about him again, felt grass against his back, arms, and legs, heard a sibilance of breeze, far-off birdsong, saw the red of light through closed eyelids.

He moved an arm, rolling toward it, thrust with all the strength in his body, and levered himself up on one elbow. He opened his eyes, looked around, saw grass, tree trunks, leaves, and a tow-headed boy, wide and squat, his mouth open in shock.

Dirk frowned and floundered, pulling himself up to a sitting position. "Hey, kid . . . What . . ."

The boy's mouth snapped shut, terrified.

Then he turned and leaped, crashing through the underbrush. Gone.

Dirk stared numbly after him, feeling sluggish and fuzzy.

His eyes wandered; he saw a body lying beside him, bright full skirt and bare back, with one wavy line of dried blood across it, shoulders shrouded in dark hair.

Madelon! He shook his head, trying to clear it, and the whole fight came back.

Her head stirred; she forced herself halfway up on her elbows. Her head turned, the face tilted up to him, pale, wide-eyed, puzzled, and—yes, a little afraid.

Small wonder. He wasn't exactly feeling bold, himself.

She gave her head a shake, squeezing her eyes shut, then forced herself up to a sitting position and pressed a hand to her forehead with a little moan.

Her blouse—or what was left of it—stayed behind on the ground. For a moment, all Dirk saw was her round, full breasts, the nipples like half-ripe cherries; all else seemed dim. He stiffened, galvanized even through the pain of his headache; then he forced his eyes up to her face.

She bowed her head forward, fingertips pressed against her forehead; black hair tumbled forward to hide her body. Dirk exhaled in relief.

She looked up at him, blinking, frowning against the pain. "How . . . what . . . ?"

Dirk forced his lethargy down and threw on rationality like a cloak. "I'd like to know, myself. The last thing I remember is a pike butt hitting me between the eyes. But why didn't the Squire take us in as prisoners?"

She nodded, then winced. "Yes . . . And where's your friend?"

Dirk shrugged. "They probably did take him in. That means . . . I'll have to find a way to get him out."

"Yes." She frowned. "How much does he know?"

Dirk shrugged. "Not much, for sure. All he knows about the rebellion is meeting the two of us."

Her eyes narrowed. "Just what *is* he?"

Dirk sat very still for a moment. So much for his story about Gar being a churl.

"A tourist," he said slowly. "A man who goes visiting places just to see what they're like. Probably a rich man's son, looking for someplace where he can Do Good."

"Then he is not a churl." Her tone was a frosted dagger.

Dirk shook his head.

Her voice trembled with rage. "Why did you bring him?"

"I didn't." Dirk looked into her eyes. "He brought himself here, and just latched onto me. For my part, I thought it was better to have him where I could watch him, than to take a chance on his joining the Lords."

She glared back at him; then her lips twisted wryly, and she nodded reluctantly. "Yes. I suppose you're right. . . . But now the Lords have him."

Dirk nodded. "We'll have to do something about that."

"Can he be trusted not to tell what he knows?"

"As to that," Dirk said slowly, "we should be finding out very soon now. . . . I think he can."

"Why should he? This is not his fight!"

"He's made it his. And there's something about him . . ."

Her frown turned to brooding. "Yes. He is strange."

"He's no novice with the quarterstaff," Dirk said slowly. "You don't expect a rich man's son to be skilled with a churl's weapon. And he claims to have been here for a month; surely a Sniffer would've found him out in that much time."

"How did he escape them?"

"Yes." Dirk leaned back on one elbow, slowly and carefully. "And how did he just happen to be near here when I, uh, came down from the sky? Sure, given that he was around here, I can understand how he could've figured out where to find me—but why was he *here*, and not fifty miles away?"

Her brooding sharpened into suspicion. "This is a strange visitor you have taken up with, sky-man."

"Dirk," he said absently, turning to look at her. Then he smiled bleakly. "You might want to make yourself decent."

She looked down. Her eyes widened. She caught up the remains of her blouse and pressed them to her.

But Dirk wasn't watching; he was frowning, looking off into the leaves. "I had a strange dream while I was out . . ."

"I trust I wasn't in it." She knotted the ends of the rags around her neck.

Dirk shook his head. "Just a huge white face, with blue-green eyes and floating white hair. He said he was the Wizard of the Far Tower."

Madelon froze, her eyes widening.

"Yes." Dirk turned to her, nodding gravely. "DeCade's Wizard."

"Who shall return," she whispered, "when the time has come to tear down the Lords!"

They were both silent, the words of the Lay running through their minds:

For when my far towers drop down from the skies,
And DeCade calls you out, then all churls, arise!

Dirk shrugged off the mood. "Only a dream. We can't hope for magical help; we'll have to do it ourselves."

"Per—" Her voice broke; she moistened her lips. "Perhaps not. There have been rumors—"

"Of what? You're not going to try to tell me the Wizard's been seen; he's been dead for five hundred years! I should know. His name was Nathaniel Carlsen, he founded our company, and—" He broke off, his eyes widening. "Of course! 'For when my far towers drop down from the skies . . . Towers from far away, dropping down—our gigs and ships! Flareships dropping down from the skies!"

"You see," she whispered, "the rumors are true! He *is* moving again!"

"Only his spirit," Dirk said irritably, "his Dream and his Plan. The man himself is dead!"

"But rumor says he walks again among us. And DeCade is dead, too; but he shall rise again, to lead us."

Dirk clenched his jaw in anger; it gave him the strength to force himself to his feet in spite of the pain. "Your living, human leaders are quite capable of running a successful rebellion by themselves, without supernatural aid—and it's my job to find them and find out what they want us to do!"

Madelon started to answer, but the underbrush rustled, and they both whirled around.

A Farmer stepped out from the leaves, broad and massive—but with a lurking apprehension in his eyes, and something like awe. "You were dead," he whispered.

Dirk stared.

Then he leaned back on his staff, head cocked to the side. "Oh, were we, now? Seems nobody bothered to tell us!"

"The Soldiers felt for your pulse; they held the feather to your lips," the Farmer said doggedly. "You were dead."

Dirk suddenly got the point. "But Gar—the big man who was with us—he was alive?"

The Farmer nodded. "Alive, and awake—though he was bleeding badly. They took him away to the castle, and the Soldiers bade us throw your bodies on the dunghill. But we did not. We bore you away to the forest, here, to come back and bury you properly, at night . . ."

Madelon nodded. "That was fortunate for us. You did well."

"Very," Dirk agreed. "And thanks for the offer, but we don't really need the burial."

"But your friend must be rescued." Madelon stood, turned to the Farmer. "How can we get into the castle?"

The Farmer stood impassive, only his eyes widening at the impudence of her words, and the danger.

Then he nodded slowly. "My sister's husband's cousin's son is a Butler; he is a footman there. I shall ask a man who shall ask."

Madelon nodded curtly. Then she remembered her manners and gave him a dazzling smile. "Do so."

The Farmer nodded, turned away.

"And good Farmer—" She boosted the smile a few degrees Kelvin—"Thank you."

The Farmer looked back, nodded. "The word shall run," he whispered. "It has begun. The dead have come alive . . ."

Then he was gone. Dirk stood staring after him, stupefied.

Then he turned angrily on Madelon. "There! You see how rumors begin? In two days it'll be all over the kingdom as some sort of supernatural miracle! And all it was, was . . ."

Madelon raised her eyebrows politely, waiting.

"Just a simple case of suspended animation," Dirk finished weakly. "Uh . . . Just that . . ."

"And pray, sir, how was this done?"

Dirk turned away with a snarl.

"You dreamed of the Wizard," she reminded.

"Coincidence," Dirk snapped.

She watched him a moment, then turned away, smiling gently.

But Dirk didn't notice; he was carefully avoiding her eyes.

Damn it, there was no reason for him to feel

like a fool! Suspended animation was a common phenomenon; it happened to billions of animals every winter! It even happened to people occasionally; they called it "catalepsy," or something like that.

But it didn't happen to two people at the same time in the same place—did it?

He shrugged it off. It was just a coincidence— but why did that word have a superstitious ring to it, suddenly?

Somehow, without any reason for it, he had a hunch Gar would answer that question.

The Farmer came back as dusk was blurring the forest. "He is in the dungeons," he explained, "and had not yet been harmed, an hour ago. The Question waits for a visiting lord."

Dirk frowned; that had a very ominous ring. "You mean they won't start till the guest gets there?"

The Farmer nodded.

"Lord Core," Dirk said thickly. "Name your odds—it's Lord Core."

Madelon frowned. "Why should it be?"

Dirk shrugged. "He's Privy Councillor—and he was at the field where the sky-ships land, warning us not to try dropping anyone—meaning me. It stands to reason, doesn't it?"

"Of a sort," she agreed dubiously and turned to the Farmer. "Can you get us in?"

The Farmer nodded. "I shall lead you to a man who shall lead you. Come."

They went the way messages went among the churls—from hand to hand, and surprisingly quickly. The Farmer took them into the village again, where a second Farmer was waiting near the common. He fell into step beside them; their first guide disappeared into the darkness.

"I am Oliver," the new guide said. "I bear word from Felice."

Madelon nodded. "Is she safe?"

Oliver nodded. "She looked back once, to see her house in flames, and never looked back again. She and all her children are safe with the outlaws. Word was brought to her husband while you still were fighting; he laid down his hoe and went straight to the forest. He is with them now."

Dirk kept his face carefully impassive; but he was, as always, floored by the efficiency of his own people. They each knew what to do in any given situation, and did it, without question or hesitation. Inbreeding couldn't account for it; he wasn't sure what could.

Oliver led them up to the castle and around to the side. Dirk looked up at the frowning granite pile, looked down at the slimy green of the moat, and felt his own grim dedication renewed. Eighteenth-century France—the culture the Lords imitated—had favored chateaus of the elegant-palace sort, not medieval fortresses. Of course, they hadn't had radio, or radar, or laser pistols, either. The Lords made a few concessions here and there; they seemed to be very much aware where the loyalties of their subjects really lay.

Oliver fumbled next to the bank, came up with a rope, and yanked on it. A log floated out from the bankside toward them. Oliver lifted its bark off, revealing a long, narrow canoe. He gestured; they climbed in, carefully. Oliver took up a paddle and sent them across the sixty feet of moat with five slow, even strokes. He turned the canoe broadside and grappled the bank while Dirk and Madelon climbed out, and a postern gate opened in the shadows. Madelon went toward it, and Dirk turned to thank Oliver; but he was already halfway back across the moat.

Chills chased each other up Dirk's back as he turned back to the gate. They acted like parts of a machine, with perfect timing and perfect coordination—and in a situation like this, it was a fair bet they hadn't had much rehearsal.

He stepped through the postern, and it closed behind him as a hand closed on his arm. The pressure was gone as quickly as it had come, and a slender, liveried silhouette was moving away from them. Dirk followed, and glanced down to see Madelon cloaked in a black, hooded robe. Again the sense of eeriness shimmered over him; they thought of everything.

They moved silently across a courtyard in the shadow of the wall. When they reached the keep, their guide opened another shadowed door; they stepped through into darkness, and the door closed behind them. Then Dirk heard the chink of flint on steel, and light flared in a tinderbox, revealing a young, fine-boned face under a powdered wig. The footman took a candle-stub from his pocket, lit it, and handed it to Madelon while he doused the tinderbox. The candle wavered, and strengthened as Madelon cupped a palm around it.

The footman slipped the tinderbox back into his waistcoat. Over it he wore a pinch-waisted, burgundy, velvet coat—dark enough to blend into shadow. "We can speak here, in whispers, while we go down the stair—but then you must be silent as the dead." He took the candle and started down the steps.

Madelon followed him; Dirk brought up the rear. "Where is our friend? In the dungeons?"

The footman nodded. "Of course."

"Has the other Lord arrived?"

"Nearly an hour agone. He dined quickly and lightly, and went to the dungeons. They have been putting him to the Question for perhaps fifteen minutes."

Dirk swallowed. He knew these Soldier torturers; they could do a lot of damage in that much time.

"How shall we rescue him?" Madelon murmured.

"That I shall tell," hissed a voice from below.

Dirk froze; the harsh accents were those of a Soldier. Then he reminded himself sternly that anyone helping them was laying his neck on the line. All right, it was a Soldier—but they could trust him.

Which, Dirk decided, was something decidedly new. He started walking again.

The bobbing pool of candlelight picked out the gleam of a steel helmet and the chain mail beneath it. A few steps more, and it showed them the face—rough-hewn and scarred, with a mouth like a snapping turtle. Even if he was an ally, Dirk didn't like meeting him in a dark alley.

The footman stepped to the side, let Dirk and Madelon step past him, then turned back up the stairway, taking the light with him. Dirk fought down the panic of being alone with a Soldier in a dark hole, and hissed, "What do we do?"

"There is an alcove off the torture chamber, with a squinthole and a door," the Soldier muttered. "The Lords can rest there if they wish to watch the torturing without being seen."

"They are not using it now?" Madelon demanded.

"They are not," the Soldier confirmed. "No lord has, for many years. The door-latch is rusted. But I have brought oil. It will take some time to work, and then we must use main force to open it. Then I will leave you. I must remain, trusted, until De-Cade calls."

Dirk swallowed a surge of annoyance at the superstition. "I did not know Soldiers would fight for the rebels."

The stairwell was frighteningly quiet for a moment, and Dirk cursed himself mentally, bracing his hands on his quarterstaff.

"We, too, are churls," the Soldier growled, and somebody breathed a quiet sigh of relief. Dirk wondered if it was himself.

But he couldn't let it rest. "How many of you will rise when . . . when DeCade calls?" The words tasted bad; but he had to use their idiom.

The Soldier hesitated. "No man may be sure. All

other churls hate us; how we will fare if they win, none can know. Nor can any know if they *will* win; so each Soldier's thoughts are hidden, even from his brothers. Each man must decide for himself—when DeCade calls."

"We waste time," Madelon hissed.

Immediately there was a slight grating noise, and light speared in as a door cracked. The Soldier oozed around it and was gone; a moment later, his hand came back, beckoning.

Dirk bit down on his courage, narrowly missing his tongue, and followed Madelon out.

The Soldier was moving away in the wavering torchlight. They followed, as silently as they could, heading for a grated door fifty feet away.

A hoarse bellow of pain and rage cut the stillness.

Dirk froze, eyes automatically leaping toward a grated door a little way behind him.

Then the jangle of mail sounded, faintly, far down the corridor. The Soldier beckoned frantically, and Dirk leaped forward to him and through the barred door.

The Soldier slipped in behind him, pulled the door to; a few moments later, steel clashed and jangled outside as a sentry walked past.

A strained whine of agony lanced through the chamber. A man trying to hide pain. Madelon turned away from the squint-hole; by its pale light, Dirk saw her face, white and bloodless.

Silently, he stepped up to look. Behind him, the Soldier moved silently to force oil into the latch.

Two torches flared on the far wall, and fire

leaped in a brazier in front of them. It lit Gar's huge form, stripped except for a breech cloth, chained to a reclining board. Two muscle-bound figures, alike enough to be twins, shaved bald and stripped to the waist, stood near him, one of them watching him with arms folded. The other lifted a glowing iron from the brazier, inspected it, and, satisfied, turned back to Gar.

Between Dirk and the brazier, silhouetted against the fire, were two men, in velvet coats and powdered wigs. One was short and stocky, the other tall and slender.

Dirk's breath hissed in; he recognized the taller man's aquiline profile—Lord Core!

"So, then," Core mused, "you have had a taste of our banquet. Would you like to progress beyond the hors d'oeuvres? Or would you prefer to tell us what we wish to know?"

"If I know the answers, I'll tell them," Gar rasped.

Behind Dirk, Madelon gasped. Dirk tensed.

Core inclined his head in polite surprise. "I must confess I did not look for such ready cooperation. May I inquire the reason?"

"Certainly." Gar gave him a sardonic smile. "I am quite certain that I know nothing—or at least, nothing you don't already."

Core was still a moment; then he turned to Lord Cochon. "Perhaps I mistake his tone, but I think the words smack of insolence."

"Remind him to whom he speaks," Cochon answered, in a voice like a gravel-crusher.

The glowing iron came down against Gar's bicep. His body arched; his jaws clenched with the effort of suppressing a scream. Core gestured and the iron came away.

Dirk's jaw tightened.

"A mild taste only," Core murmured. "There are far more sensitive portions of the body."

Gar relaxed convulsively, gasping and wild-eyed, glaring at Core. But he didn't speak.

"Well enough, then," the Lord said easily. "Now I believe we may begin . . ."

"Where is your King?" Gar demanded, gasping. "Does he care nothing for his people's suffering?"

The torturer turned for a fresh iron, but Core held up a hand, staying him. "Your words betray you; anyone native to this planet would not need to ask."

Gar shrugged impatiently. "All right, I'm from off-planet. I should think that was obvious."

"But it is of interest to me to have it confirmed." Core's eyes had become gimlets. "What is your birth and your station?"

"Noble," Gar snapped.

Core stood immobile.

In the alcove, Dirk whirled to Madelon. They stared at one another, appalled.

"Of what house and line?" Core snapped.

"A d'Armand, of Maxima." The sardonic smile was back on Gar's face.

Core relaxed visibly. "I know of Maxima. It is a miserable asteroid, and all who live there claim to be noble."

"They are, and more noble than you!" Gar

barked. "They do not enslave men for their servants—they build robots!"

They? Dirk pursed his lips, musing.

Core's smile was a thin sneer. "The essence of nobility is power over others, child of innocence—as I now have power over you." He glanced at the second torturer and motioned; the man bent to crank a huge wheel. The chains on Gar's wrists and ankles tightened; he gave a whining, agonized grunt.

Core strolled over beside him, fully into the light. "I believe you will find this posture more conducive to our current discussion."

Dirk frowned; Core hadn't caught the "they." Apparently Gar didn't think of himself as a member of Maxima society. Dirk settled himself for an instructive example of the art of speculative fabrication.

"Who sent you?" Core demanded.

"No one," Gar snarled. "I came on my own. And don't bother asking the next question; here's the answer: I've been bumming around this star sector for a couple of years, trying to find a cause I could devote myself to—something worth any sacrifice. Even my life, if necessary." He glared defiance.

Core's lip twisted with contempt; he nodded at the torturer. The man held a pair of thumbscrews before Gar's eyes.

"The truth, please," Core purred.

"That *is* the truth. Don't you recognize the symptoms?"

That gave Core pause. He stood, glowering

down at Gar. Then he spoke through drawn lips. "I do. It is a deplorable condition of the young—even our young. We must go to great pains to root it out."

The Games! Dirk's belly twisted. Core was right—they did go to great pains. But the Lords weren't the ones who were hurting.

"But you are well past your teens." Core frowned, perplexed. "Surely you have lived a grown man's life long enough to be done with children's games of ideal and reform. Why do you stoop to it?"

Gar shrugged. "Ennui."

Core stared. Then he turned away, seething, but he did not call for the torturers.

Dirk began to wonder if Gar might not be noble after all. He certainly knew what to tell a Lord in order to be believed.

Dirk turned, glancing at the Soldier. Very gently, the man put pressure on the latch; then he relaxed, shaking his head.

Dirk pressed his lips tight and turned back to the torture chamber.

Core was turning back to Gar. "There could be truth in what you say. But we are reasonably certain that the freight company that serves our planet landed a man near here last night, and we have reason to think that man is a rebel."

"I already told you I was after a Cause."

Core's eyes burned, but he restrained himself with visible effort. "If you are the man who was landed, then you can tell me: how deeply are the spacers involved with the rebels?"

"Not at all," Gar said promptly. "I had to pay through the nose to get them to do it."

Dirk turned to Madelon, eyes wide in surprise. So were hers; she gave a slow nod of approval.

Core's lip writhed with contempt. "So, of course, you would have no idea about their activities."

"Of course." Gar watched him as though he was a cobra.

"And the fellow who traveled with you—I suppose he, too, was merely a tourist?"

"No, he was a local. When I heard a search party coming after me, I ducked into the nearest cover, a ruined hut. He was in there, hiding, too."

Core smiled in polite skepticism. "Didn't you wonder why he was hiding?"

"No." Gar smiled. "With that kind of racket behind us, it didn't seem at all out of line."

Core frowned, pursing his lips. "So you decided to travel together."

"No, I hired him for a guide."

Core was silent for a moment, eyes narrowing. "What did he tell you about the rebels?"

"Nothing." Gar's smile turned sardonic. "But he did give me a lot of very interesting background information about your society."

Core froze and Dirk took a deep breath. Sure, it was a good way to get Core's mind off the investigation—but wasn't it a little risky?

Core straightened slowly, eyes hooded.

"He cannot let a stranger leave the planet with such knowledge!" Madelon's whisper shook.

Core lifted his hand, and the torturer turned toward a huge cutlass hanging on the wall.

The Soldier tested the latch, caught Dirk's eye, and nodded.

"I think not," Core murmured.

The Soldier started, staring toward the Lord's voice, the whites showing around his eyes.

But Dirk gave his head a quick, tight shake, held up a cautioning palm, suddenly realizing that, if Core realized Dirk was alive, it'd mean more torture all around.

On the other hand, if the torturer took down that oversized switchblade . . .

But the torturer was turning back empty-handed, scowling, disappointed.

"No, I think we will have some amusement from him." Core's smile returned. "Since he wishes to learn our ways, we would be most ungracious if we did not afford him every opportunity."

Gar frowned, puzzled, and Dirk braced himself while foreboding twined around his spine.

"We will let him participate in the Games." Core gave Gar a warm smile. "I'm sure you will find the experience instructive."

Fingers bit into Dirk's arm; he looked down into Madelon's appalled face. He glanced back through the squint-hole; the torturers, disgusted, were unchaining Gar while Core murmured softly to Lord Cochon.

Dirk turned back to Madelon, shaking his head, and stepped back into the most shadowed corner of the alcove.

Madelon stared at him, unbelieving. Then anger kindled in her eyes, and she stepped up to him.

Dirk clapped a hand over her mouth and breathed into her ear. "If we charged in their right now, we might win, but we'd probably lose. Either way, the Lords get tipped off by a latent rebellion turning active. More to the point, if they win, Core realizes we're still alive, and he'll want a few more answers—and not just from us."

The anger in Madelon's eyes faded. Dirk lifted his hand from her mouth. She turned away, biting her lip.

"Gar handled him beautifully," Dirk breathed. "Let well enough alone."

Madelon stood unmoving; then, reluctantly, she nodded.

Dirk looked up at the Soldier, who stood waiting, impassive. Dirk shook his head. The Soldier nodded once and withdrew his hand from the latch.

Dirk drifted up to the squint-hole again. The torturers were hustling Gar through a door in the far wall, while Core and Cochon turned, still talking, to the door to the corridor.

Dirk nodded, satisfied, and stepped back into the shadows, leaning against the wall with his arms folded, to wait until the way was clear.

He heard one door boom shut, then another. Madelon darted to the squint-hole, looked out, and swung back. "They're gone—we can talk."

Dirk nodded. "How soon till the Games?"

"Perhaps a week," the Soldier rumbled.

Dirk scowled. "He can't learn a whole new style of fighting in a week. They'll slaughter him."

"That might be what they intend," Madelon said dourly.

The Soldier frowned. "It is always slaughter. What difference how well he can fight?"

Dirk bit his lip. "Yes. Of course. You'll have to pardon me—I've gotten used to a polite fiction called a 'sporting chance.' . . . . All right, how do we work it?"

The Soldier scowled. "Work what?"

"Rescue, of course. He stood by us, we stand by him—especially since he might still prove useful."

Madelon nodded. "A point. If Core wants him dead, he must be an advantage to us."

The Soldier nodded thoughtfully.

"Well, how do we do it?" Dirk demanded.

"Talk to the outlaws, arrange a small ambush," Madelon retorted.

Dirk shook his head. "That's like hanging out a sign saying, 'Watch this space for further news of that great, new, once-in-a-lifetime peasant rebellion! Due at your castle wall any day!' Maybe I'm just a cynical pessimist, but I do think the situation calls for something a little more subtle."

Madelon bit her lip. "I think you have reason . . . Very well: one in the cages, to show him the way out."

"*What* way out? That place is kept tighter than a husband with a paranoid wife!"

She tossed her head impatiently. "We have no chance at all till the day of the Games, of course.

Then one in the cages, to tell him the plan, and one in the stands, to show him the way."

Dirk chewed it over and found it palatable. "Of course, that's going to be a teensy bit chancy all around. The one in the stands is as likely to get caught as the one who's trying to break out."

"*Neither* will be caught, if they know what they're doing! It's all but impossible to get a woman into the cages, so the stands are my place."

Every protective instinct in Dirk reared back up bellowing; but reason won out, sour though it might be. "If there were any choice . . ."

"But there's not."

Dirk sighed; he knew a losing hand when he held one. "Okay. How do we go about getting me into the cages?"

CHAPTER 4

There was an easy way, of course—Dirk could go into a tavern, pretend to get drunk, start saying nasty things about the Lords. This system was guaranteed to produce five stocky Soldiers on a moment's notice, who would be quite amenable to hauling Dirk off to the nearest Reeve/Gentleman, who would send him off to the Cages with all due alacrity and expedition. Dirk was all in favor of alacrity and expedition, they'd been his companions in trouble before; but he wasn't too happy about the chance of being brought to Lord Core's notice. It is extremely difficult to explain the presence of a dead body, especially if it's yours. Nonetheless, Core would no doubt be rather insistent on getting answers, and his forms of insistence were not likely to be conducive to Dirk's future well-being. So lawbreaking was out.

That meant Dirk had to be smuggled into the cages—and that meant the Guild.

He and Madelon made it to Albemarle, the capital, in two nights and four Soldiers. Dirk hoped their Lord would put down their disappearance to outlaws, which was almost true.

They rode into town right after the gates opened, cleverly disguised under a heap of cabbages. The churl driving the cart was understandably disconcerted when, at the first hidden corner, his vegetables heaved and erupted, spewing out a Gentleman and his Lady (Madelon had procured new clothes somewhere along the way; Dirk had carefully not asked how). But he recovered quickly and turned his eyes front as they dropped to the ground and hurried off; churls acquired selective perception rather early in life.

Dirk and Madelon turned a corner and slowed down, breathing a little more easily. Dirk's interest perked up as he looked around him at the narrow land and half-timbered buildings. He'd been a country boy, so the towns didn't awake that haunting sense of alienated familiarity that troubled him in the villages. Also, there was more variety, even at this early hour, as they turned into the main street—a Butler from the castle on an errand; a Hostler leading horses out of a Lord's town house; a Tradesman in front of his shop, throwing a pot; a party of Merchants en route to the counting-house. Each was distinct, obviously a member of his Guild—after all, occupations were chosen for them by looks—but there was a strange sameness to them, a blending, as the blending of several colors produces a muddy gray. They all had the same color hair—dun, sparrow-colored; they were all round-faced, all of medium height and build. In the towns, all the genotypes mixed together and produced a hybrid—but only one hybrid; the genepool was sharply limited.

The light-headed delight of the morning passed, leaving sullen, smoldering anger. Dirk muttered, "And even if the Lords had known this would happen, they probably still would've done it."

Madelon looked up, puzzled. "Done what?"

Dirk started to answer, then clamped his mouth shut, remembering that the churls didn't know what a clone was.

And if they learned, what would it do to them?

"Set up the Games." And, quickly: "All right, we're here. Now where do we go?"

"In there." She pointed to a tavern.

Dirk looked up at the sign. "There'll be Soldiers."

"We are dead—don't you remember?" She pushed him through the door.

The common room was paneled in dark wood and greasy smoke. They found seats at the long central table, and Dirk tried not to breathe too deeply. It was early; there were only a few other people at the board, eating what passed for breakfast.

"What do we do now?"

"Eat," she replied sweetly. "Or aren't you hungry?"

Dirk's belly answered her with a sudden, mutinous rumble. He remembered their last meal—an overly optimistic chicken who had foolishly gone out for a stroll; it had really been too young to go out alone—and fumbled in his purse, relieved to find all his money still there.

The innkeeper came up, wiping his hands on his apron—a fat Merchant type, with a smile pasted on for the gentry. "Your pleasure, Gentleman and Lady?"

"The best of whatever you have to break fast with." Madelon gestured airily with two fingers.

The smile vanished. Its owner peered more closely into her face, while he said, much too casually, "There is roast fowl and wine, Lady. All else is too coarse for the palate of Gentry."

Madelon nodded judiciously. "That will do. Bring the wine quickly, please."

The innkeeper bowed and turned away, moving as calmly and deliberately as though he'd seen nothing out of the ordinary.

Dirk pitched his voice low. "Whose is that sign?"

She stared at him a moment; then she smiled sweetly. "If you do not know it already, you have no right to."

Dirk's eyes narrowed; but before he could speak, the innkeeper was back, setting two wineglasses and a bottle before them, then bowing and turning away.

Madelon filled the glasses and handed one to Dirk. "For a man who claims to be of us, you seem to know little about us."

Dirk glanced uneasily down the table; which one of the other customers was the Lord's spy? But he'd have to have an amplifier to hear more than a low murmur. Not impossible—but Dirk didn't see any hearing aids.

He turned back to Madelon. "You don't learn very much about rebels when you're ten. You certainly don't meet any—except the ones who smuggle you out, and they don't tip you any secrets."

"Of course," she murmured. "Then you *have* met the Guild?"

"You could say so," Dirk said slowly. "But even after I was away, it was several years before I realized what they meant when they said *the* Guild. I mean, when the men helped me escape, I saw their guild-patches on their arms—but they were all from different guilds. And when I was a boy in the village, I knew the local Tradesmen were members of different guilds, and I got a hazy impression that there was a guild governing each trade, keeping up the quality of the product and doing the paper work—but never trying to improve the lot of their members, or doing collective pushing on the Lords. . . ."

Madelon's eyes widened. Then she propped her chin on a fist, musing. "An interesting thought, that . . ."

"Yes." Dirk smiled wryly. "Bizarre new concept, isn't it? . . . So after I was . . . 'away' . . . it took me a while to realize that since anybody who wanted to oppose the Lords couldn't do it through his guild, they'd set up another, secret Guild for the purpose.

"It *is* confusing." She smiled sweetly. "We hope the Lords find it so, too. But do not your people deal with the Guild?"

"Oh yes, quite often—but mostly just to smuggle the occasional child off to us, or to assure them we're still working for them. They always keep us at arm's length—deal with us, but don't trust us."

"Small wonder, since you take only children. Why do you not take grown men and women, too?"

Dirk shook his head. "If we started doing that, every churl on Melange would be trying to join us—and with that kind of rush, the Lords'd be onto us in no time and shut us down. Escaping children are rare—and a child can learn more than an adult. Learn faster, too—and our operations require a lot of book knowledge. An awful lot."

"So you take only the brighter children," Madelon said crisply. "The others must stay with the outlaws, in the forest—and you wonder why we do not trust you! One would think you know nothing of us, had no idea of our sufferings!"

Dirk stiffened, "I know. I know well. My mother died in the dead of winter because Lord Core wouldn't give my father the medicine—even though he stood outside the portal all day in the snow. Then Lord Core rode through the village and spotted my sister and gave orders that she be brought to his castle. My father hustled her off into the forest before the Soldiers could get there, and I never saw her again. But Core had him whipped to death for it—and he made me watch with the rest of the village."

She stared into his eyes, surprised by the hate in his voice. Then her gaze softened. "And that is when you ran."

"Yes—before my father was buried, while they thought I was still too numb to do anything. But I vowed to come back and avenge them."

"And now you are back."

Dirk nodded. "And we're working on the other part."

Her eyes were wide, staring into his—and, Dirk realized, not black, but a very deep violet. Very deep—he seemed to feel himself losing hold of the hard wood beneath him, being drawn into those eyes, very deeply . . .

Her lashes fluttered, and broke the spell. She dropped her eyes. "The tale of your sister is . . . familiar."

Like her own, Dirk realized; and it hit him like a pile driver. Pity and tenderness welled up in him; outrage surged. If they had dared touch her, he'd . . .

Whoa! He hauled himself back, shaken as he realized the emotions he'd just felt. What *was* it with this girl, anyway?

She looked up at him. "I cannot doubt you now, Dirk Dulain. You tell your tale with too much will; only one who has suffered as we have could feel so much hate." She reached out and took his hand. "I have helped you only with an ill will, so far; but now, we will be together in this, with all my will—and, I think, my heart."

Dirk sat, frozen by the spark-gap of her touch, fighting to contain the sudden surge of elation, to clear the subtle distortion that seemed to have come over the room.

Then he remembered that Gar wasn't around at the moment, and reason returned.

The innkeeper came up with the two roasted birds, and Dirk dropped Madelon's hand—with, it must be admitted, a little relief.

The fowls were small and they were both very hungry, so conversation lapsed while they both paid tribute to the cook. When the bulk of the meat was gone, Dirk shoved his plate away with regret—picking the bones wasn't seemly for gentlefolk. Madelon looked up, caught on, and, for once, followed his lead.

Dirk reached forward and refilled both glasses for the third time. "Next?"

"We wait." Madelon sat back and sipped. "It shouldn't be long."

It wasn't. A wiry, fox-faced man with a bolt of cloth materialized at their table. "Here are the goods you wished to see, Lady."

Madelon looked up with only the slightest trace of surprise. She recovered quickly and unrolled a yard or so, spreading it out over her lap and feeling, pinching, running her hands over it. "Yes, it is excellent stuff, but the color is not quite right. I wish a little more red in it."

"Ah!" The tailor nodded vigorously, as though she had confirmed a personal opinion of his own. "I know just the bolt, Lady—but it is at my shop. Will you come?"

Madelon rose and headed for the door, the tailor at her elbow. Dirk lingered long enough to drop several gold coins on the table—far more than the cost of the meal, but revolutions need financing— and jumped to catch up.

They went down the street, Madelon and the tailor side by side, chattering happily about cloth, cutting, and draping in a jargon that meant about as much to Dirk as a language of supersonic emanations put out by silicate life-forms. He followed after, totally bemused.

A hand shot out from an alley to touch Madelon's elbow. Without the slightest pause, she turned into the alley, as though she'd planned on it all along. So did Dirk. The tailor hurried on by.

As Dirk turned the corner, their guide was turning away—a stocky sandy-haired youth with the badge of a smith's apprentice on his sleeve. Dirk regained some measure of self-confidence; the pattern was familiar. "I will lead you to a man who will lead you . . ." The tailor would never be able to say where his two charges had gone because he didn't know; he'd be able to say only where the next guide had picked them up. He couldn't even tell who the new guide was.

As they came to the end of an alley, another hand shot out of a doorway, touching Madelon's elbow; again she turned and followed without breaking stride. Dirk followed her while the second guide went on by. The door opened onto a stairway, and they went down into a basement. Their guide shoved a hogshead aside, revealing a hole in the wall. Madelon stooped and went through, Dirk right behind her; behind him, the hogshead rolled back into place. Their next guide was waiting with a candle.

They followed, Dirk slightly stupefied by the Guild's coordination. True, they'd had centuries to lay out this route and rehearse the system; but still it was eerie, as though the guides could read each other's thoughts. But Dirk knew, from statistics, genetics, and his own experience, that there couldn't be *that* many intelligent telepaths on the planet—or at least, not in one town.

Four guides, one alley, two cellars, and a tunnel later, they emerged into a large granite chamber with tapestries on the walls, a rich carpet on the floor, and a finely carved, polished set of table and chairs in the middle. A chandelier with four oil lamps hung over the table, lighting the room brightly (by local standards).

Dirk looked around, frowning. There was no guide, so presumably this was the end of the trip; but who were they supposed to talk to? "Where's our host?"

"He will come presently." Madelon sat down at the table and reached for the bottle of brandy in its center. "Don't fret so, Dirk Dulain—we've five days yet."

Dirk wavered, glaring at her; then he threw himself into a chair and reached for the brandy.

He was beginning to feel remarkably peaceful by the time a hidden latch clicked and their host walked into the room.

Dirk eased around in his chair, smiling affably. He saw a tall, stout Merchant in a long burgundy robe over an ochre tunic and pale blue hose. He was round-faced, jowly, with small, hard eyes and a grim, puckered mouth. Over the robe, he wore a baldric embroidered with arcane symbols.

Dirk's smile vanished; he recognized that insignia. He was looking at the Grandmaster of the Guild.

Madelon came to her feet. "I am Madelon; my home village is Marcire, on the estates of Lord Busset. I am ..."

The Guildmaster nodded, cutting her off. "I know you, Madelon; I have word from those who have met you. You bear word between the outlaws and the women of the houses. But who is he?"

Dirk stood slowly, as Madelon said, "He is from our friends in the sky ..."

" 'Friends?' " The Guildmaster mocked, turning to Dirk. "What do you here, sky-man?"

"We're not just friends, we are kin." Dirk held his anger carefully. "I am Dirk, son of Tobin, born in the village Dulain on the estates of Lord Core."

The Master's mouth quirked with impatience. "I know it well; I have helped enough of you escape when you were children. But it is in my mind that *you* forget *us*. You go away and come back only rarely, with the signs of good living upon you; and we never have any good of you."

"You shall," Dirk said, breathing ice, "when The Day comes."

"So you say."

"So we shall prove—and, I think, soon."

The Master's scowl deepened suddenly, to troubled brooding. "Yes . . . so it would seem. It is in the air. . . ."

"What signs have you seen?" Dirk pounced.

The Master shrugged, irritated. "Signs? Who would see signs? If the Lords saw any sign—even hope in a churl's eyes—The Day would be doomed before it began. But everyone knows it; everyone feels it."

Only what he already knew, and no more. Dirk felt disappointed. For a moment, he let his mind reel into fantasy, imagining psionic transmitters, broadcasting a steady emotion of Something Big Coming, goading the churls to frenzied revolt. Then he jolted himself back to reality.

Which the Master promptly yanked out from under him. "There is rumor the Wizard walks among us again. . . ."

Superstition! Dirk pressed his lips tight to hold back the anger. "Anything else?"

"Each churl is digging up his ancestors' weapon-hoard, and testing the blades, then reburying them." The Master shrugged. "And there is rumor that two outlaw couriers were slain by Soldiers, then waked to life again."

Dirk stood a moment, galvanized; then he realized that, if he had to put up with superstition, he might as well make use of it. He opened his mouth, but Madelon was ahead of him. "We are those two."

The Master's head snapped up, staring. *"You?"*

Dirk nodded.

The Master slid a hand inside his doublet—clutching a holy medallion, at a guess. White showed all around his eyes. "Were you truly dead?"

Madelon hesitated.

Dirk shrugged. "Who can tell? The churls said we bore no sign of life. For myself, I can tell you I dreamed."

The Master's eyes swung to him like a compass needle to a magnet. "A dream? What of?"

Dirk swallowed, then forced it out: "The Wizard of the Far Tower."

The Guildmaster's eyes widened their last possible millimeter. "In what way may I serve you?" he whispered.

Dirk came down with a sudden attack of conscience, so Madelon leaped into the breach. "A man of ours has been taken and sent to the Games. We must get him out, if we are to have any hope for The Day."

The Guildmaster turned to her in surprise, then frowned, musing. "It is indeed strange to take a man from the Games—once there, he will not be questioned, and at least will have a quick death. But if you say it must be done, then it must. . . ."

"Dirk must go into the Cages, to take him word of the plan," Madelon said quickly, "and I must be in the stands, to lead them out. It is for you to choose the route and to have it cleared before us and blocked behind us."

The Master nodded. "Simple enough. It is also for me to smuggle your friend in?"

Madelon sighed with relief and nodded.

So did the Guildmaster. "That is more difficult, but possible, quite possible. Let me see. Alphonse is a trainer there, and the Master of the Cages is a cousin to . . ." His voice trailed off into mumbling as he turned away, chin in his fist, pacing the chamber.

Madelon caught Dirk's eye and gave him a glowing smile, lips parted in joy.

Dirk swallowed hard and tried to dig his toes into the carpet. He managed a weak smile back.

The Master strode up to them, clasping his arms behind his back, nodding vigorously. "It shall be done, Lady and Gentleman—yes, it shall be done! I must go and see to the doing—will you abide here, to rest and refresh yourselves? One will come in good time to lead you to one who will lead you."

It was a command, for all that it was phrased so politely; but Madelon gave him her most dazzling smile. "We will be delighted, Guildmaster—and will do it quite gladly, for, to tell truth, we are sore wearied. I thank you for all your great kindness."

The Master actually blushed. "It is nothing, Lady; I delight in the doing of it. Do you seat yourselves now, and leave all else to me."

He whirled about, ducked behind a tapestry, and was gone.

Madelon turned to Dirk, glowing. "You were magnificent, sir! You knew just what to say!"

But in this case, Dirk didn't.

CHAPTER 5

In the heat and bustle of the noonday crowd, no one took any particular notice of another brown-robed monk with a butcher's apprentice at his elbow.

"Not far now," the apprentice muttered. "We'll be at the beginning of the downgrade in a moment. The arena lies below us."

Dirk peered out of the brown wool hood. "I'll be glad to get there, strange as that may sound. This sack itches like an army of fleas."

They came to the rim of the hill, and Dirk stopped, appraising the stadium with an eye to a quick escape route.

Offhand, he didn't see any. He looked through an iron-barred door in a ten-foot cellucrete wall, and stared down—a long way down. The Lords had been thrifty; they'd built their local coliseum in a natural bowl between the hilltop that held the town and the higher hill that held the King's castle. Tier upon tier of seats fell away in a beige giant's staircase, to a circle of white sand a hundred yards across and twenty feet down from the innermost tier of seats. That wall—and the whole stadium for that matter—was cellucrete: an unholy molecular alliance between cellulose and silicon, tough as armor, hard as tool steel, and slick as glass. A grappling hook might get a purchase on granite, but not on this stuff. Once a man was down in the circle of sand, he was there to stay. Oh, there were doors in its walls—a set that led to the Cages, and another set that led to freedom—but only the Lords passed through those last.

"No churl has ever escaped from there," his guide informed him.

"Pleasant thought, isn't it?" Dirk turned away. "Well, I always did want to set a precedent. Shall we go?"

They wound their way down to the bottom of the hill, where the street opened out into a cobblestoned plaza before a huge iron door in the cellucrete wall. It was for wholesale transactions; it could be cranked up to admit a whole cartload of convicts, and often was. For the retail trade, there was a smaller, hinged door set into it.

The butcher's apprentice ambled up to it, and on by, leaving Dirk standing by it in contemplation, like a moraine deposited by a glacier.

The ice, at the moment, was in Dirk's feet. He folded his arms to keep his hands from trembling and propped his chin on his chest, reflecting that it was one thing to contemplate a damn-fool risk, but another to take it. But—the die was cast, and Dirk should've had his head thumped.

He glanced up at the sun—just about high noon. Something was supposed to happen about now. Just what, the Guildmaster hadn't informed him—but something, any minute . . .

Suddenly, through the small iron gate in the door, he heard a melee of bellowing, screaming, and the clash of steel. Then the lock growled, the door slammed open, and a brawny arm shot out to yank Dirk inside. The door crashed shut behind him—not that Dirk could hear; the fight was much louder in here.

He found himself facing a Soldier tastefully attired in crossed lether belts and breechcloth. Without a word, he yanked Dirk's robe off, almost taking his arms with it. Dirk had to grind his teeth against pain—and to keep them from chattering; it was *cold* in here! After all, all he was wearing was a breechcloth, himself!

The guard grabbed him by the shoulder and hustled him away, shot a key into a lock, slammed open a door, and shoved him through. The door boomed shut behind him, and Dirk was in.

He immediately wished he wasn't. By wavering torchlight, he saw a near-naked crowd of yowling devils battering at a wall of bars. Shrill whistle blasts answered them, and spears started poking through the bars. Strangely, each man seemed to step just a little aside a split-second before the barbed head came through.

Then—suddenly—the howling slackened, groaned, and ground to a halt, like a record shut-off halfway through. The prisoners turned away, shuffling toward Dirk, muttering. On the far side of the bars, the guards relaxed and strolled away, growling to one another.

"What made 'em go like that?"

"Happens all the time . . ."

Dirk's ears pricked up. "Happens all the time?" What illicit operations were the prisoners covering up?

Then he saw the earthenware bowls they were all shuffling back toward, saw the thin gruel they contained, and understood. Not covering up anything. Just a food riot.

The prisoners were sitting down on the filth-strewn floor and taking up their bowls. Dirk's gaze zeroed in on the huge bulk of one man still standing—Gar! Dirk started toward him.

The steel door crashed open, and a monolithic guard strolled in, absentmindedly flicking a bullwhip. "All right, you hoghounds! You hate your grub so much, we won't make you eat it! Line up and file out—we'll start the afternoon session a little bit early."

The prisoners bellowed profanity with one voice and rose up, arms swinging back with bowls poised.

The bullwhip cracked like a gunshot, building echoes into a cannonade.

When the echoes faded, the prisoners were standing slack, facing the guard.

"You'll all be dead in less than a week. What difference does it make if you go a little early?"

The bullwhip twitched.

The prisoners were silent, eyes glued to the flicking tip.

The guard nodded, satisfied. "All right, then. Line up."

They put their bowls down and queued up in a silent, dispirited line. Gar waited till the others had shuffled into position, then tailed onto the end of the line.

He would, Dirk thought. He couldn't have said why, but it seemed in keeping with Gar's character.

Dirk moved out of the shadows and slid up behind Gar. He reached up and tapped the giant's shoulder. Gar turned around with a slight smile of polite amusement—and froze, staring down in disbelief.

Dirk had to press his lips tight to squelch a laugh. It felt good to be one up on the big guy for a change.

Gar recovered, and smoothed the urbane smile back on. "Delightful. I trust you'll explain how you managed it?"

Dirk frowned. "Managed what?"

"Being so nimble. You must remember that, when I saw you last, you were scarcely in any condition to be walking about. In fact, if I remember it rightly, you weren't even in condition to breathe."

"Oh." Dirk pursed his lips. "Well, I don't know. Matter of fact, I was hoping *you* could tell *me*."

He saw the flicker in Gar's eyes and knew he'd struck pay dirt. But then why the look of shock when Gar saw him?

Acting, of course—and not a bad job, either. But why? What was the big guy trying to hide?

"How did you manage my 'death'?" Dirk murmured.

"I?" Gar's eyebrows shot up in mock horror. "My dear fellow, how could I have had anything to do with it?"

"I was hoping you'd explain that."

Gar frowned, but just then they came up to the door, and he had to cut off the conversation to turn and file through. Dirk stepped through right behind him, and a pair of boxing gloves slapped him in the midriff. His belly sucked in with the slap, and he looked up into the eyes of the guard who had let him in. There was a grim warning in the man's eyes. Dirk straightened up and shuffled ahead.

"Put them on," Gar muttered over his shoulder. "These are just for practice; they tell us we'll get really nice ones for the big day—lined with lead and faced with iron."

"Glorified brass knuckles," Dirk growled, slipping the boxing gloves on.

They filed through a second door into a vast, slant-roofed room. The other churls had already paired off, trading half-hearted swipes.

"Not brass knuckles, really." Gar turned to face Dirk, bringing up his gloves. "Cestas—the iron boxing gloves the Roman gladiators wore."

Dirk nodded. "Probably straight out of a history book. They have a penchant for that kind of thing." He eyed Gar's huge, leather-covered fists and brought his own up warily. A corner of his mind wondered why Gar was being so very polite. Defense mechanism, certainly—but what was Gar hiding?

Then a leather-covered cannonball drove at his face, and he had to stop thinking to slap it aside.

It didn't slap too well. In fact, it drove right on through and slammed the side of his head. Dirk staggered back, shaking his head to clear the distorted glass that had suddenly come between him and the world.

"Sorry," Gar muttered, "but we have to make it look halfway good, or they're on us with the whips."

Dirk glanced at the guards strolling around the edge of the room, bullwhips snaking lazily behind them. "Perfectly all right. I just haven't quite gotten into the spirit of the thing." If that was Gar's idea of halfway good, Dirk was definitely going to have to go all out.

He jabbed at Gar's face. The giant blocked it, moving so quickly Dirk scarcely saw it. Then the leather cannonball was in his face again. He threw all his strength into a block and was partly successful; the glove whistled past his ear. But Gar's left was already hooking up. Dirk rolled back by pure reflex, just barely in time.

"Nothing wrong with your coordination." He came back with his guard up.

Gar smiled. "Yes, that's the mistake people usually make—because I'm so big, they expect me to be clumsy. But you're not bad, yourself—you're the only one here I haven't been able to hit when I wanted to."

Startled, Dirk stared, then glanced quickly at the other prisoners. A few of them were taller than he was, well-muscled and lithe.

"It seems they don't know much about boxing," Gar explained. "Only what they've learned since they've been here."

Dirk nodded. "Of course. The Lords won't allow churls to learn or teach anything to do with combat, even the unarmed kind. Anyone caught trying to work out a system on his own . . ."

". . . is sent here," Gar finished grimly. "Yes, I know. I've had some highly elucidating conversations in the last few days. Surprisingly good, really—they all show an amazing degree of intelligence."

Dirk gave him a malicious smile. "Feeling inferior?"

Gar's smile became a glare.

One of the guides caught sight of them and started over, gathering in his whip.

"Too much talk and not enough action," Gar growled and swung a haymaker.

It was easy to block, and for the hell of it, Dirk tried. He caught Gar's swing, all right, just before it caught him. But he did have the satisfaction of seeing the guard turn away, mollified. He saw it from a very low angle, with sand against his cheek and a ringing in his ears.

He pulled himself to his feet, shaking his head, and found Gar gazing at him in consternation.

Dirk's lips thinned. "Now you're going to try and tell me that wasn't full strength."

"It wasn't. I'm sorry; I guess I'd better pull my punches a bit more."

Dirk just stared at him. Then he nodded. "Yes. Please do. If you expect me to be any use to you at all."

"Use?" Gar frowned, jabbing lightly.

Dirk ducked—no more of this blocking nonsense. "Yes, use. I came in here to help you break out. What'd you think I was doing—taking a break from a busy schedule?" He tried an uppercut.

Gar blocked it absentmindedly. "I took it for granted they'd caught you. Well—my thanks."

Dirk smiled sardonically. "Did you think we were going to leave you in here to get killed?"

"Frankly, yes. I'm not exactly a key figure in your plans, you know. I didn't suspect you of so much sentiment."

Dirk's smile turned sour. "I wouldn't call loyalty a sentiment."

"But I would." Gar glanced at their local efficiency expert and threw a punch. Dirk leaned back from it, but not far enough. As he picked himself up off the sand, he heard Gar muttering, "If revolutionaries take time for luxuries like loyalty, they lose."

"Not always. Sometimes they save a valuable man." Dirk lashed out with all his strength.

Gar batted it aside impatiently. "Only by risking another one—or several. I don't know how elaborate this scheme of yours is. In addition to which, it tips off the opposition." He swung another hay-maker.

Dirk dropped to a squat and felt the breeze as Gar's fist went by. "It's nice of you to be so concerned; but don't worry, we'll try to make it look like a plain, ordinary, everyday riot that got out of hand." He lifted his fist and drove up like a ramrod.

Gar caught his wrist and lifted; Dirk's face hovered in front of his. "How often do riots happen at these Games?"

"Never," Dirk admitted, "but we feel obliged to go out of our way for a visitor."

"So thoughtful of you," Gar murmured, and let go.

Dirk landed in a crouch and danced around Gar, weaving in and out.

"Be careful," Gar admonished, turning to follow him. "You'll make me feel like a V.I.P."

"Well, there is something to that. We do feel a certain responsibility for you."

"Of course," Gar murmured. "You wouldn't want my father to feel you'd been careless with me."

"That, too." Dirk leaped in, feinting with his right. Gar blocked it, and Dirk hooked with the left, caught him under the chin. Gar's head snapped back and Dirk bounced out, feeling a warm glow of accomplishment spreading through him.

Then he bounced—period. He shook his head and saw Gar looking sheepish, but he couldn't hear what the big man was saying. His ears were ringing too loudly.

". . . just a natural reaction," Gar apologized, as the ringing faded.

Dirk nodded, though groggily. "That's okay —we all have our conditioned responses. And judging from yours, we should find you very useful."

Gar shook his head. "Not enough to justify the first escape from the Games in your history. I'm just another fighter, albeit a good one." His smile was tinged with irony. "As to my father—do you even know who he is?"

"Only that he's rich enough to give you your own space yacht, and has time to go bumming around the galaxy—unless there's some truth to that line you fed Core."

Gar's eyebrows shot up. "Your intelligence system isn't too bad. And yes, there's *some* truth to it. I am a d'Armand, but have you ever even heard of Maxima?"

Dirk scowled. "Yes, some. That's the robot house, isn't it?"

"Well," Gar said judiciously, "the automated factories there do make very good robots. But I wouldn't say that was a tremendous distinction."

"Enough." Dirk hid a smile. "I should imagine it's a very lucrative trade."

"Somewhat," Gar admitted. "Enough for everyone there to live in some luxury—but not enough for private yachts." He jabbed halfheartedly.

Dirk leaned aside from it. "Where did you get the money?"

"On my own." Gar wore a puckered smile. "There are certain kinds of salvage that pay very high figures—especially if you're a good cyberneticist."

"Salvage?" Dirk hoped his dismay didn't show.

But it did. Gar's smile went flat. "Salvage. Yes. I'm a junkman. So you see, your whole charade is a waste."

"No," Dirk said slowly, looking straight into his eyes, "I think it'll prove to be very much worth it. You're still you, you know."

Gar's gaze held steady, but his face drained.

Sandals slapped earth, and the guard came toward them. Gar glanced at him, irritated; then his fist lashed out, blocking the world, and Dirk had the rest of the afternoon off.

So it went—boxing practice all morning and all afternoon, with brief breaks for meals, then doused torches and deep, almost-drugged sleep. The prisoners gained some skill, but they made up for it in increasing exhaustion.

"If they keep this up, they'll be easy meat for a pussycat," Gar growled over his evening bit of porridge.

Dirk nodded, swallowing. "I think the Lords're aware of that."

"But we'll look excellent for ten minutes," the Butler next to Dirk said brightly.

"Yes indeed." A Tradesman finished licking his bowl and lay flat on his back in front of them. "For the first ten minutes, our good brother churls will see a real battle. Then we'll weaken, and the young Lords'll gain an advantage, then more and more—and our kinsmen will see the Lords triumph slowly but surely, as men of their birth must inevitably do."

"Yes." The Merchant on Gar's far side rubbed his knuckles, smiling softly. "But those first ten minutes . . . Who knows? I might even cave in a helmet."

"Never happen." A Farmer ambled up, shaking his head. "No man's strong enough, by the time they get you to the games."

"No *ordinary* man." The Tradesman cocked an eyebrow at Gar. "But we're counting on *you*, friend."

Gar gazed at him a moment; then he smiled wolfishly. "I think I may give you some slight satisfaction."

The words induced a prickle of warning in Dirk. What did the big man have in mind?

" 'May?' " A lantern-jawed Fisher sat on his heels between the Merchant's and the Tradesman's feet. "Only 'may'? Is that the best you can offer us?"

Gar leaned his head back against the wall, smiling lazily. "What did you have in mind?"

The Fisher suggested, "A mild massacre, perhaps. Fifteen or twenty Lords would do."

"Twenty! My two poor fists against plate armor and swords? Twenty?"

"Your two poor fists will be leaded and steelshod," a Woodsman pointed out, joining in. "And, too, I think we could promise you something of a diversion, allowing you ample time to develop a deep and meaningful relationship with any one opponent."

Gar sighed, gazing up at the ceiling. "It's tempting, gentlemen. Almost, I could let myself be persuaded to it. But there's a small matter: my conscience. It'd be needless bloodshed."

"Conscience!" The Woodsman snorted, and a Hostler scowled. "Needless? How can you think that?"

Dirk glanced up and saw, with a shock of surprise, that most of the prisoners had gathered around them, and the last few stragglers were coming up.

Gar laced his fingers behind his head. "If what you say is true, we'll all die anyway, but all the lordlings will live. So, if we kill any one of them, it's a death that needn't have happened."

"There *is* a need for it," the Butler assured him grimly; and the Hostler said, in a voice soft as flame, "*We* have a need for it, Outlander. Great need. We cannot accept death tamely; we cannot accept having our lives count for nothing."

Gar lifted an eyebrow. "So that's how you manage to stay so cheerful. I was wondering."

The Farmer grinned like a bandsaw. "What would be gained by moping and trembling?"

But the Tradesman laughed and rolled up on one elbow. "Do not think we are so courageous as that, Outlander. When I came here nearly a year ago, I was so sick with fear I could scarcely hold water. But after a time, I began to see that I would have died young in any case, even if I had not been caught out."

The Merchant nodded. "Only Lords die old, here."

"I know the day of my death now; and that is all that has changed," the Tradesman continued. "I might have had a day or two more otherwise, perhaps a year. . . ." For a moment, his face bleached to bleak; then he shrugged it off and grinned. "But never much longer—and I would have died with no purpose, with nothing accomplished, nothing changed by my life so the world could look and say, 'Here! Here is the sign that a man lived!' But now, here . . . I have purpose now, a chance to kill a lord. Only a chance, perhaps, and a poor one—only steel gloves against sword and plate armor, with the sun in my eyes—but my chance nonetheless! Any chance at all is more than I had before—and perhaps . . ." His voice sank low, caressing; he brought a hand up, clenching it slowly. "Just possibly, I might, by some wild freak of chance, kill myself one of them. . . ." His fist clenched in a spasm; he nodded, eyes glistening. "Yes. That is worth a death—even a certain one."

Gar had lost his smile. His gaze held on the Tradesman, very steadily.

The Tradesman brayed laughter and threw himself flat on his back again. "Why, Nuncle! Do I amaze you?" He rolled a droll eye at Gar. "I think you know nothing of hate."

"I thought I did," Gar said slowly.

"Welcome to school," said the Hostler, amused.

Gar turned his head slowly from side to side, unbelieving. "You're incredible. A band of men, eagerly awaiting certain death, for the minuscule chance it brings of chopping down a few minor enemies."

The Farmer shrugged elaborately. "We are not particular. Any of them will do."

Gar still shook his head, smiling now. "If I had an army of men like you, I could conquer a world."

"Why, here is your army," the Tradesman said lightly, but his gaze held Gar's. "Where is this world you would conquer?"

There was a silence then, stretched out like the skin of a war drum.

Then Gar laughed. "It is outside the walls of this jail, coz. Shall we stroll down to the river? Or perhaps you know a tavern where we might sit down to discuss fates of kingdoms."

The Tradesman's mouth pulled slowly into a sour smile, against his will.

One by one, the other men smiled, too; but the sudden disappointment weighted the dank air of the prison.

The Tradesman rolled to his feet. "We waste time in chatter. We should sleep; it behooves us to be as fit as we may in four days."

The other men rumbled agreement, they slowly moved off to find filthy straw pallets against the walls.

Gar watched them go by the wavering light of the single torch outside the bars.

"I think you almost had a revolution going there," Dirk pointed out.

"Yes." Gar nodded, eyes shining. "And I think I could have it again, anytime I called." Then, very softly; "They're amazing. You expect to find brutes in a prison, not men of wit."

"They are brutes, in a way," Dirk said slowly. "Each of them thinks only of killing."

" 'Think?' " Gar turned to him, nodding. "Yes, they do, don't they? I always thought myself an intelligent man—but I had a good education, and they've had none. Am I the lowest intelligence in the room?"

"I think not," Dirk mused. "You strike me as having no shortage of brains. But you certainly find yourself in congenial company."

Gar nodded. "What kind of anomaly *is* this planet? Do only the brains turn to theft?"

"They aren't thieves," Dirk said softly. "Not a one of them."

"What, then?"

Dirk looked up into his eyes. "You really haven't figured it out yet? The whole purpose behind this gladiator's charade?"

Gar frowned down at him a moment, then rolled his head back against the wall, lips pursed in thought. "I've figured out that the purpose of it is to cull out the brainy ones—but I haven't gone too deeply into the mechanism. This is one place where you don't ask a man about his background. Why *are* they here?"

"They're rebels. Any man who's here was overheard speaking against the Lords—maybe just a joke, or a drunken curse. Or both. And most of them have good senses of humor—they would've pulled a large audience."

"Including Soldiers?"

Dirk nodded. "And didn't particularly care. Because, of course, there was a lot of anger behind them—to make them lose their heads that way."

"I'm surprised all they did was talk."

"If they'd actually *done* anything, they wouldn't be here. If they'd tried to kill a Lord, or stake out the local squire with a set of sickles, they'd have been strung up by the heels and beheaded right there. No, this place is for the ones with sharp wits and hot blood—too smart to do something instantly fatal, too hot-tempered to be able to hide their anger and hatred."

"It comes to the same thing," Gar said slowly. "Instantly fatal, or fatal within the year—what of it? Dead is dead. There must be some with more brains and cooler blood."

Dirk shrugged. "If a man looks intelligent but doesn't make waves, they put a robe around him and call him a priest. They have to have a few churls who can read or write, after all—and who can preach resignation and humility to the masses."

Gar raised his eyebrows. "You've got a religion?"

"Oh yes. Eighteenth-century Christianity, with all the trimmings. The Lords thought of everything. And they preach patience, all right—but the Lords don't know that, with most of them, the patience they preach is just a matter of waiting for DeCade to come back to life. They're the focal points of the communities—priests always have been. But the Lords don't know what they're focusing the churls on."

Gar nodded slowly. "And, of course, they have to be celibate."

Dirk nodded. "The penalty for fornication is death —for both parties. And any children born of it."

Gar scowled, nodding. "So the hot-tempered intelligent ones get killed off in the Games, and the cool-tempered intelligent ones don't pass on their genes. Either way, smart genes get filtered out— but only the ones smart enough to be troublesome, of course. Couldn't have a population of idiots. . . . Yes, very neat."

"Not completely. These berserkers may be smart enough to stay unmarried, but they *are* passionate. They've usually passed on a gene or two before they got caught."

"So," Gar said slowly, "the filtering never ends. It's got to be continual, a regular event."

"Yes, and they do make quite an event of it. They gather all the available churls together to watch it."

"That should have a very salutary effect."

"Oh, it does," Dirk said softly, "but not quite the one they expect. The whole mob comes away every year, more determined than ever to turn out for a bloodbath"—his mouth twisted—"as soon as DeCade rises again."

"Yes, there is that little problem," Gar mused. "How do you plan to start the revolution if DeCade doesn't rise?"

"We haven't quite got that one figured out yet," Dirk admitted.

"And who's going to figure it out?" Gar smiled wryly. "By your account, all the brains get killed off or culled out."

"No," Dirk said slowly, "not all. Not the *really* smart ones, no."

Gar frowned, puzzled; then his face cleared, with something like shock. "Of course. The really intelligent ones would be smart enough to hide it—successfully. They'd never be caught or found out."

Dirk nodded. "All we're left with is geniuses. And, with the kind of inbreeding we've got, there're a lot of them—almost as many as there are idiots. The Wizard was no accident."

"Yes. The Wizard." Gar chewed at his cheek, thoughtfully. "Most of your boys—the spacers—made it off-planet because they had to leave their homes rather suddenly, didn't they?"

"Most of us, yes. Which means we were found out while we were still very young. So, in answer to the question you're polite enough not to ask, surprisingly. No. We don't consider ourselves geniuses. Smart, yes, most of us—but not that smart."

Gar nodded. "So where do you find them?"

"A few in the forests, with the outlaws—they got sick of pretending. But most of them are in the cities, in the secret organization."

"The secret society." Gar's eyes widened; he nodded slowly. "Yes, of course. It has a long and honorable history."

"Well, not exactly honorable; I can think of quite a few that weren't. But, shall we say, effective?"

"Let us hope so, in this case." Gar raised a skeptical eyebrow. "And just how do these geniuses of yours plan to start the revolution without DeCade?"

"I don't know," Dirk said slowly, "and I'm not sure they do, either."

CHAPTER 6

For all their good cheer, the prisoners' nerves began to fray as the days slipped by. The tension was partly fear, of course; but it was partly eagerness, too. The boxing practice became more feverish, less deft. They began to bark at one another during the slivers of free time, after supper; there was an occasional quarrel.

Their last dinner, the night before the Games, was better than usual—they actually had a few ounces of meat each. But afterward, they sat around the walls of the great chamber, turned in on themselves, occasionally muttering to one another—or, more often, growling.

One of the Merchants sat idly throwing a pebble against the wall, catching it on the rebound, and throwing it again. *Chink, chink!* It began to get on

Dirk's nerves, even though he was fairly sure of living through the debacle tomorrow. Oliver, the Farmer, paced the chamber, back and forth, back and forth, like a caged gorilla—huge, lithe, and deadly, and ready to erupt into snarling fury.

"Cease that infernal pacing, Farmer!" one of the Woodsmen rasped. "It's bad enough in here tonight, without you winding it tighter!"

Oliver whirled, his fists coming up; but before he could speak, Gar snapped, "Hold!"

His voice wasn't loud, but it stopped Oliver—or at least changed his direction. He turned toward Gar slowly, eyes narrowing. "And who are you to command me, Outlander?"

Gar lifted his head, raising his eyebrows. "Why, I am myself. Care to debate the point?"

Oliver started toward him, fists coming up.

Hugh, the big Tradesman, growled, "Oh, stop it, the pair of you! Isn't it bad enough the Lordlings'll be hacking us to bits tomorrow, without our tearing at each other now?"

Oliver slowed, turned toward him, puzzled. He looked back at Gar; his mouth tightened in a quick grimace, and he turned away, to take up his pacing again.

The Woodsman glared at him and started to speak; but Hugh caught his eye and he subsided.

Oliver began to beat his fist into his palm in time to his pacing. "Something's got to break. It's got to."

"It will," a Hostler growled. "Tomorrow."

"Don't speak of tomorrow." Hugh snapped. His mouth tightened in chagrin. "Damn! I'm doing it too, now." He looked about him, glowering. "We need a song."

The room fell suddenly silent. They all knew which song he meant—and they also knew the penalty for singing it. Death. Instant.

Dirk raised his head and looked slowly about the room, saw the naked craving in each face, but also the fear that overlaid it.

So slowly, softly, Dirk began to chant the Lay.

> When DeCade was young, he fell in love,
> As even churls may do;
> His lass was bonny, bright, and gay;
> For them the world seemed new.

Heads came up slowly, all around the room. They stared at him, startled, a little shocked. Then the hunger rose in their faces, and their eyes fastened on him, greedily.

Dirk sang on:

> When you take joy, remember price—
> Each pleasure must be paid.
> Before they wed, the charge came due—
> A Lord espied the maid.

He sang the whole tale—how DeCade had wakened at midnight, hearing the screams of his love, had caught up his staff and bolted from his hut to fall on the band of Soldiers who were stealing her away—a huge bear of a man, nearly seven feet tall, three hundred pounds of silent homicidal muscle, with a hardwood quarterstaff as heavy as a bar of iron, laying about him in fury, not counting the tally of dead. The leader of the party held a knife to the girl's throat, and DeCade broke the man's skull and spilled his brains. But the leader was quick—he sliced her throat as he fell—and De-Cade stood, numbed, staring at his love, lying dead in a pool of her own blood, all trace of pity and forgiveness pouring out of him as the blood poured out of her. Then, only when she lay emptied before him and only a hollow, frozen void remained within him, did he turn his eyes to the leader, and realize it was the Lord's son.

So Dirk sang the tale; and Gar looked down, staring at him as though he were insane. Dirk took a breath and took up the ballad again.

DeCade fled to the forest that night and hid for some time, living on poached meat and killing any Lord or Soldier foolish enough to come in under the trees, alone or in company.

And, finally, the outlaws found him and took him for their leader.

Then churls began to escape to the forest—a few at first, then more and more, hundreds, thousands, who never would have thought of escape before, risking their lives to come join the Lord-killer in the forest.

And the Wizard found him, too—some unnamed genius with magical powers, or so the legend said, who had appeared out of nowhere and given De-Cade an enchanted staff. With it, DeCade took on a small army that came to clean out the forest—a band of a hundred—and he slew them all, by himself, alone.

The word was brought to the King, in his castle at Albemarle. At last, he realized that a vast churl army lay hidden in the huge forest that was nearly at his doorstep. So he summoned his Lords from the length and breadth of the kingdom and their armies with them, to raze the forest, if they had to, to wipe out the outlaws.

But DeCade didn't wait for His Majesty. On the Wizard's advice, he marched out of the forest with a horde at his back, to storm the nearest castle and take it, by surprise and sheer weight of numbers. He armed his men and moved on, his army swelling into the tens of thousands as he marched. He stormed and took castle after castle—until the King moved out of Albermarle.

The King marched out with a hundred thousand well-armed Soldiers at his back, and five thousand Lords with laser rifles to watch the Soldiers. He met DeCade at the field of Blancoeur and raised a clamor that clawed at the sky and brought vultures down; for, at the end of the battle, DeCade retreated, leaving a third of his men dead or dying. The King marched after him and met him again at the foothills of Mont Rouge. DeCade lost half his men before night; but darkness and a heavy overcast saved him, covering his retreat up the mountain to Champmortre, the bone-white, sun-bleached plateau high in the mountains near Albemarle. There he stationed his remaining men in a human parapet, armed with spears, bows, and a few captured laser rifles. The King, in a rage, marched up against him, and the churls mowed his army down—till the archers ran out of arrows and the rifle power-packs ran dry. Then the King scaled the heights and drove DeCade back to the center of the bald plain with his men grouped around him, fighting a last, desperate, doomed battle with no quarter given or asked, knives and swords against swords and lasers, each churl thinking only of how many Soldiers and Lords he could take with him, killing and dying in an orgy of blood-lust and vengeance, till the setting sun threw the long shadow of a ring of dead churls on the plain; and, within the ring only DeCade and the Wizard stood alive, back to back, with a circle of King's men outside the rampart of dead. Then the King shouted the command, but the Soldiers stood, surly, unwilling to attack DeCade. Laser bolts crackled; the rearmost soldiers fell, screaming, and the rest pressed forward, flowing over the heap of corpses to press in. Then DeCade's staff whirled, threshing out a crop of death, and hundreds of Soldiers died before they buried him under sheer weight of numbers. Then the Lords broke his neck, broke his back, stripped his body and cut his flesh into ribbons, tore out his entrails to prophesy that the churls would never rise again, broke each separate bone in his body—and took up the golden staff, and broke it in two.

Then, as the shouting and madness subsided, they looked all about the plain, and found it filled only with dead. The Wizard was gone. They searched, but did not find him. They never did.

Sated, the King and his men marched away, leaving DeCade's corpse to the vultures. But the next day, the King realized that even DeCade's bones could threaten his peace. A host of churls might rally around them. He sent men to take the bones away and burn them. But they came too late. The giant body was gone, and the golden staff with it, never to be seen by Lordling or Soldier again. Only the churls knew where he lay, beneath a great hollow mountain, the mountain from which the Wizard fled into the sky. But he would return—oh yes. He would return when the churls' time had come; he would return, to waken DeCade. Then DeCade would ring the bell and march out to challenge the Lords, with new and magical weapons and a churl army behind him. They would crush the Lords then; they would free all the churls . . .

Dirk took a long, deep breath; then, more loudly, he began to intone the last verse; after a few words, Hugh joined him, his voice a low chant; then Oliver joined, then the Merchants, then more, till all the prisoners together roared out the last lines, shaking the chamber around them:

Each worn knife and blade
   you must bury and save,
For when DeCade wakes and
   comes out from his grave,
Then dig up the weapons that you have laid by,
And sharpen their edges and do not ask why—
For when my far towers drop down
   from the skies,
DeCade shall call out, and all churls shall rise.
For Freedom!

The echoes faded; the chamber was still. Each churl looked at his fellows, eyes glowing, filled with the fire of a Cause.

Dirk leaned back, drained and satisfied. It was worth the risk.

Then armor jangled in the hall, a harsh voice bawled out, and he suddenly wasn't so sure.

The guard came into sight on the other side of the bars, carrying an ugly, short-barrelled weapon—a laser pistol. He shoved it through the bars and glared around at the prisoners, eyes probing their faces. "All right. Who started it?"

Fifty-odd pairs of eyes swiveled toward him, chilled holes in hating masks. The room was as quiet as a sepulcher.

Gar straightened, seeming to gather himself, his gaze becoming remote, abstracted. Dirk took notice of it and frowned.

"Somebody talk!" the guard snarled. "Talk, or we'll pound you flat. Oh, you'll be able to totter out into the arena tomorrow—just barely!"

His voice rang off the granite walls and was swallowed up in the cavern of fifty united minds.

The guard's lips writhed back with his snarl; the pistol rose . . .

"And what will you do to the man who sang it?"

Dirk looked up, startled. The voice had come from Gar; but it was deeper, more resonant, almost seeming to come from someplace else.

The pistol tracked toward him, steadied. "Who asks?"

Slowly, Gar stood—unhurried, easy: And ready.

"What will you do? Kill the man? Will that hold the song from its ending?"

The guard's eyes narrowed. "Are you saying you began it?"

"Why, no." Gar moved toward him, easily, almost causally, slow movements hiding the speed of long strides.

"You lie!"

"Why would I do such a horrible thing?" He was halfway to the guard.

The pistol flicked upward toward Gar's head. "Stand where you are!"

"Why? Are you afraid to speak to my face?" Gar kept moving. And suddenly, somehow, something clicked together in Dirk's mind, and it all made some sort of crazy sense. Nothing he could say, but . . . He rose to his feet and paced after Gar.

"Stop!"

"Why? I can come only as far as the bars," Gar said reasonably. "Are you afraid of me even behind bars?"

The prisoners watched—tense, ready.

Gar was a stride away from the bars. The guard took a step back. "If you did it, say so!"

"But I didn't," the strange voice purred. Gar took the last stride and raised his fists to clasp the bars at shoulder level. "Would I be fool enough to talk this way if I had?"

"Then tell me who did!" The pistol rose level with Gar's eyes. "Or I promise you, you'll die in his place!"

Dirk ducked around between Gar and the bars. "I sang it!"

The guard's eyes flicked down to him, startled; the muzzle wavered.

Gar's whole body went rigid—and the bars bent.

The guard looked up, saw, and wild terror spread over his face. The gun muzzle jerked upward—Dirk leaped through the bars and slapped it aside. The searing light-lance spat wide, shearing through four more bars as Gar's huge fist closed around hand and gun both, squeezing. The guard's face went white; his mouth stretched in a silent scream as he dropped, unconscious.

Gar stood over him, his body slowly loosening. Dirk could almost see him changing back to his normal self. It was as though something were lifted off of him, out of him . . .

The prisoners rose as though one string pulled them all upright, with one massive shushing hiss of straw sandals on stone.

Dirk looked up, ducked back through the hole in the bars, sure of what to do without knowing why, as the prisoners began moving toward him like a single enormous machine. "Oliver, Hugh, Gaspard!" he called out softly, but the prisoners paused while the Tradesman, the Woodsman, and the Merchant stepped forward to Dirk.

Dirk whirled back to Gar. "It's your party. What do we do?"

Gar shook himself, looked up, frowning. He gazed at the churls, seeming to see them for the first time. He nodded. "The guards should be gathered in the wardroom by the main gate. But we've made something of a noise, so they may have a patrol out checking the halls, and they may have put a guard on the armory. Divide into three parties—one to the armory, one to the arena gate, and one to the wardroom. That'll cover all the halls, and the trouble points, too."

Dirk swung back to the three churls. "Oliver, go to the arena gate. Gaspard, to the armory."

They didn't even wait to nod—just slipped through the hole in the bars and split, Oliver to the left, Gaspard to the right. Two-third of the churls stepped after them like a wave and filed through the hole in perfect order, half turning to the left, half to the right, following Oliver and Gaspard, moving with the precision of drilled soldiers without command or question—like zombies or robots, Dirk thought—till he looked in their eyes and shuddered.

He turned back to Hugh. The big Tradesman just stood there, watching Dirk and waiting, with seventeen churls waiting behind him.

Dirk turned to Gar and nodded.

The big man let out a long, hissing breath, set his jaw, nodded, and turned away. Dirk followed, and behind him, Hugh stepped through the bars with seventeen silent churls behind him.

"Mind telling me how you did that?" Gar growled down at Dirk as they led their squad down an empty hall.

"Sure!" Dirk smiled brightly. "As soon as I figure it out."

There were two doors to the wardroom. Dirk

split off from Gar and Hugh and padded silently
through the hall that led to the far door. Once he
glanced back over his shoulder, saw eight churls
following him. Eight—just about half. He turned
away with a shudder; not so much because of their
unthinking precision—he was almost getting used
to that—but because he'd known what he was going to see *before* he looked. *That* bothered him.

He rounded a corner and stopped just short of
the opened door, waiting. He didn't know what he
was waiting for, or how Gar would let him know
when to charge—but he knew it wasn't time yet.
The other eight churls had stopped behind him and
were waiting with a stone's patience; he knew
that—he didn't bother to look. On the other hand,
he probably didn't dare . . .

Suddenly, it was time. Dirk leaped through the
door and saw Gar and Hugh burst through the door
opposite him. And he saw a startled guard whip
around, staring. Dirk dove, reaching for his throat,
and saw a huge fist coming up at his face. He
twisted in mid-air, felt a boulder the size of a
house crush his shoulder, and felt his hands close
around a flexible tree-trunk. Then body slammed
body; the guard staggered, overbalanced, and went
down. Dirk whiplashed the head, cracked the
guard's skull on the stone floor, let go of a limp
body, and leaped to his feet as his churls charged
into the room in perfect unison. The guards were
surging to their feet, catching up weapons, but Gar
and Hugh's churls whooped, and the guards looked
back startled, as the first wave of churls hit them
from the east. A moment later, the western wave

poured in, and the sea closed. There were nineteen prisoners and twelve guards. The troubled waters spewed up jetsam.

Some of the guards died trying to raise their weapons. The ones who just laid about them with their fists lasted a little longer. Dirk threw a punch and danced back out of range; the guard charged him, roaring, and a silent fury landed on his back, slamming him to the floor. Dirk heard something crunch as he turned away, but he didn't have time to think about it; a guard was backing toward him, retreating from two Merchants. Dirk dropped to hands and knees; the guard tripped on him, bellowing, as the Merchants moved in.

It was all over in three minutes. Dirk climbed to his feet and saw Gar standing, glaring down at the still bodies; but there was something bleak about him. Dirk recognized the look; he got over to Gar fast. "You don't have time for a conscience now, Blunderbore. We still have a small problem of a full arena tomorrow."

Gar looked up, frowning. He closed his eyes, nodding, then turned to Hugh. "Pick up the live ones and lock them up somewhere. Set someone to doctoring the ones who might make it, but give him a strong guard. Then get down to the armory and break out weapons."

"Ho!"

Dirk looked up, saw Gaspard coming through the east door with fifteen churls behind him. The big churl looked down at the carnage, shaking his head sadly. "Too late for the party, hey?" He looked up at Gar. "Fortune was against us; they were all here."

Gar nodded, then turned as Oliver appeared at the west door. "There were two of them guarding the armory," the big Farmer reported. "Bertrand Hostler is dead."

Gar nodded. He didn't bother asking about the guards.

Fifteen minutes later, the churls assembled in the wardroom, armed and somewhat armored. There was an occasional moan from the punishment cell down the hall, where the live ones were locked; but it was blocked by the chink of mail and the quiet, exultant laughter of the prisoners.

Hugh and his men swaggered back into the wardroom, fresh from a trip to the armory. Hugh held up a short sword and slapped the pistol at his side, grinning. "It's astounding how these lift your spirits."

Dirk couldn't help grinning. "Just don't lose your head, Tradesman. There's still tomorrow, and an arena full of guards to get through."

Hugh shrugged and thumped Gar on the chest. "What matter? With a brute like this to lead us, who could stop us?"

Gar looked down with a bleak smile. "So I'm appointed permanent leader, eh?"

Hugh looked up, surprised. "Why, so you were before this coil began. Did you not say you could conquer a world with us, Outlander?"

* * *

The holiday dawned bright and clear. The churls arrived with the sun, carrying baskets of food; they were expecting a long day.

Dirk and Gar peered through the portcullis at the arena gate, watching the huge beige bowl fill from the top down. Gar frowned, quizzically. "Little quiet for a holiday crowd, aren't they?"

"I assure you," Dirk said sourly, "that this is one holiday during which all the workers wish they were back at their drudgery."

The Master of the Games arrived about that time, too, banging on the wicket door and striding in, bedecked in finery—yellow waistcoat and breeches under a scarlet coat, gleaming linen, and a huge cocked hat. He strutted up and down between the cages, filled with self-importance, watching the prisoners eating breakfast in the pen, as they always had; he saw nothing out of the ordinary. On the other hand, he wasn't looking for suspicious bulges. "It seems as though there were more of them yesterday."

"Why, that's only because 'tis the day of the Games," the guard beside him explained easily. "They've shrunk in on themselves, don't you see." He was the only real guard left free; the rest of the day shift were behind bars, unconscious, where they'd been dumped as soon as they came through the wicket door. But Dirk had recognized Belloc, the man who'd smuggled him in, and had realized the value of having one genuine Soldier among them.

The Master of the Games nodded, apparently satisfied. He swaggered up and down the halls for half an hour, slapping at the guards with a riding crop, barking out last-minute instructions. He didn't seem to notice how much his guards' faces had changed overnight.

When Belloc had closed the door behind the Master, he turned about and collapsed against it with a sigh of relief.

"When will we see him again?" Gar appeared from the watchman's booth.

"Not until after the Games." The rebel Soldier pulled himself up. "Which means never, I hope. For a while there, I was afraid I would have to kill him."

Now it was Gar who strode through the barred halls, checking to be sure each churl had at least one weapon hidden on him somewhere. All the "guards" had laser pistols. Gar tucked the last one into his loincloth, snaked out a hand to catch Belloc by the shoulder, and headed for the arena gate. "Where do you boys usually stand during the Games, Belloc?"

"Up there." Belloc pointed through the portcullis as they came up to the gate. "Atop the wall, all around the Arena—in case of accidents."

Dirk smiled sourly. "Which means, in case three or four churls manage to gang up on one lordling."

Gar nodded, peering up to the stands. "Lot of brass up there, too."

Sunlight glared off the armor and bared weapons of the Soldiers, fifty feet apart, forming interlocking squares all through the stands.

"Castle Soldiers," Belloc explained, "there in case of trouble. We never had anything to do with each other."

Gar nodded, lowering his eyes to the glare of full plate armor at the other side of the arena. "These, I take it, are our worthy opponents?"

Dirk nodded. "With ten years of tutoring behind their swords and full plate armor for a womb. The young sons of the noble houses—not a one under eighteen or over twenty-one."

Gar scowled, squinting against the sun. "What is this—their rite of passage?"

"You could call it that," Dirk said slowly, "though no lordling could live this long without getting a taste of blood. Whipping churls, or killing one who tried to escape. For most of them, this is the first time the churls fight back. But that's only part of it."

Gar transferred his scowl to Dirk. "Would you mind explaining that?"

"Our lords and masters are very efficient; anything they do has to have at least two purposes." Dirk turned away, looking out at the arena. "You see, in spite of everything they can do with education, youth does tend toward idealism. Somehow, in spite of everything they can do, a few of their sons always wind up with horribly humanitarian ideas—churls are human, justice for all men, sympathy with the underdog, all men should be happy—downright subversive."

Gar looked down in surprise. "Liberals? You mean these dinosaurs are actually capable of producing an open-minded man?"

Dirk nodded. "Far too often for their comfort. Happens to every noble family at least once in every generation. So they bring them here, put them in the arena against churls who're armed enough to be dangerous, and just possibly lethal, even to a man in full plate armor. And these churls are the hotheads of the nation, drilled and primed to come out craving blood and howling hate."

"Like killer wolves," Gar said tenderly.

"It seems to be singularly effective. What chance is there of a young man coming out of that with any thoughts of gentleness left—fifty steel-fisted churls charging down on him, screaming for his blood."

"It *would* tend to cool idealistic enthusiasm," Gar agreed.

Dirk twisted on a smile. "Moral: Kindness to churls is lethal. And that's how you make a reactionary out of a young radical."

"How many come through it with any shred of an ideal left?"

"One," Dirk said judiciously. "I'm no historian, mind you—but I know of only one."

"Oh?" Gar raised an eyebrow. "What happened to him?"

"He started treating his churls decently, and the neighboring Lord didn't like that—it might give his own churls nasty ideas. So he declared war, and the King lent some of his own troops to help out."

Gar nodded slowly. "I take it there wasn't too much of him left by the time they got through."

"His daughter managed to escape, with her grandfather. We smuggled them out; now he's lobbying for us with the Tribunal."

Gar nodded. "And the liberal?"

"He stayed on the planet—or *in* it, I should say. Six feet down."

A trumpet blew in the arena, and Belloc reached up to touch Gar's shoulder. "Gather them, Outlander. It is time."

The churls were pacing, impatiently swinging their lead-clad fists and growling at one another. Dirk slammed the iron door open, and every head in the room snapped around toward the crash. The muttering cut off, and every eye fastened on Gar as he stepped in. He ran his gaze over them in a quick survey and nodded, satisfied. "All right, now's your chance. Come out howling, they expect that—but don't get carried away. Keep sight of me, whatever you do. Follow me wherever I go, and I may bring some of you out of this alive. Don't stop to pick off a tempting lordling along the way—just follow."

Their cheer went up, and Dirk's spirits dropped. They wouldn't remember.

But Gar nodded, satisfied, and turned away. The churls streamed out after him, down the halls to pile up against the portcullis like a human flood.

The Master of the Games strutted about in the center of the arena, calling out the opening amenities in a clarion tone. When he finished, he turned away toward the safety of the arena wall, walking very quickly. He stepped on a stairway, and it retracted as he climbed, telescoping in till it swung away into a recess in the wall.

The lordlings stepped forward, swinging their swords and glancing at one another nervously, stretching out into a line across the far end of the arena.

A trumpet blasted. Gears clashed, iron grumbled, and the portcullis slid up. Gar bellowed and charged out. Dirk leaped into place beside him, glancing back to make sure; Hugh, Bertrand, and Oliver were following, and the three separate groups of churls were following them. He looked back just in time to avoid slamming into Gar as the giant skidded to a halt, facing the steel-clad line fifty feet away. Dirk stopped and Hugh snapped dead still just behind him. Bertrand and Oliver leaped to the sides, and the churls fanned out behind them into a solid, charged line, like a condenser about to spit.

A murmur rippled through the arena, rose in a wave. The gladiator-churls had never been organized before.

The lordlings stood frozen, galvanized.

Then Gar paced forward slowly, bringing up his mailed fists—a panther with brass knuckles. Dirk followed; Bertrand, Hugh, and Oliver followed him; and the line of churls ground forward like a steamroller.

The lordlings lifted their swords and crouched down behind their shields.

A trumpet snarled, kettledrums bellowed, and a clarion voice cried, "Hold!"

Gar only grinned and paced forward faster.

The lordlings glanced at one another, clanked uncertainly, nodded, and stepped forward, snarling.

The churls quickened their pace.

A laser bolt boiled the dust between them.

Gar's head snapped back with a frown, nose wrinkling. Dirk agreed; ozone stinks. The churls hesitated while Gar thought it over; then his mouth tightened in disgust, and he relaxed, resting his mailed fists on his hips. The churl ranks rustled in a sigh, and came to a halt.

The lordlings relaxed, lowering the swords, and the grandstands subsided, muttering.

"They smell something," Dirk growled. "They're stopping it before it gets out of hand."

"Aye." Hugh grinned like a wolf, right behind him. "Come, Outlander! Let's get out of hand!"

But Gar held up a palm, shaking his head slowly, a slight smile touching his lips. "There isn't much they can do now except shoot us down; if they were going to do that, they'd have done it. No, let's see their reason for stopping the show."

A ladder swung out from its recess and telescoped down to touch the sand.

Gar's smile widened to a grin. "Oh yes. I was hoping they'd do that."

"Sorry to disagree," Dirk grunted, "but right now, I don't like anything out of the ordinary."

"And you claim to be a liberal?"

A tall, lean figure in plum-colored coat and white waist-coat, breeches, shirt, and stockings came down the stairs, followed by twenty Soldiers with laser rifles ready.

"Core!" Dirk hissed.

"I believe we've met," Gar murmured.

CHAPTER 7

As Core came up to them, Dirk could see that the white clothing was sweat-stained and dusty; Core had had a long, hard ride. "What's happened that we don't know about?"

"Don't worry, he's the soul of politeness." Gar smiled, never taking his eyes off Core. "I'm sure he'll inform us directly."

Core strode up, glaring, and halted ten feet away, drawing his sword.

Gar tapped his chin with a steel fist and murmured, "Good day, milord."

"I should have been harsher with you," Core spat. "It seems I have once more been misled by my pity and kindness."

Dirk nearly choked.

But Gar only smiled quizzically. "How so? All that I told you was true."

"Then how do you explain a ship dropping into orbit around this planet early this morning! A geostationary orbit, over this very spot!"

Gar's smile widened. "Quite simply; it is my ship. I wanted to have it on hand today; I had a notion I might have need of it."

Dirk's stare swiveled to Gar, unbelieving.

Core glared, seething. "And what of your bribing the freight company to land you?"

Gar shrugged. "You've caught me—I did tell one lie."

Core set his teeth. "How many men have you on board that ship?"

"None." Gar's smile returned.

"Do not jest, fellow." Core stepped forward, sword coming up to guard. "Your death in this arena will be quick, but I could make it last for a week."

"Why?" Gar's smile broke into a grin. "I told you truth; there is no one aboard that ship."

Core's lips writhed back. "Do you take me for a fool? What would guide it, if there were no one—" He broke off, staring.

Gar nodded. "I told you we make good robots." He laid one steel-clad hand over his biceps, massaging it. Dirk noticed there was a wide bronze bracelet on the arm, under the glove.

Core scowled, face thunderous. "A computer? Is that your pilot?"

"Its name is Herkimer," Gar said helpfully.

Dirk could've sworn he saw steam coming from

Core's ears. But the Lord held his temper and turned away to look about the arena, slapping his leg with his sword, considering a decision.

His eyes lit on Dirk.

Dirk suddenly wished devoutly that he had hidden behind Hugh. But too late; Core's eyes widened, and he lifted a trembling sword, pointing at Dirk. "This—this—"

Gar glanced at Dirk, frowning, then turned back to Core with a polite smile. "Well, yes, I apologize for its condition—but you must remember, we weren't fed excessively well."

"Still your fool's chatter," Core snarled. "This is the man who accompanied you before you were arrested—the one who you claimed was your hired guide!"

Gar stood still for a moment; then he nodded gravely. "Your Lordship's memory is good."

"Then he is also the man whose dead body I saw!"

Gar nodded judiciously. "Now that you mention it, I do remember something of the sort."

Core gave him a tight-lipped smile of contempt. "And how do you explain his sudden resurrection?"

Gar shrugged. "Frankly, I can't. But I'm willing to consider any reasonable hypothesis."

Core stared at him, frozen.

Dirk glanced at Hugh, Oliver, and Bertrand. Each caught his glance and nodded almost imperceptibly.

Core smiled abruptly. "Politely said—in return for which, I'll afford you the same courtesy." He waved his sword, beckoning his guards. "Take him to the castle; we'll listen to his reasonable hypotheses there."

The laser rifles leveled, centering on Gar.

Gar twisted a stud on his armlet.

Dirk threw himself forward and slammed into the backs of Gar's knees. The big man toppled as laser bolts spat where he'd been. Hugh leaped over them, and Dirk hugged the ground as fifteen churls hurtled after the Tradesman. Out of the corner of his eye, he saw Oliver and his men closing in on Core's troop from the right, Bertrand's from the left. Startled, the guards swung laser rifles to cover the horde, but too late; leaded fists crashed against rifle stocks as flame-darts crackled, then swung up to crush bone, and the Soldiers dropped. So did a few churls, but the rest of the troop converged on Core. He backed away, sword up, eyes darting about wildly—and the lordlings came out of their trance with a howl and a clank, and went into action like a troop of sardine cans striking for higher-grade fish. The churls paused to scoop up fallen rifles, and Core darted free. But Hugh came hard after him, and the Lord turned at bay, chopping and thrusting. Hugh blocked the sword cuts with metal fists and swung like a threshing machine. Core danced backward, just out of reach.

All Dirk's childhood memories boiled up into hate and lust for revenge, and he surged up with them, charging like a bull. Core leaned back, away from Hugh's fists, and Dirk slammed into him, bowling him over. They landed flat, Dirk on top, grappling for Core's throat. The Lord screamed and chopped down with his blade. Dirk blocked it with a leaden fist; the sword glanced off, cutting. Pain seared Dirk's forearm, and he roared, chopping down at Core's throat, seeing the blood flowing from his father's back. Core jerked his head to the side, and Dirk's fist slammed down into sand. Core twisted and heaved himself clear of Dirk, leaping to his feet. But Dirk rolled to his feet, too, and paced toward the Lord. Voices clamored in his ears, steel rang on steel in his head, but it seemed far away, unimportant somehow; only the sneering face in front of him was real, and the smell of his father's blood in his head, and all that mattered was smashing that jeering face . . .

A huge hand snaked out of nowhere, caught Dirk by the neck, yanked him around, and Gar's huge, ugly face filled his eyes. "Snap out of it! Look—there!"

Dirk turned to look where Gar pointed, and Core leaped free, running toward the arena wall. Dirk started after him with a bellow, but Gar caught his shoulder, yanked him around, clamped steel fingers on the back of his head, and pointed his eyes toward a large white cloth flapping at the top of the arena wall. "Do you want to live—or have your cause die here with you?"

Something wrenched inside, and Dirk put Core out of his mind. He was himself again. His head was clear—one Lord didn't matter, it was all of them that counted. He turned toward Gar, but the big man was loping away toward the fluttering white square. Dirk remembered a girl and a signal. He ran after Gar.

Halfway to the wall, he looked back and slewed to a stop. Core stood at the base of a telescoping stair, hulking guardsmen standing over him with lasers. More Soldiers were leaping to the arena floor, springing into the melee. Above them, guards stepped up at the top of the arena wall, raised lasers, and fired—and, below them, the Soldiers fell screaming. Belloc and the boys, Dirk thought with savage satisfaction. Core was scrambling up the stair, and the churl gladiators were locked in combat with Soldiers and lordlings. Young Lords and churls both lay bleeding on the sand already. Above them, the death struggles went on. Good, and a delight to the eye—but Gar was right, it was time to break up the party. "To me!" Dirk screamed. "Away!" But the human jumble churned away, indifferent to him. Dirk set his jaw against the sudden grip of panic and dashed back, seized the nearest shoulder, wrenched at it. Hugh slammed back against him and pulled away, snarling. Then he recognized Dirk, and his eyes cleared. The guard he'd been fighting raised his sword for a chop at the neck. Dirk leaped forward, swinging his cesta into the man's face. Bone crunched, blood spurted; the Soldier went down, but Dirk turned away before he hit the ground. "Follow!" he bellowed and leaped away. It was all he could do.

Fifty paces, and he glanced back over his shoulder. Hugh was following, with five or six churls behind him—all Tradesmen. The rest struggled on in the blind passion that Gar had torn Dirk out of, their worlds bent inward till nothing existed but themselves and their enemies. Nothing else mattered to them. Dirk had a momentary vision of caterpillars marching around a lampshade; he shuddered, shaking it from him, and turned back toward the white flag.

In front of him, Gar was almost to the wall. A rope ladder cascaded down. The giant leaped, caught at rungs, and was halfway up before it touched sand. Dirk hit the hemp right behind him—and heard a roar from the arena, a spitting blast of heat past his cheek. He glanced back—more Soldiers were pouring into the arena, and the front rank knelt, rifles trained on the fugitives.

And a huge golden sphere swooped down on the arena, sinking to a stop ten feet overhead. Blisters opened on its sides, and beams of ruby light lanced out, gouging holes in the arena walls, walking down in a strafing row toward the ranked Soldiers. They dropped their weapons, and ran—and, above them, the crowd let out one massive scream, rose up, and crashed down on the Soldiers stationed in the stands.

That was all Dirk saw before he scrambled on up the ladder and over the wall. Before him, the white flag trailed away with Gar right behind it. The spectators were surging up through the stands like a tide; the way was clear. Dirk sprinted after Gar and took it on faith that Hugh and the boys followed him.

Up into the stands ran the flag, into an exit tunnel jammed with fleeing spectators. Gar bellowed, slashing out with anvil fists, and the way cleared.

Dirk followed, lashing out to left and right to keep the way clear.

Then, suddenly, the screaming was behind them, and they were pounding down through dark, cool shadow, echoing, down a curving ramp toward the exitway on the far side of the arena. Gar disappeared around a bend in the tunnel; Dirk skidded into it after him, kicked out running downhill toward a rectangle glaring with sunlight. They went rattling down a long, steep flight of stairs and out into daylight.

Out across a plaza, heavy feet pounding behind him. Ahead, Gar disappeared into an alleyway between two tall buildings. Dirk bolted in behind him and slammed on the brakes as he saw it was a dead end. At the end of the alley, Gar stood, chest heaving, wiping his brow, looking down at a tall, slender, skirted figure. Dirk pushed himself into a trot just in time to avoid being trampled by Tradesmen, jogged up to the couple. Madelon glanced at him once, then turned back to pounding on a door in the side wall. Dirk shuddered to a halt, gasping for air, suddenly noticed the searing pain in his lungs. He forced himself to long, steady breaths and finally spared time to look back as Hugh and his half-dozen came pounding up behind, panting and blowing.

The big Tradesman grinned, mopping a forearm across his brow; then the door grated open, and Madelon led the troupe through the doorway, into sudden gloom, blinding after sunglare. Dirk raised his fists, groping, could scarcely hold them up, the cestas suddenly unbearably heavy. Then a wall jolted him to a stop, and he let his arms fall with a sigh, and leaned against cold granite, and breathed.

Suddenly he was shuddering, his whole body relaxing as cold stone drained adrenaline. The door boomed shut and the darkness was complete. Echoes faded, and, in the sudden silence, Hugh laughed softly, exulting.

"Aye," Gar rumbled. "We are free."

"Aye, outside those walls." Hugh almost seemed mocking. "Now! Where is this world you would conquer, Outlander?"

CHAPTER 8

The guide led them to a guide who led them to a guide, also incidentally leading them through a route laid out by a drunken snake in a moment of ecstatic delirium, through a maze of cellars and finally down a long, dank tunnel which, logically, should have run under the city walls. Since it was logical, Dirk was faintly surprised when they straggled out into daylight and moist, knee-high grass, and, turning to look back, he saw the city walls in the distance. It seemed strange, somehow; things weren't supposed to work out logically on this planet.

"One will come shortly to find you," the latest guide informed them. Then he turned and was gone. Dirk stared after him, at the brush and grass disguising the hole in the side of a hummock, feeling strangely removed from the whole thing; it seemed vaguely unreal.

"So Core lives." Gar dropped down to a seat in the grass, leaning back against the hummock. "And he'll be out after us with a troop of Soldiers."

"No, not too quickly." Hugh sat on his heels in front of Gar, grinning. "The town will be merry chaos for quite a time, I think. Lord Core and his fellows'll have their hands full."

Gar pursed his lips. "Yes, it will be a little confused, won't it?"

"The churls will be in turmoil." Madelon shivered. "Small wonder. I almost ran, myself, when that great golden ball came dropping down."

"Oh yes, that." Dirk smiled whimsically. "Yours, I presume?"

Gar looked up, too quickly. "My ship, yes. . . . Does it matter?"

Dirk shrugged. "Probably not. Just wondering why you didn't climb aboard—that's all."

Gar frowned. "There was a small matter of fifty churls to try to save. I'm not in the habit of deserting my fellows."

"Aye, and good for us you didn't," Hugh said soberly. He cracked his fingers thoughtfully. "I'd have liked to kill a few more—but all in all, I'd rather be alive."

His handful of Tradesmen muttered agreement. "That thing was yours?" one of them said, awed.

Gar suddenly seemed wary. "What matter?"

"I'd thought it was the Wizard's tower, dropping

down," another answered, staring at Gar as though he were something supernatural.

Gar smiled feebly. "Just the thing to start a riot."

"And a riot's just the thing to bring the Soldiers out in force," Dirk chirped, "guarding every by-way and highway."

Madelon gave him a black look. "Yes, of course. We'll have to be careful."

"Why?" Hugh asked, staring at Gar. "We've our own wizard with us, now."

"Belay that!" Gar surged to his feet, paced out toward the forest wall. "He said the new guide would come soon! Where is he?"

Dirk watched him, marveling. Why be upset? It wasn't real, anyway. He pointed to the lip of a trail poking out into the clearing. "If you're really all that eager, there's an exit off that way."

Gar's head swung about, eyes riveted to the trail.

Madelon glanced at him, then at the trail, back at Gar, looking worried.

"Why not?" Gar grinned, shrugging. "Our new guide must know the woods. He shouldn't have any trouble finding us."

Madelon still looked worried, and so did the churls. "There are times when personal initiative is singularly inappropriate," Hugh pointed out.

But Gar only laughed and strode toward the trail.

Dirk shrugged and shoved himself away from the hummock, following. Why not?

The churls followed automatically, but also slowly.

Madelon stared after them, shocked. Then she pressed her lips tight in exasperation, and ran after them.

As he came in under the leaves, Dirk glanced back toward the city. The sun was touching the tops of the towers, coloring the whole landscape rose and magenta. Dirk pursed his lips; the day's carnival had taken more time then he'd realized. "Night's coming down, Gar. Any idea where we sleep tonight?"

"Why, with us," said a voice from the shrubbery.

The whole party stretched to a halt. "Who said that?" Gar asked carefully.

Everyone looked at Dirk. Dirk looked at the bushes. "It didn't sound like a man's voice—and it certainly wasn't Madelon's."

"I'm rather aware of that," Gar said sourly. "Now, mind you, I'm not one to turn down an invitation—but I do like to have a look at its source."

"Look, then," the contralto answered, and a huge tub of a woman waded out of the underbrush with two archers to either side of her. Gleaming chestnut hair fell unbound to her shoulders. Her eyes were small, almost hidden in folds of fat, as was her mouth. She had a pug nose, scarcely noticeable. She wore a hooded robe, the color of walnut juice, over a beige tent of a dress. But her step was firm, and she spoke with the authority of a general. Her archers wore brown leather jerkins and tan hose, plus well-stocked quivers and longbows—nocked, at the moment.

The woman stopped a few feet from Gar and searched his face, frowning. Then she nodded, satisfied. "I am Lapin. You are welcome to our poor hospitality, though I'd rather you'd waited our coming."

"So would Lord Core," Gar said sourly.

"Gar, be still!" Madelon hissed. But Lapin's eyes turned hard and opaque. She turned her head toward Dirk. "I believe I should resent that."

Dirk stared back, at a loss for words; but a voice behind him said, "No need, Mother Lapin," and Hugh stepped toward the huge woman, grinning. "Forgive him; he is an outlander and knows little of manners. But he is a good man for all that, and has brought me back to you whole, with several worthy recruits."

Gar frowned. "My thanks, Hugh—but I have a tongue of my own."

"It is so rude you had better not use it," Lapin retorted. "I think you have need of an advocate, and you could scarcely ask for a better one than my own fellow captain."

Dirk and Gar stared, poleaxed.

Hugh smiled at them, amused. "Come now, fellows. You knew I was not in the Cages for the theft of a chicken."

Hugh saw them outfitted when they reached the outlaw camp. It didn't do much for the handy collection of thorn scratches they'd picked up on the way, but it was definitely warmer than the cold night air of the forest. They wore sparrow-brown tunics, rather thin at the elbows, with a few major tears, and breeches of the same ilk. Hugh came back about the time they were done dressing— transfigured. Now he wore leather jerkin and tan hose, like the rest of the forest outlaws, and a grin a mile wide. "It is good to be back to mine own place to bide," he confessed, slinging an arm around each of them. "Now for some honest feeding."

He led them out of the bushes toward a large fire in the center of the forest clearing, with a spitted carcass roasting over it. Dirk sniffed, recognized venison, and wondered about the "honest" part. His stomach, however, informed him that the issue was academic. Hugh gave him a wooden plate, an outlaw turned around from the fire to slap a steaming, rare slab of meat on the plate. Dirk stepped back, found a convenient log, sat down, and tore into the food.

After the fourth bite, when his mind had room for other matters, he looked up and surveyed the camp, chewing thoughtfully. The huge fire was the only light, aside from a sprinkling of starshine. The outlaws were gathered around the huge blaze in groups of four or six, fletching arrows with crow feathers, making bows, sharpening arrowheads; and the women, scraping hides, patching garments, grinding meal—or, men and women alike, simply sitting and gossiping, while a few children ran about with bubbling laughter and joyful shrieks.

Beside him, Hugh was explaining to Gar,

"Lapin escaped from the Houses some years ago and came here alone. The few outlaws in the wood gathered about her—then a few more, and a few more; there are always a few who escape the Estates. But, about a year ago, they began to come in greater numbers, and more frequently, till now we have twelve-score here in our pleasant forest hideaway."

Dirk frowned. "How come the sudden increase? Did they say?"

Hugh turned to him, grinning. "Oh aye; it was they who brought us the news—that the Wizard is abroad in the land again, to bid all churls to make ready."

Dirk choked on a piece of gristle.

"The life is not easy," Hugh went on explaining to Gar while he pounded Dirk on the back. "There is constant toil, and always the danger of Soldiers. But there is no need to bend our backs to any man. And, though there is little enough to feed on, we all share equally in what we have; no man holds back the bulk for himself, as the Lords do. No one starves."

Gar nodded slowly. "Then no one owns anything, but all of you own everything."

Dirk glanced at him, irritated, and Hugh looked puzzled. "Why, what nonsense is this? Every man owns his clothes and his weapons; each woman her clothes and the goods of her household. These they have made for themselves; who is to gainsay them? Do you think we are lordlings?"

At least Gar had the grace to look embarrassed.

But he plowed on: "The women own the goods of the household? Not the men?"

Hugh cocked his head to the side. "How could they? Would they know how to care for such things? I do not understand your questions, Outlander."

But Dirk suddenly did. The outlaws were a free churl society, the only one on the planet. Their economy and social organization would be the template for whatever grew up after the Lords were thrown out. Of course Gar was curious.

And, come to think of it, so was Dirk. Let's see— economy, a form of socialism. Sex roles clearly defined, but with equal rights under custom—which would, presumably, grow into law.

But what about government?

Suddenly Dirk was very curious about the power structure in this outlaw band.

"I notice everybody seems to take orders from Lapin," he said slowly.

Hugh turned to him, more puzzled than ever. "She is Keeper here, aye."

"I thought you said no one bent their backs to anyone else."

For a moment, he thought Hugh was going to hit him.

But the big Tradesman set his jaw and visibly forced himself to unclench his fists. He took a deep breath, turning his face toward the fire. "Lapin governs, but only by the approval of the whole band. When they do not like what she wishes them to do, they complain and protest, bitterly and loudly—and if enough join in the protest, Lapin gives way, and forgoes her wish."

Dirk nodded, and Gar rumbled, "What if enough of them wished someone else to lead?"

"There are those who have wanted to lead," Hugh said slowly, "and the band has discussed it, and wrangled, and argued; but in the end, all but a few called for Lapin."

"But if it went the other way around?" Dirk pressed.

"It has not happened." Hugh gave him a very cold stare. "But I believe in Lapin. She would step down."

"Would she have a choice?"

Hugh watched for a moment. Then he began to smile, shaking his head slowly. "Perhaps not. As I said, none here bow their backs."

"And I'll wager they are on the watch, to be certain no man asks them to." Gar put down his plate, still chewing, and rose, wiping his hands with a tuft of grass. "I have a sudden desire to speak with this paragon of yours, Hugh. Take me to her, if you will."

The big Tradesman looked up, startled. Then he grinned, and rose. "Aye, gladly! This should be worth the watching—if you seek to match wits with Lapin!" He looked back at Dirk. "Will you come?"

"No," Dirk said slowly, "I don't think I'd learn anything new."

Hugh frowned. "How's that again?"

"Nothing. But tell me this, Hugh . . . from whom does Lapin take orders?"

"Why, no one." Hugh grinned. "Till DeCade arises."

Dirk nodded sardonically. "That's what I'd thought, somehow. No, I think you can get by without me."

Hugh shrugged. "As you wish." He turned away and led Gar off around the fire.

Dirk sat watching them go, chewing the last mouthful. There was no point in talking to Lapin; he was looking for the top rebel leader, and she wasn't it. No one was.

Except DeCade . . .

"Good evening, Outlander."

Dirk looked up, instantly wary.

A lean old man with a tonsure and a monk's robe sat down beside him, turning a friendly smile toward him. In spite of himself, Dirk smiled back. "A good evening it is. But I'm not an outlander."

The smile was still friendly, but the monk shook his head with certainty. "There is the touch of the alien in the way you say your words, in the way you bear yourself—a thousand small things. Any man can see it—you are not completely one of us."

Dirk bit down on bile and nodded reluctantly. "You're right. I'm a churl—but I'm a churl from the skies."

"Ah." The old man nodded, satisfied. "From the Wizard's towers. Yes, there would be strangeness in the way you say your words—and the words themselves strange, I should think."

"Strange words?" Dirk frowned. "Oh—you

mean words like 'molecular circuit,' 'monofilament,' 'nuclear fusion.' "

"Exactly." The old man smiled, pleased, but there was a watchful look in his eyes. "Words of wizardry, I fancy. Surely you who have followed the Wizard into the skies would have far more such surface wisdom than any others of our people."

Dirk frowned. " 'Surface' wisdom? How do you mean?"

"No doubt these words give you great powers." The old man smiled gently. "But will that help you live your life more fully and happily, my friend? To understand the Riddle of Life?"

"I suppose not," Dirk said slowly. "I take it any other kind of wisdom is 'surface'?"

The monk shrugged. "By my beliefs, at least."

"And you may have a point," Dirk admitted. "At least, that kind of wisdom is about all that could let these people stand to live at all, let alone happily. I was wondering how a guerrilla army could manage having children around, when they have to be ready to split up and run any minute."

The monk nodded. "But the children understand it as a fact of their life and dismiss it as easily as the adults do—more easily perhaps."

"When they have to run, they do. Till then, they don't think about it."

"Quite so," the monk agreed. "So they have no need to worry for their children. The mothers carry the infants, the babes ride their fathers' shoulders—and all the others can go to ground and stay hidden as well as any rabbit."

"Oh." Dirk's eyes widened. "So that's why the

top banana calls herself 'Lapin.' I was wondering why they called their chief 'Rabbit.' "

"Of course." The old man smiled, amused. "They have great respect for rabbits, I assure you. In fact, they surpass them when it comes to hiding and lying still till the King's hunters have passed them. But these rabbits have teeth, and very sharp ones."

"I believe it." Dirk's eyes strayed to an outlaw who sat near the fire, making arrows. "Didn't I notice you playing that game with them earlier, Father?"

The old man glanced at the arrowmakers, then nodded. "Aye, I must admit I have some skill at it. For that reason, they call me 'Father Fletcher.' "

Dirk frowned at the chagrin in the old man's voice. "That bothers you, eh? A man of the cloth, making weapons of war?"

"Somewhat," the old man admitted. "But Our Lord said to love our enemies and forgive them; He did not say we should not fight them."

Dirk cranked his head around to try to swallow that one, but found he couldn't. "I—ah—don't quite think that's—uh—an accurate reflection of the—ah—gist of His preaching."

The old priest tried to shrug, but it bowed his shoulders. "We do what we must, Dirk Dulain; and if my conscience wakes me in the night with screaming, that is my concern and no one else's."

But Dirk had suddenly lost interest in the topic. "You know my name."

"Aye." A smile touched the old priest's lips again. "So does the whole of the camp, by now.

None ever escaped the arena before; you are men of some moment."

"I'm overcome by the honor," Dirk said dryly. "Are you chaplain to this merry army, Father?"

"Only a wandering guest, like yourself." The old man looked out over the camp, and Dirk thought he saw a certain yearning in the lined and weary face. "I am a hedge priest, my friend—a clergyman without a parish or a flock, wandering wind-tossed over the earth, bringing words of hope to all the people."

" 'All . . .' " Dirk rolled the word over his tongue, wondering whether he liked its flavor. "How many bands like this are there, Father?"

"A dozen more within this forest, and at least another dozen in every other forest in the kingdom. After that, who knows? There's scarce a woodlot in Melange without its score or more of outlaws."

Dirk nodded. "Seven major forests—that's eighty-four bands right there. And each Lord has his hunting park. Figure fifty people per band on average . . . about five thousand archers, trained and armed, and ready . . ."

"You're quite the pessimist," the priest assured him. "I'd estimate at least twelve thousand."

Dirk nodded. "And which is the largest band?"

"Why, this one." The priest smiled, amused. "Would you not expect it, nearest the King's own town?"

"Ordinary outlaws, no," Dirk said judiciously. "But people with a folklore culture aching for guerrilla warfare revolution . . . Yes, of course. Should I ask who all these bands take orders from?"

"No, you've guessed it." Father Fletcher's mouth crinkled at the corners. "All acknowledge suzerainty of this band."

"And that means of Lapin." Dirk heaved a sigh. "Quite an army to bring against the Lords, if De-Cade ever calls."

"*When* DeCade calls," the priest corrected serenely.

Dirk felt a sudden, sinking certainty that he'd never find a way to kick this patient peasant army into motion.

A sudden piercing whistle shattered the calm of the night.

The outlaws leaped to their feet, staring toward the east, where the whistle had come from. Murmurs rose and fell like surf, with a subtle undertone of rattling wood, as men and women strapped on quivers, caught up bows.

A runner came bounding into the firelight, glanced about him wildly. "Lapin!"

The leader moved into the firelight like a creasing bow wave. "Speak! What moves?"

"A hundred Soldiers, at least," the runner cried, whirling toward her. "And at their head—Lord Core himself!"

"Core!" Hugh spat, and the outlaws took up the word, passing it about from mouth to mouth, like a swollen porcupine involved in a dispute about its ownership.

"Why comes he here, himself?" Lapin rumbled.

"Why else?" Gar shouldered up beside her. "From all I hear, escape from the Games isn't exactly a move calculated to make the authorities lose interest." He looked up at Dirk. "I think we might consider a change of climate."

"We all must," Lapin said sourly, and the whole army turned to gather up its belongings.

"No, wait!" Madelon stepped up. "There's only a hundred of them; we are twice their number. Why not take them?"

"Aye!" Hugh cried. "Disperse, but only to the borders of this clearing. Then let them all come in, and when the last is here within the clearing—let fly the arrows. Cut them down!"

"Rifles," Father Fletcher murmured, but Hugh waved the objection away. "They won't have time."

"Why not?" Madelon cried. "If we take them—Lord Core! At a stroke, we've stricken out our harshest hunter!"

"Devoutly to be wished," Father Fletcher admitted. "Still, it lacks the taste of wisdom."

"Why?" Hugh bellowed. "We'd take them all; not a one could live to run! No one would learn of it. No one could know—save us!"

"Well planned," the priest approved. "But every plan can go awry; and if only one should slip away, to bear the word—"

"How?" Hugh interrupted. "What Soldier could outrun or hide, in our own for—"

"Enough," Lapin said—not loudly, but with the weight of a new bride's biscuit; and the argument was killed. Silently, they all turned to her.

"We will hide," she said.

Silence stretched a skein.

"Why!" Hugh erupted. "Odd gods, woman! How much chance is this?"

"None," Lapin said with profound calm. "But it would be war, and the Bell has not yet rung."

Hugh stood staring at her in poleaxed silence. Then he turned away, his face thunderous, and took the kettle off the fire. Madelon stayed a moment longer, glaring furiously at the older woman; but Lapin turned a granite gaze upon her, and Madelon turned away, flushing.

Dirk stared, paralyzed. Just one word from this she-leviathan, and a whole peasant army threw away a certain victory. In his mind's eye, he saw a vast and ready army, stretching across the length and breadth of the kingdom, armed and poised to strike —and frozen, immobilized in ice. Because a word had not been spoken, had not because it could not—because the lips that had to speak it had turned to rot and dust, five hundred years before.

A hand clasped his shoulder, jolting him out of his trance.

"It might be best if you would come with me," Father Fletcher suggested. "I know these woods and can lead you to a safe place."

Dirk raised his eyes, saw Gar and Madelon standing behind the priest. He looked out over the clearing, saw it almost empty, except for a few stragglers who slung packs on their backs while he watched, and a hundred brushwood shanties.

He turned back to Father Fletcher, nodded judiciously. "Yah. That might be a good idea."

Father Fletcher strode away toward the trees. Dirk glanced at Gar and Madelon, then turned and followed the priest.

CHAPTER 9

The rising sun found a party of four wandering down the King's Highway—an old hedge priest, a young woman in a dark, hooded robe, and two filthy madmen, crusted with dirt and with only a twist of loincloth for clothing. The one might have been very tall, if he ever stood straight; but he was hunched and shambling, shuffling down the roadway.

What the other lacked in height, he made up in energy. He bounded down the road capering and crowing, howling a hymn of glee to the rising sun.

"Quite well done, I'm sure," Father Fletcher said dryly, "but I think you do it with too little cause and too much will. I would ask you to remember that I am, after all, a Christian priest."

"Of course, Father," Dirk tossed back over his

shoulder, "but any good Christian would agree that only a madman would chant a hymn to the sun."

"Nonetheless, our good Father has a point," Madelon demurred. "True, we must be disguised from the King's patrols, and two madmen and a maiden bound for convent will scarcely be noticed in this land, if they travel under a priest's protection; but I would like to remind you that no Soldiers are watching at the moment."

Dirk brushed the objection away. "You don't understand the art of it. The true histrionicist must always be in character; you never know when you're going to have an audience."

"Ordinarily, I wouldn't find that argument too compelling," Gar demurred. "But, since three horsemen have just come into sight ahead of us, I must reluctantly grant it a certain validity."

Dirk looked up, startled, Far down the road, half-obscured by the morning mist and the sun behind them, three riders stood in silhouette.

"Be easy, my children." Father Fletcher seemed relaxed around a core of tension. "We are only two poor madmen and their grieving sister, journeying to a Bedlam house under the protection of a priest."

Dirk filed the fact for ready reference, and whirled around to begin the next act of "Salute to the Sun."

Halfway through the second stanza, a voice cried, "Hold!"

Just in time, too—Dirk had almost run out of lyrics.

He whirled about, one hand poised over his

head like a fountain-statue, staring wide-eyed at the Soldiers.

Father Fletcher came to a halt and looked up, mildly inquisitive. Gar kept shambling on; Madelon tugged at his arm, and he stopped, then turned, slowly, to gaze at the Soldiers with a vacant bovine stare.

The sergeant scowled down at them. "What have we here, Friar? Three geese, plucked bare by the parish?"

"Only two poor madmen, Sergeant," Father Fletcher intoned, "newly orphaned; and their saner, grieving sister."

Saner. Dirk wondered about that.

One of the troopers leaned down to yank Madelon's cowl back; rich auburn hair tumbled down. The Soldier whistled.

"Under my protection, of course," Father Fletcher murmured. The sergeant glared at the trooper, and the man drew back. Dirk was amazed; he hadn't realized the clergy had so much influence.

"And where would you be traveling to, Father?" The sergeant was measuring Gar with his eyes.

"Why, to the nearest Bedlam house, of course," Father Fletcher said easily. "The Hospice of Saint Orthicon, at Chambray."

"Three, they are," the second trooper growled, "and, if you straightened out the big one—"

"Pray do not attempt it," Father Fletcher murmured. "He becomes violent if you touch him."

The trooper eyed Gar's bulk, and moved his horse back a little.

"Well, what of it?" the first trooper growled. "Do we arrest them?"

Father Fletcher looked up in mild puzzlement. "What for? Surely these poor unfortunates could have harmed no one."

"I'm sure they could not have." The sergeant's sarcasm was thick. "But, ridiculous as it may seem, we Soldiers are bound to consider that even you, a man of the cloth, might be trying to smuggle dangerous criminals past us."

"No!" Father Fletcher was appropriately scandalized. "Is there really so little faith left among your superiors?"

"Even so," the sergeant lamented. "But—ours not to question why, Friar."

"Sergeant," the priest reproved him gently, "I am a man of peace."

Dirk thought about arrows and kept his mouth shut.

"My superiors, I fear, are not," the sergeant pointed out.

Father Fletcher's tone became more severe. "Sergeant, if you meddle with those under the protection of a priest, you earn the displeasure of the Almighty."

"There's some truth in that," the sergeant said thoughtfully. "But if we don't, we earn the displeasure of Lord Core—which is apt to come a little sooner than God's."

"But it doesn't last quite as long."

"There's some truth in that, too." The sergeant glowered down at Dirk, who had fallen into a rapt study of the grains of dust in the roadway.

Madelon looked up at him wide-eyed, almost adoring.

The sergeant straightened in the saddle, with an air of decision. "Well enough, then, Father—we won't interfere with the clergy. We'll let you take your charges to the Bedlam house."

"I thank you," Father Fletcher murmured.

"In fact," the sergeant went on, "our respect for your cloth is so great that we'll even escort you."

"Oh." Father Fletcher pursed his lips, thinking that one over for a moment. "I thank you greatly, but ... surely that is too much bother to ask of you."

"Not at all, not at all," the sergeant said affably. "After all, we couldn't have you being set on by outlaws, now, could we?"

The sun was setting as the priest brought the madmen to the Hospice of Saint Orthicon—with three steel-clad Soldiers behind him. Their sister kissed them a fond, tearful farewell at the door—and muttered between kisses, "Keep your hearts up, as well as you can. We'll get you out somehow—I just can't promise how soon."

Then she stood back, hand raised in parting, while the priest blessed them, and the attendants ushered them in, out of the sunlight—and into a dank, chilly gloom, filled with the smell of unwashed bodies and excrement.

They stopped in the doorway, involuntarily pulling back as a pandemonium of moans and wails hit them. Dirk's eyes fought to adapt to the gloom; there was only a little light, from a few small windows way up high on the walls—barred windows, set in granite thirty feet above them. By the time this modicum of sunlight filtered down to the floor, it had spread out to a sourceless, uneven murk, out of which rose islands of pallid bodies clothed in rags and filth. Some of the islands moved in a constant, slow churning.

The attendants pulled them forward, and, as they passed between rows of poor madmen lying on straw pallets, Dirk saw an occasional one whose movement was hurried, frenzied—and totally aimless; a kind of threshing pantomime of violence. Dirk tried to shrink away, inside his skin, away from them all; they filled the long, narrow room, standing, sitting, or lying against the walls. Each one had a chain, some on the ankle, some on the wrist; the other end of the chain was driven into the wall. He stared about him, horrified, following the attendant, feeling as though he was wading through a sea of groans, walls of despair, cries of rage, and shrill, gibbering laughter. Suddenly, he doubted if he could even make it through one night here. He could only stare, horrified, as the warder riveted a chain around his ankle and went away, leaving both of them chained between a Tradesman who crouched against the wall, glaring at an unseen persecutor and cursing steadily in a low, even voice; and a Farmer, squat and flabby, who sat hunched against the wall, munching slowly at a sore on the back of his hand.

"It's a madhouse," Dirk whispered, stunned.

"Yes." Gar swallowed heavily, his eyes bulging. "Not a mental hospital, not an insane asylum. A madhouse. The real, genuine medieval article. A Bedlam." He swallowed again, thickly.

"I don't know if I can even make it through one night here."

"Shut up," Gar snapped, his eyes burning. Cold sweat stood out on his brow.

Dirk frowned up at him, puzzled—and felt a sudden hollow fear, as he watched the anger bleach out of Gar's eyes, leaving only agony. The big guy looked like a wounded man fighting against a burning pain clawing inside him, able to hang on only because he knew the doctor was coming. "What's the matter with you?"

Gar swallowed thickly again and muttered, "The walls . . . agony . . . despair . . ." He turned on Dirk furiously. "Shut up, can't you? You're tearing my ears out!"

Dirk shrank back into a crouch, staring up at the big man as fear scooped out his entrails and jellied his legs. He hadn't been saying anything.

As the light faded, Gar sank back against the walls, lower and lower into a crouch, back plastered flat against the rough stone, staring bug-eyed up at the little, high window across from him, sweat trickling down his face in the chill.

When the sun had set, and the huge stone room was cloaked in twilight, a warder came by with bowls of food—a hunk of stale brown bread, a cup of water, and a bowl of gruel for each man. There were no spoons; the inmates ate with their fingers and drank the gruel, or spooned it up with their hands—or turned it upside-down over their heads.

Gar wouldn't touch his food. He sat on his heels, jaw clenched tight, eyes bulging, sweating. Dirk watched him, and wisely held his peace. At least, he thought it was wisdom.

Clank of keys; a warder stopped in front of Gar. Dirk looked up at a miniature gorilla, obviously chosen for the sensitivity and delicacy of his feelings. He scowled down at Gar. "Come, then—eat! We'll not have you wasting away, and robbing us of the penny a day the King gives us for you!"

But Gar just sat on his heels, staring off into space.

The attendant looked worried. With a shock, Dirk realized the Neanderthal actually had some dedication. He sat on his heels, staring into Gar's eyes. "Come, come, it's not so bad as that. Only eat, and hold onto life, and all will grow better."

Gar's throat muscles worked, but he stayed silent.

The warder scowled, and Dirk remembered that even the finest empathy can be blunted by the wrong environment. He screwed up his courage and reached over to give Gar a shake. "Nay then, coz! Will you not do a king's bidding? His Majesty bids you to eat—why, then, glad fellow, you were ever a man for the trencher! Come, 'tis a fat pullet, and wine from the King's own table!"

The warder's brow smoothed; he nodded approval. "Aye, there, good fellow, talk him into it, if you can."

"To be sure, Majesty, to be sure!" Dirk salaamed, turned to hiss into Gar's ear. "Come out

of it, idiot! What're you trying to do—get yourself
force-fed?"

Gar's head turned, slowly, almost mechanically,
as though it were separate from his body. His
voice was a hoarse, grating whisper. "The
walls . . ."

"Yeah, the walls. Well, the hell with the walls!
Eat the damn food, man, or they'll ram it down
your throat!"

Gar's eyes stayed glassy.

Dirk scowled to hide abiding fear. "Come on!
What's the matter with you?" He slapped Gar's
cheek and cried, "Wake, coz! For the moon, that
startled into flight, the sun before him, from the
lake of night . . ."

He hoped Khayyam's ghost wasn't listening; but
it seemed to work. Something seemed to click behind Gar's eyes; they seemed to focus suddenly.
He turned, frowning, to stare at the bowl of food,
Then he shuddered and began to eat.

The warder nodded approvingly, climbing to his
feet. "You're a proper man, though a daft one," he
said to Dirk. "Care for your brother, then. You
seem to have wits enough for that, at least."

At the far end of the chamber, a man screamed,
rearing up to claw at the air, straining against the
chain harnessing his shoulders. The warder looked
up in alarm and leaped over to him. Another attendant slammed into the man from the other side.
They grabbed the ancient's arms, wrestled them
down around behind him. "Come then, old Jean,
come," the warder growled in a tone that was

meant to soothe. "It'll pass, Jean; it always has.
They'll go away . . ."

Dirk turned away, stomach rebelling, as the old
man collapsed, sobbing, sliding back down the
wall, drooling and trembling. Dirk looked up at
Gar, and felt alarm grab him. The big man had frozen again, into stone, eyes squeezed shut, lips
parted, breath hissing in and out. Sweat dripped
from his temples.

Dirk scowled. "Hey, then! What's the matter
with you?"

"I can't . . ." Gar swallowed thickly. His eyes
opened; he gave his head a quick shake. "I can't
. . . not much longer . . ."

With a heave, he rolled forward to his knees,
rolled back to sit on his heels with only the soles
of his feet in contact with the floor. "The stones,
dammit! I can't take them! The clamor in here is
bad enough, but the stones! Ten times worse—it's
too much! They . . . the emotions . . . screaming
. . . rage, despair, the . . ." He swallowed, and was
stone again, his mouth moving as though trying to
force sound out.

Dirk felt a thrill of panic, and under it, the dread
certainty that, if Gar hadn't been crazy when he
came in here, he would be when he went out. This
was just the place for it.

He tried to calm himself—maybe it was all an
act. *Too good an act,* something inside him prod-
ded. He'd heard of such cases—actors who really
began to believe they were the characters. And if
the character was insane . . .

The gloom in the chamber deepened into night.

A single lamp burned at the far end of the hall, where two warders sat playing cards. The inmates lapsed into slumber—most of them, at least. A few began to moan, rocking themselves from side to side. Several lay huddled against the wall, sobbing with the tearing agony of total despair. Now and again one sprang to his feet with a scream, arms windmilling as he fought invisible demons. The two warders were at his side almost before the first long scream was ended, hedging him in and keeping pace with him as he turned, so he couldn't harm his neighbors, until the spasm passed and the patient sank into a sobbing puddle.

It was a night of nightmare, lit only by the flickering rays of one feeble lamp, filled with wails and the howling of demons—and Gar reached over to slap Dirk on the arm. "Talk—anything! Give me bits, anything to chew on."

Dirk stared.

Then he shook himself; he could remember when he'd needed distraction. "Okay. Obviously there's no psychology here, not even an attempt to understand any of what's in their minds; the authorities stick on the label 'mad,' and don't question any further. After all, everyone knows there's absolutely no understanding of a madman's mind, right?"

Gar nodded. "Right. But—common sense, at least? Her!"

He jabbed a finger out into the gloom; Dirk looked across the way, and saw a girl, maybe twenty, who would have been beautiful anywhere else—hair golden under the crust of filth, heart-shaped face, high, full breasts and a tapering waist, which were easy to see, because her gray tunic was ripped in a dozen places, shredded. Her eyes were glazed, vacant; and Dirk might have been wrong, but he thought Gar winced as he looked at her. "Don't they wonder why a beautiful girl would despair?" Gar grated. "Can't they see why—"

The girl erupted in a sudden, soundless fury, her face contorted in a silent scream, ripping and tearing at her clothes as though they were on fire.

Gar snapped his head down, huge fingers digging into his scalp, eyes squeezed shut, body rolled into a tight ball balanced on the balls of his feet, until the girl had relaxed into silent, shuddering sobs. Then, slowly, he looked up, breathing hoarsely.

"What's the matter?" Dirk said gently. "Couldn't you even stand the sight of her?"

Gar shook his head, looking up wide-eyed, gasping. "No. It was . . . what was going on in her mind."

Dirk frowned. What kind of figure of speech was that?

"It gets worse." Gar waved vaguely toward the right, past Dirk, not looking. "There's a man down that way who's watching her like a gorgon, and his tongue is thick in his dripping mouth."

Dirk turned and looked, frowning. He could just barely make out the humped body of a Merchant who sat tailor fashion, leaning elbows on knees, staring at the girl in rapt fascination, lips parted, a thin thread of saliva hanging from his lower lip.

Gar hadn't even looked. How had he known? Noticed the guy earlier, probably.

"Don't they see what she's doing to him?" Gar rasped. "The fantasies he's building around her, the constant tension she keeps him at?"

Dirk turned back to him, scowling. "How do you know that?"

Gar shook his head impatiently, went on as though he hadn't heard. "And there's one down beyond him, gene damage—from inbreeding?— with only the stump of a leg, and it's not amputation, born that way—and with a piece of his mind missing, too; born without a left frontal lobe."

Dirk peered through the murk, but this one he couldn't see at all. Could Gar have *that* much sharper eyes?

No. Impossible.

He turned back to Gar. "You can hear their thoughts, can't you? And you can't shut them out—not this many, this strong."

Gar shook his head, staring, glassy-eyed. "That's not what's doing it. Not just that much, alone. It's the stones, you see." He rose into a crouch, shifting from foot to foot, picking first one off the floor, then the other, in a sort of shuffling dance. "It's been stored in the stones of this place, year upon year, agony and despair, piling up into centuries, and *I can't get away from them*!"

Dirk glanced nervously at the warders. "Keep your voice down."

"If I just didn't have to touch them, if I could get something between me and them, a good thick board maybe, but no, that wouldn't help, they're coming at me from all sides, pushing and shoving into my head, and I can't . . . can't . . . *I can't take it!*" He whirled about, clutching at his head, spinning around against the chain. "Stop them, damn it, stop them; shut them up! *I can't take it!* I've got to get . . . *out of here!*" He grabbed the chain in both hands and set his foot against the wall. *"I can't take it!"*

Dirk jumped to his feet, remembering the bars in the arena, as the warders came running up. Gar's body convulsed, straightening out against the chain; metal groaned, screeched—and the warders piled onto him. One threw an arm around his throat, the other bear-hugged his arms to his sides. The giant whirled about, roaring, shaking them like a terrier with rats; then three more warders out of the bunk-room piled on, bearing him down under sheer body-weight. Dirk plastered himself back against the wall, staring, horrified. Then he shook himself, and dived into the churning mass of bodies, throwing his arms around a warder, yanked him loose—and Gar surged up with a bellow, spewing warders out like a volcano, blasting out one huge, blood-congealing shriek that lanced through Dirk's ears down his spine. It echoed, and faded, but the dim light showed a huge, stiff silhouette bowed over backward, mouth gaping, vacant eyes staring up. Then, slowly, the human spring uncoiled, and slowly, slowly, folded in on itself, crumbling; then, in a sudden cascade, collapsed, sprawling trembling limbs and bowed head to the floor.

The warders stood back, watching, faces locked in lugubrious tragedy.

Dirk stepped forward, knelt, reached out a hand toward the huge body.

"Does he live?" one of the warders rasped.

Dirk touched the massive shoulder tentatively, then grasped, shook it.

The huge body lifted itself up agonizingly, one leg straight out, the other folded under him. The torso lifted up, leaned back, backward, until shoulders and head fell back against the wall. The great arms lay limp, hands upturned and empty on the floor. The eyes stared upward, blank.

The warders stood in a silent semicircle, their faces grave. Then one frowned, leaning down, and slapped Gar's face. "Now, then, answer—do you hear me?"

The face rocked to the side with the blow; the eyes stayed empty.

"Gone," another warder muttered thickly. All their faces seemed to gel; they turned away, slowly, back toward the light. The warder who had spoken stood over Gar, then turned to Dirk. "He's gone, then, lad. Do you know what that means?"

Dirk remembered he was supposed to be mad. His eyebrows shot up in surprise; he managed a smile. "Aye, Nuncle! Why, 'tis my brother!"

For a moment, the warder's face seemed to soften. "Aye, poor idiot. But is he here, still?"

Dirk turned to look at Gar in surprise. "Why, wherefore not? He is as he has always been, since the day of his birth. Except . . ." He rolled forward onto his knees, thrusting his face to within an inch of Gar's, peering at him from every side while he fought down a sudden surge of nausea. Then he looked up at the guard with a delighted, beatific smile ". . . except he is bigger now."

The warder stood silent for a moment, his mouth working. Then a sad smile won over his face; he turned his head from side to side. "Aye, lad. Aye, he is bigger now. Aye, that is all." He started to reach out to Dirk, as though to pat his head, but thought better of it, and pulled his hand back. "Aye, care for him, then. He is your brother." He turned away, going back to the light.

Dirk watched after him, staring at the feeble glow of the lamp—anything to avoid looking at Gar. Yes, Gar was his brother now. There was a bond between them—now, when it was too late.

And the warder was right again—Gar was gone, or his mind, at least. Catatonic, probably—he wasn't an expert. He couldn't be sure.

And, now that it was too late, he understood. Gar was a telepath; he could "hear" other people's thoughts; but not just that. He could "hear" the thoughts of the dead, too—if he was in the room where the dead had lived. There was a word for it, "psychometry," and even a theory to back it up— that strong emotions made minuscule changes in the electrical potentials of objects within range; and a special kind of mind, "scanning" those objects even centuries later, could still resonate tiny echoes of those long-lost emotions and, through them, of the people who had held those emotions. A really good psychometrist was supposed to be able to pick up a rock, or a cup, or anything, and describe the personality of the person to whom it belonged and the main events in that person's life.

And here, in a room that had never held anything but the mentally ill, and had held generations of them, for centuries ... A room in which there had never been anything but strong emotions, and most of them negative ... For a moment, Dirk felt a touch of what Gar must have gone through and shuddered, automatically pinching the sensation off, closing it away from his mind. Gar must have thought he had walked into hell. Presumably a telepath—or any kind of a psi—built up automatic defenses against psionic input, a kind of blocking or closure that would automatically shut out any signals he didn't want to hear, the way most people can be in a room where music is playing and never really be aware of it, until the music stops. But even the strongest dam can be breached. Or overwhelmed ...

And what happens then, when the floodwaters come booming in, and the storm churns throughout the land? Why, you find yourself a bolt-hole, some watertight place in the bowels of the earth, and you go lock yourself in and pull the key after you, so that nothing can ever get to you, ever, ever again.

Somewhere, some cul-de-sac corner of Gar's brain, the giant's mind had retreated into, pulling the hole in after it, leaving the rest of his brain clear, for the demons to play in ...

Suddenly, frantically, Dirk ached for daybreak.

CHAPTER 10

At long last, the huge cell began to lighten with false dawn, gray light filtering down to soothe shuddering forms with cool lucidity. The warders stretched, grumbling, ready to strike out for home as soon as the day shift came in.

A huge, booming knocking sounded from the outside door.

Dirk looked up, hope suddenly spurting in him. Was this it, so soon? But how could they possibly have pulled the army together so quickly? And what about the Bell not having rung?

The chief warder scowled and gestured to one of his men. The attendant turned away, into the tunnel leading to the outside door; Dirk heard the huge bolts grind back, the hinges grate open.

There was the murmur of voices; then the attendant came back, looking singularly baffled. He muttered something to the chief warder, who scowled, puzzled. The attendant held out a sheet of parchment; the chief warder spread it out flat on the desk, scowling over it, lips moving to silently piece letters together. Then he looked up, shrugged in resignation, and nodded. The attendant motioned to two others, picked up a maul and a cold chisel, and strode down the room toward Gar and Dirk.

Dirk's heart hammered. Never had he wanted out of a place so dearly as he wanted out of this one.

The warders came to a halt in front of Dirk and Gar, and Dirk went limp with relief. Two went to stand to either side of him, ready to catch hold, while the third kneeled down, set the chisel against the chain, and cut through it with two blows. He stood, shaking his head, mystified. "Why His Lordship wants them is more than I can see."

" 'Tis not for us to question," one of his mates growled. "Come, let's get it done." He turned to Dirk, jerked his thumb. "Up on your feet, fellow."

Dirk stood, not understanding what was going on, but not about to worry about it, either. At the last moment, he remembered the act. "Praised be the sun, moon, and stars! The ransom is paid; the King wanders free! Praised be the deliverers, praised be—"

"Yes, yes, I know," the warder soothed. "Stand there like a good fellow, while we get your brother free."

The first warder set his chisel against Gar's chain while the other two watched warily. The maul swung, the chain dropped free; but Gar still sat like a statue, staring forward.

"Up!" The man with the chisel scowled down at the giant, braced for anything—but nothing happened.

Dirk dropped down beside the big man. "Why, come then, Brother! We must up and away! The night is gone; the sun wheels toward day!" He slung the giant's arm over his shoulder, braced himself for a hard haul, and pushed himself to his feet—and almost fell over backward. He'd expected to have to haul the giant up by main strength; but impulse was all the huge body needed; it rose by itself, willingly. But, standing, it just stood.

Dirk looked up at the warders. "Come now, I'll lead my brother. Take us out to the Lord of the Ransom; take us out from the castle of durance vile, ere the ogre returns."

The warders traded a commiserating glance and turned to escort them out.

They went down between the two rows of inmates. The ones who were awake looked up, saw two of their number going toward freedom, and set up a chorus of howls, wailing for liberty. The warders stiffened, but their steps never slackened. Inmates surged to their feet, clawing at the air and bellowing, but the warders plodded on at the same even pace, past the chief warder and into the passageway to the outside door. Dirk breathed a silent sigh of relief, realized he was shaking. He wondered how the warders could take it, and realized it was a miracle they'd managed to keep so much human feeling.

The warder wrenched back the bolts and swung the door open. Dirk squinted against the dazzling sunlight, let them lead him out. As his eyes adjusted, he looked up . . .

. . . and saw a young page with five Soldiers, in Lord Core's livery.

Suddenly the Bedlam seemed a very pleasant place to be, warm and secure . . .

Then his eyes finished adjusting; he looked more closely at the page's face and recognized Madelon. He took a deep breath and decided he'd never been so glad to see a woman in his life.

Dirk turned to look more closely at the five horsemen and recognized Hugh and a couple of his other old acquaintances from the arena. He was sure he'd seen the other two around the campfire the night before.

"Get them up on their horses, lad," Hugh growled. "The Lord grows impatient."

"Aye, right quickly." Madelon turned to the warder. "I thank ye, goodmen. I shall bear word to His Lordship of your excellent night's lodging for his guests."

The warder looked a little worried, but he shrugged stubbornly. "We do what we can, young Gentleman. We are not, after all, given overmuch to do it with."

Public institutions were the same everywhere, Dirk decided.

"I will speak to His Lordship of it," Madelon promised. "Thanks, and farewell."

She led Dirk to a waiting horse as the warders shrugged and went back into the Bedlam. The door slammed shut with a hollow echo as Dirk swung into the saddle; he breathed a huge sigh of relief.

Then he looked down and saw the giant standing, blankly, in front of a Percheron. The horse eyed him and snorted uneasily.

Madelon frowned. "Come then, mount! Drop your pretense; no one watches but us."

"Don't worry about that part," Dirk said dryly, "he's not faking." He dismounted and went to Gar, picked up a huge foot, and set it in a stirrup. Then he lifted the two, massive hands—he hadn't known a human arm could weigh so much—and balanced them on the saddle-horn. He stepped back to survey his handiwork; the huge body still stood, unblinking, poised on one foot. Dirk sighed, went around behind, and gave him an upward shove. Reflex took over; the giant body swung up. Dirk caught the right leg and swung it up and over the horse's rump, and Gar sprawled down onto the horse's back. Dirk scurried around to the far side, secured the right foot in its stirrup, and came back to Madelon and Hugh, mopping his brow. "I think he'll do now. Once he's in position . . ." He broke off, seeing the looks on their faces.

Then Madelon turned away and mounted. He followed suit, thinking about the look on her face. Stricken, he could understand—but devastated?

"Away!" Hugh growled. He swung his horse about. The party turned away after him, toward the forest. Dirk looked back over his shoulder, at the gloomy, granite building, reflecting that, if the revolution succeeded, he had an excellent purpose for Lord Core's chateau.

As they reached the shade of the trees, a mule trotted out from a thicket to join them. Dirk nodded to its rider with a smile of thanks. "A timely rescue, Father. How did you manage it?"

"I? Not at all." Father Fletcher smiled, amused. " 'Twas Madelon's scheme."

Dirk glanced at the topic of discussion and decided she wasn't in a mood to explain. "Where'd she get the uniforms?"

Hugh pursed his lips and looked up at the leaves. "Why, as to that, a few of Lord Core's men seem to have lost their way in the wood t'other night; and, taking pity on the poor lads, we thought to give them a home . . ."

"Under the roots," Dirk suggested.

Hugh shrugged. "It may have been something of the sort. Of course, I would know nothing of such details. Naetheless, there were their liveries and armor, doing no good to any man, being far too cumbersome for forest travel. So our lasses worked quickly with their needles, and we had a page's suit to fit our likely lad, here. . . ." He nodded toward Madelon; she looked up, frowning, seeming to notice them for the first time. "For the rest . . ." he shrugged. " 'Twas nothing at all to draw up a letter and draw Lord Core's seal on it. After that, you know the tale yourself."

"But *I* do not," Father Fletcher said ruefully. "You shall have to tell it to me, friend Dulain, when we have more leisure—or perhaps yourself, my great friend?" He rode ahead to catch at Gar's arm, gave him a shake. The great body rocked, came back to an even keel, and rode steadily ahead.

Dirk saw the sick realization coming into the priest's eyes. He nodded. "It was timely rescue, Father; you came as quickly as we could hope for. But even had you come at midnight, you would have come too late."

"But what has happened to him?" the priest whispered.

Dirk shook his head. "There was madness all about him, Father. It seeped into him, claimed him. Where his mind has gone, I do not know—but it's gone."

"Tell us the manner of it," Madelon whispered hoarsely. Dirk glanced at the agony of her face, glanced away—and despised himself for a bitter stab of jealousy. "He went into a rage, went stiff, and collapsed. Since then, he hasn't spoken a word, and he's looked—like that."

Madelon looked at Gar again and looked away, squeezing her eyes shut. "If only we could have come earlier . . ."

"He was gone by two hours after sunset," Dirk said quickly. "Any ordinary man could make it through at least a night in there. How could you have known? I certainly didn't."

She flashed him a look of gratitude, and there was something of appeal in it, which surprised him. In fact, it tied his tongue, but he managed to smile back at her. For a moment, their glances held; then she turned away, with a shuddering breath, and set her face toward the depths of the forest. "We must ride. Core's Soldiers must certainly have told him of the two madmen they left at the house of Saint Orthicon. Only good luck kept him from coming before us."

"Aye," Hugh growled. "He'll come behind us, never fear, when the warders tell him the tale."

"Yes." Father Fletcher nodded. "And he'll call for dogs when he follows our trail to the forest."

"How about it, Hugh?" Dirk said softly. "This is your country. We can run if we want to, but sooner or later we'll have to hide."

Hugh scowled. "I've thought of it—and there is only one place near to here."

The other outlaws looked up at him, startled—almost, Dirk might think, scandalized. Then foreboding settled onto their faces, and one muttered, "Hugh—desecration brings curses."

"Is it desecration to sing at the tomb of a minstrel?" Hugh demanded.

"But we bring the sound of battle," the outlaw objected.

Hugh flashed him a grin, and rode on.

From the brightness of the light filtering down through the trees, Dirk could tell it was midday.

The outlaw Hugh had sent riding back to scout the trail came crashing out of the underbrush. "They're onto us, Hugh. A mile behind, I could hear the hounds."

Hugh nodded, and reined in. "We've gone as far as we can with horses as is. Come, free your beasts—and, friend Dulain, do you lead our silent one."

They all dismounted, unbridled their horses, bound the bridles to the cantles.

"Away!" Hugh cried, slapping his horse's rump. "Be off to your freedom—and leave a good, clear trail for hounds to follow!"

The horse leaped away into the underbrush, and its fellows followed it, inspired by a chorus of shouts from the outlaws. Then they stood, silent, listening to the crashing of the beasts fade away into the quiet, ever-present rustle of the noontime forest.

Dirk looked around him, wondering where they were to hide. They stood on a slope, heavily covered with trees, but with the underbrush thinning, because of the rocky outcrops, which seemed to be growing more frequent. Presumably, there were caves somewhere about—but he certainly couldn't see any. The leafy trees were growing fewer, and the pines were more frequent.

"Up, then!" Hugh turned his face upslope, grinning. "Ye who are new to our forest, try to keep your steps as much as you can to the rock—no sense to give our hunters any more aid than we need."

One of the outlaws cut down a pine bough, and slashed and cut at a tree trunk with it. Dirk frowned, not understanding; but he followed Hugh, leading Gar, trying to guide the big body's feet to rocky steps—and saw the purpose of the bruised bough. The outlaw followed them backwards, dusting the ground behind him with a branch that oozed sap and odor. It might not fool the dogs at all—but then again, it might.

They had been climbing for about fifteen minutes when Hugh suddenly stopped, holding up a hand. "Hist!"

The whole party stopped dead, necks craned around and ears straining. Far in the distance, so faint it might have been imagination, came a burbling yapping.

"Core's dogs," Madelon stated.

Hugh nodded grimly. "They have made good time."

Madelon's mouth set. She threw back her shoulders and stepped ahead. "We had best move quickly, then."

"There." Hugh pointed upward. "That bar of shadow."

Dirk looked upward. There was an overhang of rock about a hundred yards upslope. He nodded. "They might even pass us by."

They started hiking again, with renewed vigor. Gar stumbled and slipped, but his body kept up with them. They broke out of the trees and pushed upward over scraggly grass with more and more rock. As they came closer, Dirk could make out the dim outline of a cave mouth beneath the overhang.

Then they forged in under the overhang and into the cave. It was low, barely tall enough for a man, and Dirk had to pull down on Gar's arm to make the great body stoop.

"It grows chill," Hugh grumbled. He took off his cloak and slung it over Dirk's shoulders. "Do not argue, my friend. We can ill afford a sneeze, now."

Dirk bit back a protest and pulled the cloak more tightly about his shoulders. "Thanks, Hugh." One of the outlaws took off his cloak and threw it over Gar's back.

Father Fletcher had slipped ahead and led the way with the air of a man retracing familiar ground. Dirk glanced at his companions and frowned; there was a taut, leashed eagerness about them, overlaid with awe. Just where had they come to, anyway?

The priest led the way to the back of the cave, his dark gray robes growing fainter and fainter as they went further from the cave mouth. Dirk could scarcely see him. Then he *couldn't* see him, and felt a moment of panic before he realized the old man had just taken an odd turn.

"Stoop!" Hugh muttered, standing aside; and Dirk saw a cleft in the rock, perhaps four feet high and three wide. It took some maneuvering to cramp Gar through, but they managed it, sideways. Dirk stopped and took a breath on the far side, while he waited for the others to come through, and realized with surprise that he could still see. There was light, very faint, seeping down from above.

"Up!" Hugh ordered; and Father Fletcher's voice called down softly. "The way is clear." So they set out again—climbing, this time; the floor sloped up sharply. Moreover, it was very rough; Dirk stumbled a few times, and he had quite a job keeping Gar from falling. The passage turned as they climbed in a long, shallow spiral. Then the light brightened, and the passage widened, its far wall washed with gloomy twilight. Dirk suddenly realized what a great defensive position this was; a single man could hold it against an army—while he lasted. Somehow, he suspected it wasn't entirely coincidence. He stepped up behind Hugh and turned the corner.

They came out into a sort of natural gallery—a broad, shallow cave, hung with stalactites. Off to the right, a broad limestone arch admitted a startling shaft of sunlight that charged the walls with a glory of rainbow coruscations. Dirk stopped dead, involuntarily catching his breath. "On, on!" Madelon urged behind him. Dirk frowned—there was too much eagerness in her voice—and Father Fletcher stood beside the limestone arch, beckoning, his eyes alight with something like triumph.

Hugh crossed to him, his steps quick. Dirk followed, with reluctance. He turned to look through the arch . . .

It was a natural cathedral, a vast semicircular cavern, its ceiling lost in shadows, its walls of sunlight lanced in from fissures high on the walls, meeting in a pool of light in the center of the chamber.

In that pool lay the bones of a man.

He lay on a huge stone bier, a great roughly-dressed slab of granite three feet high and eight long. The skeleton seemed almost as large as its bed. He'd been a giant of a man—seven feet tall, or nearly, and three feet across the shoulders. But he had been laid low. The left side of the skull was crushed in, the rib cage was shattered; the pelvis was cracked across, and each of the long bones of arms and legs had been broken at least twice. It was brown and crusted with age.

Beside it lay an eight-foot quarterstaff, three inches thick and bound with brass at the tips, and again where a man that size would naturally place his hands. It was broken in half; the cracked ends lay several inches apart.

Dirk stood staring, awed by the solemn, serene, natural beauty of the cavern.

Then, slowly, he moved forward, tugging at Gar's hand. The giant shambled after him. Madelon came forward past him, to kneel at the foot of the bier. One by one, the outlaws followed her; even Father Fletcher came to kneel.

Dirk came up behind Madelon, to stand brooding down, beginning to understand what he was up against. Superstition was one thing; but when it assumed the proportions of a religion, it was well-nigh unbeatable.

Madelon looked up slowly, her face grave. "You wished to find our leader. Here he lies."

Dirk stood looking down at her; then he closed his eyes and turned away.

"I guess your thoughts," Father Fletcher said softly behind him. "Be assured—this is DeCade. That word has come down to us from those who laid him here. Then, too, who else would be so great, with each bone of his body broken? And who else could lie by that staff?"

Dirk let that sink in a moment; then he turned thoughtfully to look at the staff. It was truly a staff for a giant. The brass bands that must have served as handholds were seven inches wide. Dirk's brows knit. That was strange—metal handholds wouldn't provide much friction. And the broken ends. Dirk knelt down, to take a closer look. There were little bits of something gleaming in there. He reached out a finger ...

"Death!" Hugh swore, catching his arm, and Father Fletcher seconded him. "There is a curse on that staff, friend Dulain."

Dirk lifted his head and turned to look straight into the priest's eyes. "I don't ... believe ... in curses."

"Believe in this one," the priest advised. "He who tries to bear DeCade's staff—he who seeks to join those broken halves—will die." He raised a hand to forestall Dirk's retort. "This is no idle threat, my friend. It has happened three times over the centuries. Three times, men who have thought they were worthy to take up DeCade's staff and lead us, have tried; and three times, lightning has struck them down where they stood."

Dirk started a sarcastic reply, but somehow it got caught.

"It is death," Hugh agreed, scowling.

And Dirk remembered that, even if he didn't believe in curses, these people did. If he wanted to stay on good terms with them, he'd have to observe their taboos. His mouth drew into a thin, straight line; he closed his eyes, nodding. "Don't worry. I won't touch it."

Then he bent over, to peer more closely at the ragged ends of the staff. A tiny glint of gold; another, and another ... He peered into the other broken end, saw similar metallic glints, spaced equally around the circumference, and a larger one in the center. He nodded thoughtfully. Electrical contacts, probably for molecular circuits ... No, they hadn't had those five hundred years ago, but they'd had integrated circuits, and, as he remembered, they'd even then managed them on a microscopic scale. Three inches thick, eight feet long ... Yes, you could pack a whale of a lot of circuitry in that volume—enough for a computer. Not a very intelligent one, but still ... Yes, DeCade's staff had been powerful medicine once. Very powerful.

And—suddenly—he believed in the curse. Capacitors could be pretty small, too; and so could atomic batteries. Put the wrong contact together, and ... He stood up with a shudder. "Don't worry, Father. I'll leave that thing alone."

The priest breathed a huge sigh of relief. "I am very glad to hear it, my friend; for you must stay here, you and Madelon and your great friend, until Lord Core and his troops have ridden far by."

Dirk frowned. "Won't we all?".

Hugh stood, shaking his head. "We have come only to kneel in DeCade's presence, to refresh ourselves and renew our resolve. Now we must return below to watch, so that if the hunters come too near, we can strike out across open ground and lead them away from this place."

"But if you do, they'll catch you."

Hugh looked hard into his eyes. "They must not

find this place, friend Dulain. If we die, then we die."

Dirk stared. Then he shook himself out of it. "Then why shouldn't Gar and I die with you? We're the ones they're looking for."

Hugh held his gaze. "I am not entirely a fool, friend Dulain. Of the two of us, I know which can be replaced by any man, and which cannot."

He held Dirk's eyes a moment longer; then he turned and marched out, his outlaws behind him.

Father Fletcher lingered. "I will go down with them and return to tell you when the way is clear. Do you care for the giant, your friend." Then he turned away through the stone arch, and was gone.

Dirk looked after him a moment, then found a handy boulder and sat down with a sigh, letting the worries roll off him. He looked up at Gar, where the giant sat not far from the bier, staring at the skeleton with unseeing eyes. Walls filled with the echoes of torment had driven his mind into hiding. Dirk wondered what echoes these walls contained.

A rustle of cloth, and Dirk looked up to see Madelon sitting gracefully beside him. "Yes," she murmured, watching Gar. "It tears at your heart, does it not? A man so full of life, so proud and so vigorous, turned to less than a babe in a single night."

A stab of guilt lanced Dirk; he hadn't been brooding over that one at all. "It almost seems he should've died. It might've been kinder."

She squeezed her eyes shut, nodding, and clasped his hand. Dirk felt a hot sizzle of jealousy, and wondered just how much feeling she had had for the big man.

She looked up at him. "How did it come about?"

Dirk's mouth twisted as though he'd tasted aloes. "It's an ugly story . . ." Then he looked fully at Gar, and broke off, grabbing her hand.

She turned and looked, frowning; then she stared, too. Gar had picked up a pebble, was holding it a foot from his face, staring at it. As they watched, he replaced it, slowly and methodically, and selected another.

"Can his mind be returning?" she breathed.

Dirk nodded slowly. "I think it is." He turned to her, smiling. "It's the peace of this place; it's never known anything but reverent thoughts."

"Thoughts?" She frowned, puzzled. "What has that to do with his madness?"

"I think he's a psychometrist," Dirk said slowly. "He hears the thoughts stored in the walls of a room, the feelings of the people who've been there, *all* the people who've ever been there. And, if you put a man like that in a Bedlam, where there've never been anything but feelings of rage, despair, terror, and confusion—"

"Why, most surely he would go mad!" she breathed, staring into his eyes; and he saw the horror coming up in hers.

"Not a madness of terror," he explained quickly. "I think it's more that his mind has retreated, backed off into a corner of his brain, and walled it off to protect himself until he's in a more livable environment."

"Why, yes." Her eyes widened in wonder. "And he is in such a place now, is he not? A place of peace, where generations of churls have come to pay homage. . . ."

Dirk nodded. "The peace and reverence of the place are drawing him out." He looked back at Gar over his shoulder; the big man had leaned forward to lay his hand on a giant quartz crystal.

Dirk slammed a fist into his palm. "But, damn it! I should've seen it coming! I had a dozen leads—how he managed to find me in the first place, how the questions he asked dovetailed with what I was thinking at the time, how quickly he picked up the prisoners' customs in the arena, how easily he was able to fit into their attitudes in just a few days, to the point where they chose him leader! That should've told me he was a telepath, at least—and I should've realized what would happen to him in a Bedlam!"

"No man could have foreseen that much."

Dirk looked up, startled by the warmth and gentleness of her voice. Her eyes were filled with tears, but her face had a look of tenderness that almost shocked him, and took his breath away by the extraordinary beauty it gave her. "Do not blame yourself," she murmured. "No man could have foreseen it, and even if you had, there was nothing you could have done. This is not your burden; do not borrow it."

He stared into her eyes for a long, long moment; then, slowly, he leaned forward, and took her lips within his own in a long, full kiss. He closed his eyes, blocked out the light; there was nothing except the touch of her lips under his, their thawing, responding, beginning to demand, craving, full and moist, parted . . .

Suddenly her lips were gone; he heard her scream, "No!" His head snapped up, eyes wide open.

He saw Gar on his knees by the skeleton, the two halves of the broken staff in his hands, scowling intently as he tried to bring them together, like a child with a puzzle.

"Stop!" Madelon screamed again, and Dirk broke into a scrambling run, throwing himself across the chamber, remembering just how much power a few grams of uranium could put out . . .

With ponderous precision, Gar brought the two jagged ends together.

Thunder crashed and white-hot light seared the cavern, picking the giant up like a twig and slamming him into the wall.

Then the cavern was dim and silent again, with the memory of thunder fading, and a crumpled heap at the base of a wall, lying very still.

Madelon gave a sobbing gasp and ran to kneel by Gar, chafing his wrists and moaning. Dirk came up behind her and stood looking down, his face a mask, sour guilt rising up to block his throat. Again, he should have seen it coming. For a few minutes, he hadn't watched—only a few minutes—but that had been all it took.

"He lives," Madelon said fiercely, "but for how long, I cannot tell."

"Of course he's alive." Dirk was surprised at the lack of emotion in his own voice. "The current—

the lightning—didn't touch him. It just knocked him off his feet." He scowled at Gar's hands, still clasped around the huge brass bands. Then he saw the center of the staff, saw it was whole; he couldn't even see where the break had been. And suddenly he wasn't so sure about Gar's health. If those brass bands were connected to the circuitry . . . He looked back up at Gar's face—and froze, galvanized.

Gar was watching him.

Dirk's hand closed on Madelon's shoulder like a vise. She looked up at Gar—and gasped.

The big man's face was contracted, frowning, squinting against pain, but studying Dirk through it, as though trying to decide whether he were a locust or a ladybug.

Alarm clanged in Dirk's head, bracing him for defense. Then he frowned, remembering the big man was his friend. If he had his wits back, so much the better. . . . Wasn't it?

"You are alive." Madelon breathed the words, unbelieving. "You are the only man ever to take up DeCade's staff—and live!"

Gar transferred his gaze to her. His mouth tightened into a scornful smile. "Small wonder."

Dirk stiffened; it wasn't Gar's voice. It was deeper and somehow harsher.

"In truth, no wonder at all," the strange voice went on. "For I *am* DeCade."

CHAPTER 11

Dirk stood like brass, adrenaline shooting through him. Chaotic images whirled through his mind, ragtag bits of memory; and, with a creeping sense of doom, he began to suspect what had happened. .

The giant squeezed his eyes shut, pressing a hand to his head. "My head aches as though a thousand miners were swinging their picks inside it!" He glared up at Dirk, then suddenly heaved himself to his feet. He lurched forward, swaying, propped himself with his staff, glaring down at Dirk. The glare turned to a puzzled frown. "I've a memory . . . that you are my friend. Or have done me a friend's services, at least." He turned to Madelon, who knelt transfixed, staring up at him, lips parted. "And you also," the strange voice rumbled. DeCade closed his eyes, pressing a hand to his head again. "So many memories . . . that I knew nothing of. Of a life beyond the sky, on a strange world . . . So many worlds, swarming through the night sky . . ." His eyes snapped open, glaring at Dirk. "This body was a lord!"

Suddenly Dirk was on his guard. It was all gibberish, but things had a terrifying feeling of making sense, somewhere underneath it all. He'd better move slowly, and with all due caution—or undue, for that matter. "He was not a lord of this world. And do you not also remember that he came here to help us overthrow the Lords?"

It had to be the clearest case of megalomania he'd ever seen. Either that, or . . .

Gar/DeCade frowned, fingertips pressing his temples. "I . . . do remember . . . something of the sort . . ."

"Then you must also remember that he has already struck one blow against the Lords," Dirk said quickly, "and lost his mind because of it."

The giant nodded painfully, wincing at the fire in his head. Dirk studied him carefully. The voice, the stance, the mannerisms—the whole personality had changed. If this *was* a split personality with some crazy sort of delusion of grandeur, it was an extremely thorough one. But it had to be that; he couldn't really have become invested with DeCade's personality.

Could he?

"He *is* DeCade," Madelon whispered, her voice trembling, scarcely daring to believe. Then her face lit up with triumph and joy. "He *is* DeCade—and he has come back, as the Wizard foretold!"

"The Wizard . . ." Something connected in Dirk's mind, the missing piece, and suddenly he believed, too. Completely. Implicitly. With reservations; but all in all, more thoroughly than Madelon did.

DeCade looked up and saw the huge skeleton on the bier. He stood a moment, staring; then he stalked over to it, a little unsteadily, and stood over it, leaning on his staff, staring down at the shattered bones. Then, slowly, he stretched out a finger, pointing to the crushed skull. "That I remember—but none of the rest." A sardonic smile crept over his face. "Of course—they did it after I was dead." He looked up at Dirk, suddenly grinning, like a hungry wolf. "Ah, how they must have hated me!" It was gloating, a war-chant glowing with the heat of revenge; and Dirk began to understand why Gar's body had lived through it.

Father Fletcher burst into the chamber. "What was that thunderclap? It sounded like the crack of doom . . ." He broke off, staring at them. DeCade's head swiveled, watching him. The priest fell to his knees. "Hail, Grandmaster DeCade!"

The big man smiled slowly—a grim twist of the lips. " 'Grandmaster'? I have not heard that title, but it would seem that you know me."

The priest smiled, eyes glowing. "Who else could hold DeCade's staff? Now I see the great kindness hidden in the cruelty, of depriving this poor fellow of his wits! It was to empty his mind, that it might be ready to house DeCade! To him the honor, to him the praise!"

Dirk looked up, startled. Was that just a lucky guess, based on metaphor and symbolism? Or did the priest know a little more about psis and technology than he'd let on?

DeCade turned to him with a look of skepticism. " 'Kindness in cruelty . . .' Pretty words that ring hollow. I do not trust that kind of thought; eel-wriggling, they call it." He turned back to the priest, his tone heavy with irony. "As to the 'honor' of his housing me, I have some doubt. I can only hope it will not prove ill for this poor fellow."

"They've gone by, Father!" Hugh swaggered in, with his men, grinning. "They're a half-mile away, and no sign of—" He broke off, staring at the giant.

DeCade lifted his head with a curled smile.

Hugh fell to the floor on one knee. "Hail, Grandmaster DeCade!" His men followed his example, but only stared, dumbfounded.

DeCade stood looking at him a moment, then smiled, amused, at Dirk. "It seems to be catching." And, to Hugh: "Rise, man. Rise, all of you! You must be done with one man kneeling to another!" He riveted his gaze on Hugh, half-amused. "You know me, eh?"

Hugh scrambled to his feet. "You are DeCade, returned to us as the Wizard foretold!"

DeCade nodded heavily, still half-smiling. "And who are you?"

Hugh squared his shoulders proudly. "I am

Hugh, a captain of the forest outlaws, Grandmaster."

"Be done with that title; I like it not," DeCade said sharply. "I am DeCade—nothing more." He lapsed into silence, eyes boring into Hugh. When he spoke, Dirk could hear the eagerness suppressed under his words. "You are chief of the forest men, then?"

"One of them, but our true chief is Lapin." Hugh grinned. "We are waiting and eager to do your bidding, DeCade—armed, drilled, and primed, awaiting only your word."

DeCade nodded slowly, thoughtfully, eyes glinting. He turned to Father Fletcher. "And you, Father?"

"I am only a poor hedge-priest, called Father Fletcher—and, of course, a courier between the outlaws and the Guildsmen. They, too, stand ready, DeCade. Ready, and biding in patience. If you say to do it, they shall raze the town."

"No, I think I shall not ask it." DeCade smiled. "We want something left when all this is past. And you, lady?"

"Madelon, DeCade. I carry word between the Guild and the country folk, and the girls in the brothels."

"The country folk, yes." DeCade's head hadn't moved, but Dirk could feel the sudden piercing intensity in his words. "At the last, it all depends on them—the Farmers on the land, for they are the overpowering weight. How stand these churls?"

"They are ready, DeCade—ready, and craving your word."

Father Fletcher nodded. "Each courier knows his route; each churl has weapons buried away, wrapped in oiled cloth."

DeCade nodded slowly, eyes burning. "It is with them that it rests. . . . Ships!" He frowned suddenly. "The Wizard promised me those—mighty ships, tall towers falling down upon the land!"

"They are ready." Dirk stepped forward, with an eldritch, unreal feeling prickling his skin. "They ride at your order, DeCade."

Father Fletcher and Hugh stared at him, startled. With a wrench of irony, Dirk came back down to earth; "off-worlder" or no, they hadn't quite realized he could bring down the Far Towers. "I am Dirk Dulain, DeCade. I speak for the sky-men."

DeCade squinted in pain, pressing fingertips to his forehead. "Yes. . . . I remember now; you had told . . . this body. They sent you to seek out the churl's leader."

Dirk nodded. "I have found him. Twenty tall tower-ships ride waiting behind the moon. At your word, they drop down, with fire-cannon ready."

DeCade winced again. "Yes . . . 'laser cannon' is their true name. There is pain, in this mingling of memories. . . ." His head came up sharply, eyes burning into Dirk. "And the firesticks, laser pistols? The Wizard promised those, too!"

Dirk nodded. "They are ready, hidden throughout the land. At your word, we unearth them, tell the churls where they are. And when the Towers drop down, they'll bring more."

DeCade nodded tightly, with a gleeful smile. "All is indeed ready, then. You have done well, very well. How long has this taken? How long have I slept?"

The cavern was still. Then. "Five hundred years," Madelon murmured.

For a moment, DeCade blanched. Then he began to smile again, with building warmth. "Aye, so the Wizard told me; he warned it might be centuries. But it is worth it, after all; and things could not have changed so much that I cannot hold to his plan. No, they could not change much. Not in Melange."

"Scarcely at all," Dirk grunted. He'd seen the records. "If ever there was a fossilized culture, this is it. The Lords are dinosaurs, and their Triassic is ending."

DeCade nodded, gloating; then he threw back his shoulders, grinning like a wolf. "Send the word throughout the land: in five days, we ring the Bell! All is ready!"

"Well, not quite." Dirk said it quickly, before the cheer could start.

DeCade turned to him, frowning. "What lacks?"

Dirk hesitated, but his obstinate skepticism won out. "The Wizard. The prophecy said he'd come back, too."

"But he has!" Madelon cried.

"Churls have seen him!" Hugh bellowed. "The word runs abroad!"

"Only rumors." But a strange dread trickled down Dirk's spine, because DeCade was just leaning on his staff, watching him, amused. He waited for the shouting to die, then said quietly, "Only that? Come, friend Dulain! He is here; this body remembers it. It has seen him."

Dirk stared.

And before he could ask the next question, DeCade was striding toward the archway. "Come! Enough of skulking in hiding! Raise the cry!"

The whole crew fell in behind him with a shout of joy; what could Dirk do but follow?

As they stepped out into the sunlight, DeCade grinned back over his shoulder at Dirk. "You are worried; do not be. The same weakness that makes so many of our people go mad will give them victory. Your eyes shall see it: our madness is our strength."

"Indeed it is," said a coldly amused voice.

DeCade wheeled about, and Dirk's eyes snapped forward. A ring of steel-clad men encircled the mouth of the cave. In the center, a few paces in front of the others, stood Lord Core.

Hugh and his band streamed out behind DeCade and Dirk, joking and laughing. They looked forward and froze.

"What an elegant company you make," Core murmured. "And so many of you decked in my livery, too. My faith! Quite a compliment!" He turned his eyes to DeCade. "I had some notion the truth in this tale of your madness was somewhat limited."

DeCade's lips curved into a sardonic smile. "So? And who do you think I am?"

Core frowned, faintly disturbed by the change in the giant's manner. "You are the outworlder who called himself Magnus d'Armand; and the slight one beside you is your henchman."

Dirk stiffened. Slight? Admittedly, he wasn't exactly a wrestler, but still ...

DeCade's eyelids drooped sleepily. "Have you not gone to a great deal of trouble for two insignificant outworlders?"

Core's face relaxed in a smile of contempt. "Come, sir! You know I cannot ignore any outworlder abroad in this society."

"Am I so much a threat, then? Is your world so delicately balanced?"

Core's face tightened as though he'd been slapped. He stepped forward. "Come, enough of this! You see I have the advantage of you ten times—a hundred of my iron Soldiers against poor ten of you. Surrender to me now, or meet your death—you and all your company, Magnus d'Armand."

"Why, so I might," DeCade said reasonably, "were I Magnus d'Armand still."

Core's eyebrows rose. "Oh? You have become someone else? Whom, may I inquire?"

"I am DeCade!" the giant thundered, and lashed out backhanded with the great staff.

But Core was quick; he skipped aside with the look of shock still on his face; the staff caught him only a glancing blow on the shoulder. He reached for his sword—and Dirk slammed into him and picked the Lord's dagger-sheath as the trees rained outlaws and knives flashed in the sun. A score of Soldiers fell under the weight; knives probed chinks in armor, men screamed, and the outlaws rose alone.

Then the rest of the Soldiers wakened to what was happening. They turned on the outlaws, bellowing, and the clearing turned into a melee of single combats.

Dirk stepped back from Core just far enough to free his knife hand to thrust; but Core's sword hissed out of its scabbard, turning Dirk's blade and slashing out at him. Dirk leaped backward, sucking in his belly, and Core's sword swung up to chop. It fell, and Dirk stepped back from the slash and tripped on a body. Core gave a shout of joy and wound up for another thrust; but Dirk balled his body up and uncoiled, feet-first, at Core's chin. Core ducked and stepped back. Dirk landed on his feet and lashed out with a kick at the groin; Core fell back again, staying two inches clear of the kick; then he slashed while Dirk was recovering. Dirk screamed as the blade sliced his calf, and fell. He flipped over onto his back just in time to see Core, mouth wide in a caw of triumph, coming straight down at him, the tip of his blade aimed straight for Dirk's eyes. He snapped his head to the side, and the blade slit his ear. Dirk bellowed with pain, throwing himself over to seize Core's hand before the Lord could recover. Core's lips writhed back from his teeth in a snarl. He threw himself backward, trying to break free.

Dirk let go.

Core shot back and away, stumbled, and flipped down on his back. Dirk rolled to his knees, unsure of the cut leg, and gathered himself to spring. Core rolled up to his knees, and Dirk leaped, pushing hard with the good leg. Core threw himself to the side, and Dirk went sprawling on his face. He heard Core laugh, and flipped onto his back just in time to see the sword slashing down at his eyes. Frantically, he threw up his arms—and caught Core's wrist with his left hand. By pure reflex, he lashed out with his right, catching Core on the point of the jaw. The Lord lurched back, and Dirk rolled away, up onto his knees again—in time to see Core, recovered and on his feet, slashing down.

A quarterstaff whirled down between them, cracking the sword blade in half and slamming the hilt into Core's chest. The Lord shot back, mouth gaping, and Dirk clambered to his feet carefully, testing his leg, as DeCade stalked after the Lord, murder in his eyes.

Core stumbled back, turning, caught half a breath, and broke into a stumbling run.

DeCade leaped after him.

A panicked horse fled toward them, screaming. Core leaped for his life as it passed, caught the saddle bow, and swung aboard, reeling. DeCade bellowed and leaped into the horse's path, quarterstaff swinging like a poleaxe; but Core sawed back on the reins, and the horse reared, screaming in agony. DeCade's staff whined past its belly. Core yanked at the reins; the horse swung about, came down headed toward the trees. Core shouted and kicked its ribs, hard, and the horse took off like a cannonball, slamming through the ranks of the outlaws, and disappeared into the trees.

Dirk stood staring after him, hearing the horse's crashing progress fading into the distance. His eyes glazed, and he turned away with the sunken feeling of defeat inside him.

"Fools!" DeCade bellowed.

Dirk's head snapped up.

The clearing was still, filled with windrows of dead Soldiers and outlaws. In the center, thigh-deep in corpses, DeCade bellowed in rage, slashing about him with his staff. "Idiots! Blockheads! Traitorous dogs! *You let him escape!*"

The outlaws slipped back out of his reach with battle-wariness, their faces blanched with the deepest religious fear, trembling at the wrath of their saint, not understanding.

"Spawn of jackals!" DeCade screamed and leaped at Hugh, his staff whirling. Hugh danced aside. Lapin loomed up with elephantine majesty, her face somber.

DeCade froze, staring down at the huge woman who blocked him from his quarry. His face tightened in a quick stab of pain. He said slowly, "I know you. You are chief of these outlaws."

"I am." Slowly and with great difficulty, Lapin wallowed down to one knee and bent her head. "I honor you, Grandmaster." Then her head rose again. "But why do you curse us? If we have sinned against you, surely our offense was not so great that you should be so much enraged. What hurt have we done? We came, unbidden, to give timely rescue to you and your band. All your enemies we have slain, save this one; and are we so much to blame if we have let one mere man escape?"

"But you—have—let—one man escape!" DeCade grated. "And that man was a Lord!" His voice rose; he moved back into the center of the clearing, raking them all with his eyes. "Fools! Do you not see? He will ride faster than we can follow, to Albemarle! By dawn he shall bear word to the King that I live again, that the peasants will rise—and the King will send word to all his Lords—he has magic means for it, let me assure you! When our churls rise with swords, they shall find armies against them, with fire-cannon!" His staff rose above his head, and his voice rose with it, toward a scream, trembling. "I shall not be cheated! I have waited too long in the shadows for this time! I shall not see this world lost again! *And there is no way to prevent it!*"

His shriek pierced their ears; the outlaws winced and hid their faces.

Dirk stared at DeCade's eyes. There was madness creeping up there; DeCade was going insane!

"Can you ring the Bell before morning and make it heard throughout this land?" DeCade screeched. "No, nor can I! You have let one Lord escape, and for that, our cause is lost! *But if I cannot kill them . . .*"

"DeCade!" Dirk's voice cracked like a gunshot.

The giant froze. Then his head swung slowly toward Dirk, like a hawk picking a sparrow out of the flock.

Dirk stepped forward, limping but briskly, to hide the weakness in his knees. He didn't know what he was going to say, but he knew he had to snap the giant out of it. He saw the blood-lust come into the man's eyes, saw the huge staff swing up, twirling . . . and Dirk remembered what he was here for. "Ring your Bell! I *can* make it heard by *all* churls, before dawn!"

DeCade froze.

Every eye in the clearing fastened on Dirk.

DeCade stood like stone, poised to strike, madness still in his eyes.

Dirk stood firm, staring back at him.

Slowly, the fog in DeCade's eyes seemed to clear a little. His voice was low and ominous. "Tell me how you can do this."

"There are wires woven through my belt," Dirk said, fingering the rope around his waist. "Each is a series of circuits, and the frayed ends act as a diaphragm—No matter. It is magic and will send your words up to the Wizard's Far Towers, where they ride behind the moon. They shall send your words back here, to sky-men like me, in hiding all across the land. They shall bear your word to the churls and dig up the lasers. Give me the word you wish carried, and the country shall rise before Core reaches Albemarle."

DeCade stood staring at him.

Then the huge staff flipped spinning up into the air, and DeCade split the clearing with a huge, savage yell. The staff spun down at his head; he reached up and caught it and whirled it about. "Our day is saved! We shall yet bring down the Lords! Great thanks, goodmen and goodwives all! Noble outlaws!" He leaped forward, caught Lapin and Hugh by the arms, yanked them back into the center of the clearing. "Great leaders! May all the saints who smile upon bondsmen bless you this day, you who have brought me awake, aye, cared for and nurtured the man who was to be my body, and saved us all from the jaws of the Lords! Your names shall be written in fire, to burn down the ages in glory! Outlaws, remember this hour! That your children, and your children's children, down to the twentieth generation may say, 'My ancestor was there when DeCade awoke and called down havoc upon the Lords!'"

He let go of Hugh and Lapin and leaped back, whirling his staff over his head again. "Now, ring the Bell!"

The outlaws cheered, yelled themselves hoarse. In the middle of the clamor, Dirk dropped down to sit cross-legged on the ground. He untied his belt, handed one end to the nearest outlaw. "Here! Hold it tight!" He rubbed his palm over the frayed rope-end, flattening it out into a diaphragm. Then he pulled the large garnet from his ring and stretched out the long, thin coiled wire beneath it. The stone was shaped like a button earphone; he pressed it into his ear. The belt acted as microphone, transmitter, and antenna; the ring acted as receiver, the garnet as earphone, and the wire connecting them doubled as receiving antenna.

Dirk spoke into the rope-end, feeling like half a fool. "Dulain to *Clarion*! Come in, *Clarion*!" He repeated the message while the clamor in the clearing died, until he heard a rich, resonant voice in his ear. "*Clarion* to Dulain. Receiving, Proceed."

"Holding for instruction." Dirk looked up at the outlaw. "Summon DeCade."

The outlaw scowled at the "summon" part, but he turned, waved his free arm. Across the clearing, the giant caught the movement; he frowned and came stalking over to Dirk. "What means this? If you cannot—"

"I must have the words you wish sounded across the kingdom," Dirk interrupted sharply. "The *exact* words, to be sure I make no mistake."

DeCade shrugged impatiently. " 'DeCade has rungen the Bell. Bring down your Lords at dawn; then send men to Albemarle.' "

Dirk stared.

Then he cocked his head to the side. "Just like that, huh?"

"Aye. What of it?"

"Been thinking it over, have you?"

DeCade gave him a sardonic smile. "Several hundred years, these people tell me."

Dirk thought that one over a second, then nodded and turned back to the rope-end. "Uh-huh. Right . . . Dulain to *Clarion*. Copy and retransmit to all agents—General Call, Emergency/Red Alert: 'DeCade has rungen the Bell. Bring down your Lords at dawn; then send men to Albemarle.' "

There was no reply. Dirk frowned, listening closely. No, there was ambient sound; the connection hadn't been broken. "*Clarion*—come in!"

"Copied." The voice on the other end was strained, almost unbelieving. Then the operator cleared his throat, got his voice back to business. "Hold please, Dulain."

Dirk frowned, pressing the garnet into his ear. What was the matter?

"What moves?" DeCade growled.

"I don't think they can believe it's finally happening."

"Copied, Dulain; will execute." Dirk stiffened; it was the Captain's voice. "What else, Dulain?"

"Uh—hold for instruction." Dirk looked up at DeCade. "When and where do you want the Far Towers to fall?"

DeCade's face went blank; then he frowned in thought. "They bear arms, you said?"

Dirk nodded.

"What quantity on each ship?"

"A thousand rifles and ten laser-cannon. That's portable, for the churls; the ships themselves each mount four cannon and a hundred bombs."

DeCade's face tightened as he consulted Gar's memories; Dirk wondered if he was getting used to the pain. DeCade nodded slowly, still thinking. "How many ships?"

"Twenty-one—one for each province, and two for Albemarle. Believe me, that'll be enough."

DeCade stared down at him for a long moment. Then he said, "You have your own battle plan."

Dirk nodded. "You want it in detail?"

DeCade grimaced in disgust. "Credit me with some sense, Dulain. Do as you have planned; I doubt not your strategy stems from the Wizard, as does mine; they should mesh. As to time, bring them at dawn; let all move at once."

"We can raise the land by midnight," Dirk suggested.

DeCade stared.

Then he scowled. "Why did you not say so sooner? If you can . . . are you certain?"

Dirk nodded emphatically.

"Then do, by all that is holy! Let all move at midnight; so much more will the Lords be taken unaware! Bring the ships down then, save for the two over Albemarle. Let them ride unseen till I call them!"

Dirk nodded, turning back to the mike with a gloating smile. "Amend previous message: have churls bring down Lords at midnight. Bring ships down then, too, except for the two over Albemarle."

"Copied. Anything else, Dulain?"

Dirk looked up at DeCade. "Anything more?"

DeCade shook his head, his eyes glinting.

Dirk turned back to the mike. "No more, Captain."

"Copied and over." The Captain's voice suddenly turned warm, exuberant. "Well done, Dulain! If we had medals, you'd get one! How did you ever find the leader?"

Dirk started to answer, then caught himself short. "Uh . . . I couldn't," he said slowly, "so I made one." And, before the Captain could say anything, "End contact."

CHAPTER 12

When the sun was setting on a village far to the south, the churl "elder" (he was in his fifties) was leading his work gang home from the fields. As they came, they sang a slow ballad with a heavy rhythm—a work song that any listening Lord would have thought was pure nonsense. Even the numbers didn't make sense.

> When rings the bell, and comes the call,
> (Pull steady, Jean, and slow)
> Then one will run to ninety-three;
> And they will send out three times three,
> And each will go to ninety-three.
> (Jean, run when you must go!)

As they sang, another churl in a dust-stained tunic exactly like theirs stepped out of a thicket by the roadway and fell in with them. No one seemed to notice, but the air about them was suddenly charged with tension.

The newcomer eased his way up to the headman. The "elder" glanced at the garnet ring on the stranger's hand, and looked away. "What word, Sky-man?"

"The bell is rungen. Bring down your Lords at midnight; then send men to Albemarle."

The "elder" nodded thoughtfully and fell in with the song again. The gang wound on home as though nothing had happened; and, where an outcrop of forest touched the path near the village, the stranger slipped away.

The men went on into the circle of thatched huts as though it were any other evening. Each went to his own house, but with a stony look on his face. Then the village proceeded to supper, and gossip in the doorways, and mending tools and clothes, as it always did, while the sun finished setting and the first stars came out. When the light was gone, each family went back in within doors, and the village slept—a little more than ninety souls.

A little later, young men began slipping out of huts, one by one, and out to the fields. When they came to open ground, they struck out running—the easy, regular lope of long distances. There were perhaps nine of them in all, each striking out in a different direction.

* * *

The elder of a nearby village woke in the velvet darkness, frowning. It came again—a quiet, steady knocking. The elder's face went blank; he climbed out of his pallet.

He opened the door to see a tall young churl with the light behind him, breathing heavily. The elder scowled. "Jaques Farmer-of-Thierry's son," he growled; there was little love lost between his own village and its nearest neighbor, on the next estate. "More foolish than I thought, to run about at night."

" 'DeCade has rungen the Bell,' " the youth panted. " 'Bring down your Lord at midnight; then send men to Albemarle.' "

The elder's face went blank again. Then he turned aside, murmuring kindly, "Come in. You must take food and drink, poor lad."

The lad went in, smiling his thanks; the door closed behind him.

A little later, the elder's son slipped out and went from door to door.

Not long after, nine young men struck out running into the fields, each in a different direction.

By the time the courier set off on his way home, eighty-one villages had been informed, and each had sent out nine more runners.

DeCade's band slipped through the darkened forest with no more noise than a brisk breeze makes—except for Dirk. He was feeling highly embarrassed; he didn't seem to be able to take a step without snapping a twig. He was indulging himself in feeling mortified when a tiny buzz sounded, no louder than a cricket.

DeCade stopped just before him and scowled back over his shoulder.

Dirk pried the stone from the ring, set it to his ear, and tapped an acknowledgment on the frayed end of his rope belt.

"All agents have reported back," the Captain's voice informed him. "Each has alerted at least one village—fifty villages in each province, a thousand in all."

Dirk frowned as he tapped acknowledgment; that didn't sound like much, out of 250,000 square miles. "Our agents have alerted fifty villages in each province," he informed DeCade.

Near them, Lapin nodded in satisfaction. "And each has told nine other villages; each of those has told nine more. I doubted, Dirk Dulain, but you spoke truth—they *will* all rise by midnight."

"It does rather look that way." Dirk was numb; somehow the scope of the whole thing hadn't hit him before.

"I cannot believe it has truly begun," Madelon breathed.

DeCade grunted. "You will when you see the blood."

The churls from all the villages on the estates of Louvrais had gathered, muttering and shifting nervously about, in a great meadow surrounded by woodlots, just below the Lord's castle. Now and again, they glanced anxiously at the sky; but the moon hid its face, and the stars watched, uncaring.

Suddenly a low, deep thrumming filled the air. All heads snapped up, craning back their necks to watch the stars being blotted out in an expanding ellipse. A mutter of fear and awe swept through them, their eyes bulging; then the blot on the sky was gone, and a black ship's gig pressed down on the meadow grass near them. The thrumming stopped; the churls stood, awed and staring.

Then a whispered cheer hissed from their throats, and they leaped forward, running toward the ship. As they came up, a rectangular section of the side dropped forward and out; bright light cut a swath across the clearing. The churls stopped, uncertain, prickling with superstitious fear, muttering.

A tall, lean figure in tight-fitting black appeared against the light, surveyed them, then stepped out into the meadow. Behind him, another appeared with a cube about a foot and a half on a side. He set it down and turned back to take another like it from a third man, who appeared in the hatch.

The first man wrenched open the crate and lifted out a laser pistol. He held it out, butt first, to the churl nearest him. Hesitantly, the churl took it, and the sky-man lifted out another.

With a moan of delight, the churls pressed in.

Two hundred miles away, Lord Propin finished with his concubine for the evening and rolled over on his side to sleep. The girl lay, keeping her face carefully neutral, listening. Even after she heard the deep, even breathing of sleep, she waited; but her beautiful face slowly contorted with hate and disgust. Finally, sure the Lord was deeply asleep, she rose, glided to his wardrobe, and slid a jeweled dagger from its sheath on an embossed leather belt. She glided back through a single shaft of moonlight to his bedside, and stood looking down at him. Slowly she smiled as she raised the dagger and plunged it home.

To the south, in Lord Ubiquii's tall, moated castle, two guards stood leaning on their pikes outside the Lord's bedroom door.

A Butler came discreetly down the hall and stopped to murmur in the ear of the older guard. The guard's face turned grim; he nodded shortly. The Butler bowed courteously and moved away.

The younger man frowned. "What was that about?"

"It could be trouble," the older guard said slowly, "but not enough to trouble His Lordship. Go to the guardroom and tell Sergeant Garstang to come here with five picked men."

The younger man cocked his head to one side, frowning.

"Go!" the older man barked. "Do as you are bid!"

The younger man turned away, still watching his companion out of the corner of his eye.

The elder waited till the younger man had passed from sight, waited till his footsteps had faded away. Then he turned, opened the door he guarded, and went in to murder his Lord.

* * *

In Chateau Grenoble, the kitchen drudge came to the head Butler, murmuring quietly to him. He listened thoughtfully, nodding; she turned away. Then the Butler told one of his footmen to bear a message to a certain Sergeant of Guards. As the footman went, the Butler passed among the other servants, murmuring briefly to each; one by one, they finished what they were doing and went to the kitchens, where they took up knives and cleavers.

They marched up the great stairs toward the chamber where their Lord and Lady lay sleeping, each of them remembering many humiliations, injuries, and loved ones lost. On a landing they met a troop of guardsmen. The sergeant and the Butler exchanged glances, then marched on up the stairs, side by side. Fifty Soldiers and servants followed them.

The castle of Miltrait had a lord with a nasty, suspicious mind; he'd always made sure he kept a good standing army handy within the walls of his keep, and a squad of young lordlings (mostly his own) to stand behind the Soldiers with lasers. The lordlings had stood night watch in the barracks; which was why, though the house churls had opened the gate, the rebel army wasn't making much headway.

. The courtyard was a frenzy of torchlight, hoarse screams, bellows of rage, winking laser beams, and the clatter of steel. At its center stood the Lord, armor bolted over his nightshirt, hewing and hacking about him, bellowing, "On, my bullies, on! Force them out through the gate; free this castle of vermin!" And slowly, bit by bit, the churls were being pushed back to the wall.

But, silent and unseen above them, a huge black egg drifted down, hovering over the battlements. One of its turrets swiveled downward, lining up on the Lord.

He happened to glance upward, saw the dark blot against the stars, and realized what was happening. He sprang backward with a bellow of warning—but the turret tracked him, and a rod of red fire sizzled out, strafing the long line of lordlings.

The Lord died in an instant. Some of his men survived long enough for the knives of the churls to reach them.

Lady Pomgrain fled back through the keep. Behind her, in the great hall, the air danced with laser bolts. Steel clashed on steel. Her husband fought like a maniac with the handful of gentlemen left to him, guarding her line of escape, but the churls pressed them hard; as soon as one was dispatched, another popped up in his place.

The Lady threw open a door on a spiral stair, stepped in, and bolted the door behind her. Up and up she climbed, panting heavily, till she came to a door at the roof of the tower. She leaned against it, gasping till she'd recovered a little of her strength; then, fumbling her keys in her fear, she unlocked it. The door swung open; she all but fell in.

The room was empty and clean, as immaculate as gray stone can be, except for a large metal console with a viewscreen in its center, at the far side of the small room. The Lady staggered over to it, pushed a button, and jewel-lights glowed into life. She threw a key and spoke into a grid on the console's face: "Alarm, alarm, emergency! The churls have risen on the estates of Pomgrain! They have taken the castle; they are slaying the nobles! Send help; let all men guard their own!"

The message rolled out from her castle in a huge, expanding globe. It touched castle after castle; and where it touched, receiving sets woke into life.

DeCade and Dirk had donned outlaw clothing against the chill of the dark predawn hours, but Dirk still wore the rope belt, and the garnet in his ear.

The garnet buzzed; Dirk tapped recognition on the end of the rope/transmitter. He listened for a few minutes, frowning, then tapped an acknowledgment and turned to DeCade. "The word is out; the churls of Pomgrain took their Lady too late. She sent out an alarm with her communicator. As I understand it, any incoming signal on the emergency frequency automatically turns the receivers on. All the Lords will know it by now."

"I think they knew it already, from sources closer to home," DeCade said thoughtfully.

The alarm rattled from communicators all over the land; but in most castles, they spoke to empty air; there was no one near them. Some heard, but also heard the pounding at the door.

In the King's castle at Albemarle, a young lord

jerked up out of a doze, listened a moment, appalled, then dashed from the room, to bear the word to Lord Core.

Core had just ridden in, covered with dust, choleric and choking. He listened incredulously; then he slashed out at the young Lord with the back of his hand, snarling. The lordling leaped back adroitly and was about to take offense when he realized Core was already gone, angrily pacing away, bellowing orders.

Ten minutes later, a fleet of small sentry boats with large laser cannon lifted off the roof of the palace, streaking away to all points of the compass.

The King did not hear. The King did nothing.

The small silvery boats sped out across the countryside, so high up that the first few rays of dawn turned their hulls to rose.

As they sailed, tiny black specks appeared above them, swelling suddenly into squat black ship's gigs bristling with turrets. They fell like stones flung by giants. Too late, the silvery boats detected them and swung about, to bring their single lasers to bear. Rays of fire spat, and the silvery boats fell out of the sky, burning in glory.

Occasionally the black boat would fall, and the silver would speed on alone; another black speck would appear, high above it.

On the estate of Milord Megrin, the churls from all the villages converged on the castle, scythes and flails in hand. Atop the wall, sentries saw them and cried out in alarm. A corporal came running to each of them—and sapped them neatly behind the ear.

As the churls marched up to the great gate, it swung open, and they strode on in, to be met by servants, and not a few guardsmen. Silently, the Butler led them into the great hall, where they formed a semicircle, facing the great central archway. There they waited.

Suddenly Lord Megrin, with his wife and three children, came stumbling through the archway in their nightclothes. Behind them came a score of grim-faced Soldiers, their pikes at the ready. The Lord and his family stumbled to a stop, staring about them in the torchlight, dazed. Then the Lord cried out in indignation, "What means this! Why have you gathered here without my leave!" But there was an echo of dread in his voice.

The Butler stepped forward, his face politely grave. "DeCade has risen, Lord; his Bell is rungen. Throughout the land, churls are rising to strike down their Lords."

The Lord blanched, and his wife gasped, burying her face in her hands. Then she fell to one knee and clutched her children to her.

"Have I been so evil to you, then," he said quietly, "that you must serve me in like fashion?"

"You have not, milord, and well you know it. You have ruled well and wisely over us; we have been fortunate indeed. Your punishments have always been just, and never harsh; you have never been cruel, nor taken advantage of our bodies. You have always seen that no man starved or froze, even if your family and yourself had to eat Lenten rations in the Christmastide to do it. Your wife has nursed us in our illness; you have cared for us and protected us. And, as you have served us, so shall we serve you now." ·

The Lord heaved a huge sigh of relief and relaxed; his wife looked up, unbelieving. Then tears of joy filled her eyes.

"But you must understand," the Butler said more gravely, "that what has happened now, must happen; too many of our brethren have dwelt in torture and abasement. The wheel has turned; the churls must rule. You may no longer be Lord of this manor."

The Lord stood stiffly, his face unreadable. Then, slowly, he bowed his head.

"Yet credit us with sense," the Butler said more gently. "We doubt that any one among us could administer this manor half so well as your good self; we own it now, in common, but we wish you still to oversee the running of it, to instruct us and direct us."

The Lord stared, unbelieving. Then he cocked his head to the side, frowning. "Let me be sure I understand you. You tell me that I am *your* servant now, but that the service you require of me is your governing."

The Butler nodded, relief evident in his face before he brought it under control again. "Save only this: you are no more a servant than any other here. All here are now members of the community, and servants of it."

The Lord pursed his lips thoughtfully. "That is

more than justice. If the churls have risen, as you say, you do me and mine much mercy."

"Only yours returned, milord. As you have cared for us, so we shall care for you."

"But will they let you?" the Lord demanded. "Will not DeCade, or whoever rises to rule the churls, demand our blood?"

His wife looked up, alarmed.

"They may," the Butler said grimly, "but only if they kill each one of us to reach you. You are *our* Lord, and not a man shall touch a hair of your head!"

A rumble of agreement passed through the crowd.

The Lord stood a moment, trembling; then his eyes filled with tears.

DeCade led his army out of the forest into a meadow. Dirk's head suddenly snapped up; he listened for a moment, then put out a hand to De-Cade. "Tell them to wait."

DeCade frowned, but raised a hand, signaling for a halt. The outlaws and other churls stopped, watching him, frowning.

Then they heard the low thrumming filling the air.

All eyes snapped up as the big black ship's gig floated down out of darkness. It touched earth; hatches opened, and a gang of black-clothed figures started hauling out crates.

"Your weapons, DeCade," Dirk said, poker-faced. "Handle with care."

DeCade's eyes flamed. He swung his arm over

his head, and the churls charged up to the ship with a ragged cheer. As the sky-men handed out pistols, grinning, five more ship's gigs came to land.

The army paused for instruction and target practice, on the each-one-teach-one system. Then they moved on toward Albemarle, singing softly, like a wind of destruction.

Moonlight painted swaths across the floor of the barracks room in the Lord de Breton's castle. The Soldiers snored on their pallets, a double row of gray-blanketed mounds.

A stocky figure in footman's livery appeared in the doorway.

Silently, it padded down the alleyway between the pallets and stopped next to a sergeant. He placed a hand on the Soldier's shoulder and squeezed; the sergeant sat bolt upright, instantly awake. The liveried figure whispered in his ear, then stood back; quickly and silently, the sergeant came to his feet. He took down his harness from a peg on the wall and strapped on his weapons. Then he padded down the alleyway, stopping here and there beside a sleeping Soldier. Wherever he stopped, he lifted a small bludgeon, and, remembering the Lord's rape of his sister on her wedding night, struck the sleeping man behind the ear. The Soldier grunted and went limp. The sergeant bound each one with his own harness, gagged him, and moved on to the next who might possibly be loyal to the Lord. When he had finished with the last suspect comrade, he straightened, surveyed the room for a moment, then prowled down along the alley again, shaking the remaining soldiers awake, whispering in their ears. They came to their feet, one by one, and dressed for war—chain mail and steel helmets—and picked up swords and crossbows. The sergeant stood surveying them as they drew up in formation; then he nodded, and turned to lead the way out the door.

As they marched, he beckoned to one Soldier and murmured in his ear; the man turned away, to slip across the courtyard to the gate tower.

The gatekeeper sat his post, drowsing off to sleep. The Soldier's blade chopped down, and the gatekeeper slept very well indeed. The Soldier took the windlass, cranking it carefully. Slowly, the great drawbridge came down, thumped home. A horde of churls materialized from the shadows and swept in through the gate in almost military order, with scythe-blades fixed to knife-handles, and here and there the gleam of an old, but very-well-cared-for sword.

They moved in silently, divided into Tradesmen and Farmers, each village following its elder.

At the doors to the keep, the servants waited. As the churls came up, the servants turned away and strode into the castle. The army broke up into squadrons, each following a servant.

The castle woke to torchlight, shrieks, and cries. Half the Lord's Gentlemen ran from their bedrooms, buckling on swords. The other half would never wake again; the sergeant and his Soldiers had seen to that.

The remaining Gentlemen pulled together

quickly and turned to fight the horde that pressed them; but the scythe-blades were sharp and the arms strong. Only the gentlemen in the front rank could use their lasers, and the hall was narrow. Churls screamed and died on lances of light, but their cousins behind them chopped off the arms that held the pistols. The Gentlemen fell back, retreating further and further upward, to their Lord's bedchamber.

The Lord stood in the doorway, beckoning. Quickly, the Gentlemen filed into the room, and the huge door boomed shut behind them. A moment later, the churls filled the corridor, bellowing for blood. Two Soldiers shouldered their way to the fore, attacking the oak with battle-axes.

Inside the Lord swung back a section of wall and stood back while his family and all his Gentlemen filed down a hidden spiral staircase. The Lord waited till the last man was past him, then sealed the wall behind him. When the Soldiers broke into the room, it was empty.

Half an hour later and a mile away, the Lord and his retinue filed out of a hidden tunnel mouth. The churls were gone from the village; they had no trouble stealing horses. They mounted and rode away, cantering through the night.

Dirk marched with the garnet in his ear, now; the reports were beginning to come in quickly. He looked about him and saw only darkened woodland. Occasionally, he caught a glimpse of an outlaw sliding through a moonbeam, and there was always the dark bulk of DeCade a little in front of him, and Madelon, Father Fletcher, and Lapin behind; but that small band could almost have been walking alone through the forest.

And they weren't showing any sign of slackening. Dirk wasn't, either, but it was only good acting; his legs felt like noodles. It had been three hours since DeCade had called a rest.

His earphone buzzed; Dirk lowered his head, frowning. "Dulain here." He listened silently, then nodded. "Received, with thanks. Keep me informed." Then he looked up at the giant. "DeCade! Most of the castles have fallen; only a handful still fight—the ones where we had none of the Soldiers."

DeCade nodded. "As expected. Those few will fight well into tomorrow, and some may need a full siege. No matter; we should have men to send them in plenty, by this hour tomorrow."

Dirk frowned; the giant didn't even seem to conceive of failure anymore. It could be a good thing, but . . . "In many of the castles, the Lords escaped."

DeCade nodded again. "Of course. Let them ride through the night till they come to Albemarle. Let them ride."

It didn't seem like good tactics; why go against any stronger a garrison then they had to, at the King's castle? But Dirk shrugged, and, with a sigh, relayed the order on up, then looked up at DeCade, frowning thoughtfully. "Uh . . . some of the agents saw the fighting. They were flabbergasted by its smoothness."

"Were they?"

Dirk bit down on a surge of irritation, then let it pass. "Yes. You must admit it looks a little strange—a horde of peasants who've never had any military training, falling in like the best-disciplined army, each man doing exactly what he's supposed to, without question, with perfect coordination, perfect timing."

"Why should this surprise you?" DeCade countered. "You saw it at the arena."

"Well, yes. But I didn't understand it then, either."

"Even though you felt it well enough to act on it." DeCade smiled tightly. "Still, you wish the names for it."

Dirk nodded. "We sky-men are peculiar that way, yes." Suddenly, bitterly, he felt his isolation from these people again.

DeCade sighed and came to a stop. He pressed a hand to his forehead, muttering, "I must have your words." He stood a moment in silence, stiffened. Lapin, Madelon, and the priest stared in alarm. Dirk gave them what he hoped was a reassuring nod and turned back to DeCade.

The giant lifted his head, took a long breath, then nodded and strode forward once again. "Well enough. You know our people are descended from a mere dozen, each of whom was multiplied by magic—'cloned,' you call it—into many thousands."

Dirk nodded.

"Seven hundred years go by," DeCade went on. "The blood of those twelve has mingled again and again, but with no more mingling between types than the Lords could possibly help. There are now twelve clans—but each member of each clan is as like to every other as peas in a pod."

"Genetically identical," Dirk murmured.

DeCade nodded. "That is your term. It takes sharp looking to tell one Tradesman from another. And the mode of living the Lords enforce for each clan makes all homes alike. At first each set of parents was somewhat different, probably; but as time went on, the differences damped out; within each clan, the people of each generation behaved more and more like one another. Each person had the same heredity; and, since parents and life-style are nearly identical, each person has an environment virtually the same. A Tradesman's house is different from a Farmer's, and a country Tradesman's house is different from a town Tradesman's—but town Tradesmen live in town, and have for several hundred years. Where your grandfather was born, so were you."

"Yes," Dirk murmured, remembering the family traditions his father had taught him. "For seven hundred years."

"Well, there you have it." DeCade shrugged. "Within each clan, heredity and environment are identical for every person."

Dirk stopped as though he'd run into a brick wall.

DeCade stopped, too, nodding down at him, brooding. "You told it to this body; did you realize what it meant? If heredity and environment are identical, behavior must be identical, too. Give any

Tradesman a stimulus, and he will react like any other Tradesman. We know this; we feel it; and so we know what each of our clansmen will do. All know each other's actions before they do them; each knows what must be done. However, there is still enough of human caution in any group so that no man will move until another does. But give them one man to walk before them, and all will walk behind him, do as he does—for they know, in any set of circumstances, everything that must be done."

"And the leader could be any one of them." Dirk flashed the mental picture of the caterpillars crawling around and around the rim of the flower-pot again, and shuddered. He shook his head quickly to rid himself of it. "But some clans would have natural reactions that wouldn't fit the situation."

DeCade nodded, turned away, and began walking again. "They must be made to understand that silence is necessary till the battle's joined, or you lose all advantage of surprise. So the Wizard sent directions down the ages; he set his battle-plan to rhyme and tune and gave it piecemeal to the churls to sing. Fathers teach these songs to sons, mothers to daughters—and they become a part of the environment. With those songs echoing in mind tonight, each verse called up as events cued it, no churl could set foot wrong."

"A natural army," Dirk breathed, "bred that way for seven hundred years." He had a sudden terrifying vision of what his cousins could do if they were ever unleashed upon the galaxy.

DeCade nodded. "And thus the Lords made certain their own downfall. They planned this world well and thoroughly, and made it adhere to that plan down through the centuries. But no plan can include all factors because the factors change, and no man can read the future till it's done. The human creature is perverse, is it not? We always find the road the intellect did not see, nor want."

Dirk thought of Finagle and held his peace.

The Lord de Breton galloped through the night with his family and his entourage; their hooves rumbled like cannon wheels through the moonlight.

As they came to a crossroads, another troop came galloping out, nearly colliding with them. The Lord swore, sawing back on the reins; men cursed and women screamed. Horses slewed to a stop with stiffened legs, churning up dust. The Lord grabbed at his sword; then he froze, staring at the brightly dressed figure at the head of the strangers, recognizing the Lord Montpasse.

The two troops stared at one another for a long, frozen moment; then the two troops mingled, with loud laughter of relief and friendly insults.

A few minutes later, a single, stronger band trotted through the night, with two Lords at its head.

Five miles later, they caught up with another doubled band; then another, and another. Soon a thousand horses rumbled down the King's Highway, bound for Albemarle.

Dirk's earphone clicked. He frowned and tapped out an acknowledgment. He listened for a few minutes, then pulled himself to his feet and threaded his way through the packed bodies in the huge clearing, elbowing his way toward DeCade.

It was dawn, and DeCade had finally declared a rest. It was needed. Their numbers had kept growing through the night; they'd been joined by small bands of outlaws and churls at every mile. It was a huge motley army, and it needed sorting out—by clans, of course.

It was also a very weary army. Dirk had worried about that, until the word had started circulating that they'd be at Albemarle by noon—no wonder, the way DeCade had been pushing the pace. Dirk was relieved. Okay, they'd hit Albemarle bone-tired —but everyone could get at least six hours' sleep before they had to get organized for a night attack.

DeCade looked up as Dirk snaked his way through to the giant and flopped down beside him. "What word?"

"The Lords ride," Dirk answered. "The ones who escaped are riding down the main roads toward Albemarle. And they're joining up with each other: some of the bands are several thousand strong."

DeCade nodded. "As it should be. Send word to let them ride, but not let them rest. Pick off the stragglers and outriders; that will keep them fearful and running."

Dirk frowned. "Sure you want to do that? They'll double the size of the garrison, at least."

"More, by far." DeCade smiled, gloating. "There should be at least three thousand of them come to their King for sanctuary—probably five— and the castle was built for a thousand only. The

King won't need to go outside his own house to find chaos."

"Not that he ever does, anyway." Dirk pursed his lips. "Doesn't it bother you that they'll triple their fighting strength?"

DeCade shook his head. "Better to have all the rats in one nest and destroy them at one blow."

Dirk thought of a nice, tidy little tactical bomb dropping down on the packed castle, and he shuddered. "You sure you—"

"Send the word," DeCade snapped. "This, too, the Wizard planned, Dirk Dulain."

Dirk frowned up at him, wondering if there was anything of Gar left at all in the huge body. Then he met DeCade's flinty stare and decided not. He stood up and wormed his way through to a clear space, and sent the message. Could've done it there, with DeCade, of course; but somehow he just didn't want to be near the big man right now. . . .

"He is a wonder, is he not?"

Dirk looked down toward the voice and saw Madelon. Instantly, his face lost all expression.

"I suppose so," he said slowly, "but not quite a miracle, if that's what you mean. Not quite."

She glared up at him. "How can you say that? Surely it is a miracle for a man to come alive again in another's body!"

"Not when the 'miracle' is helped a little by machines."

"Machines! What machines were there, in DeCade's great cave?"

"His staff." Dirk ignored her shocked stare and

sat down beside her. "I took a look at it while it was still broken. There are tiny wires inside it, and each of them is a string of circuits—off-world magic. I didn't know what kind of machine it was, but now I think I do."

"Oh? And what, may I ask, would it be?"

"A psionic recorder and amplifier. When DeCade held that staff five hundred years ago, it recorded his thoughts through the brass bands on it. So there they lay, for five hundred years, waiting for somebody to grab hold of the conductors and put the two broken ends together, completing the circuit. Apparently three ordinary men tried—and it poured DeCade's memories into them through their hands. Their nervous systems couldn't take two personalities at once; the men died from shock."

Madelon's eyes widened. "But did you not tell me Gar was a psycha—psychometter . . ."

"A psychometrist. Yes. He could've picked up DeCade's memories just from touching the staff, even without a recorder."

"So when he *did* touch the staff . . ." she whispered.

Dirk nodded. "He got the whole thing. Not just DeCade's memories added to his own—he got DeCade. All of him—the whole personality."

"He *became* DeCade," she breathed. Then she frowned. "But if he is this thought-reader you speak of, would not the staff have killed him more surely than the others?"

Dirk nodded. "Ordinarily, yes. But he wasn't in his ordinary state at the time, you see—his mind had withdrawn into some remote corner of his brain. His whole nervous system was clear for DeCade to charge into. He found a mind like a blank sheet of paper—so he wrote on it."

"And came alive again." She turned to look at DeCade, where he sat on a log across the clearing, occasionally visible through the weaving bodies. "But—Gar's mind is still in him?"

"Oh yes. You've heard him say it—that he has the memories of the man who owned the body. But more than that—he's got the personality, too, probably still walled off in its corner—and every now and then, I think it tries to get out. When he turns silent and just stands there, scowling as though he's got a headache, I think Gar's trying to come through. From what I've heard of DeCade, he's pretty much of a hothead—act first and think later. But Gar goes at it the other way around—when the time comes for action, he's got it all thought out and ready. No, he's still there—and, at a guess, he's accepting the whole thing—for now, anyway. He knows this is his one chance to get a revolution going on this planet—and that it won't succeed without his thinking backing up DeCade's actions."

Madelon stared at him, scandalized by heresy; then she frowned thoughtfully and turned to gaze at the giant where he sat, head bowed, hands on the brass bands of the staff laid across his thighs. "Are they speaking to one another now, inside his head, where none can see or hear them? Are they working out a plan together—or warring?"

"I don't know," Dirk frowned down at her, noting the look in her eyes—awed, worshipful—and realized he'd made his own case worse. DeCade alone she might worship, but she'd never have thought of touching him; you don't try for an affair with a god. But now Dirk had put the thought in her head that DeCade wasn't quite infallible—and, worse, that there was an ordinary, accessible mortal inside his body. And one, moreover, that she'd been extremely interested in, anyway. Resentment tightened into resolution; Dirk stood up. "I don't know," he said again, "but I think I'll find out." And he strode away across the clearing, ignoring her startled protest.

DeCade still sat silent, frowning in concentration. Dirk hesitated as he came up to the giant, then sat down slowly and waited.

After a time, DeCade shook his head and closed his eyes. Then he opened them and looked up at Dirk. "What troubles your mind, Outlander?"

Dirk frowned back at him thoughtfully, trying to find a place to begin. What did you say to a man of two minds? "Hi, there! Can I speak with your better half?"

"You are not sure of me, are you?" DeCade said suddenly.

Dirk stared for a moment, taken aback. Then he smiled slowly. "No more than you are of me, DeCade—and you aren't, or you wouldn't call me 'Outlander.' "

DeCade held his gaze a moment, then nodded slowly. "Yet you would not deny that you are an outlander."

Dirk shook his head. "I'm a churl born, like the rest of you. From my tenth year I've lived among the sky-men, true; but I'm still a churl."

DeCade shook his head, too. "Not like the rest of us, no. You know the secrets of the sky-men, and you have known freedom. You are apart from us, Dirk Dulain—no matter your birth and your childhood."

Dirk bit down on his anger. He knew the cause: DeCade was right.

"So much for yourself." DeCade stared intently into his eyes. "Why do *you* doubt *me*?"

"Oh, I don't. I believe you're DeCade—but . . ." He pursed his lips, staring back into the giant's eyes. "Did you sleep well?"

DeCade shrugged impatiently. "What is a sleep? The light goes; then it comes again and you wake. There were no dreams, Dulain—only three spots of light, down the centuries: Fools—petty, ambitious, grasping fools—who took up my staff in hopes of becoming kings. They were small men, and weak; they could not contain me within them."

"But this man—Gar—can," Dirk said softly.

DeCade nodded. "He is truly a man, as great as ever I was." A shadow of doubt crossed his face. "Perhaps greater . . ." He shrugged, irritated. "No matter. We are two strong men; we have two sources of strength to guide this people now." His eyes had become compelling, almost hypnotizing. "We are both here, you see—both in this body. I speak now, my will rules—but only because this fellow—Gar, as you call him—is wholly behind me and with me."

Dirk heaved a sigh of relief, which surprised him; he hadn't realized he was that uncertain about

Gar's survival. "Well . . . I'm glad you two worked things out between you . . ."

DeCade grinned. "Oh, there was something of trouble at first—a few seconds only, to you, but hours to us. Both of us were startled, alarmed— and very ready to fight. Your friend came boiling out of his hole to crush the invader, and we locked horns almost eagerly, and strained, feinted, countered and struck—till, from the wrangle, he realized whom he was fighting and why I was with him. I shocked him out of a sleep, too, you see; but presently he knew me."

"Yes," Dirk said slowly, "he would be good at reading people, wouldn't he?"

DeCade frowned. "How much did you know of this man?"

"A lot—though I didn't realize it soon enough. I figured out he was a mindreader, and a man who read minds from their artifacts—but only when it was too late. . . . So you're both there, both within the same body, both still alive?"

DeCade nodded. "Yes. And because of that, I trust you more than any of these others."

Dirk frowned. "Would you mind explaining that?"

DeCade turned, looking out over the camp. "I know I can trust them, in that they will do whatever I say; the Wizard did his work well—better than he promised me. But they are loyal to a legend, a rumor, to a thing greater than human that the Wizard's songs have built down the centuries. Theirs is blind, unquestioning obedience and faith—and the part of me that is like them is warm with their love and trusting. But . . ." His eyes swung back to Dirk. "There is another part of me now, with memories I never lived through; and that part is like you: an outlander."

Dirk nodded slowly. "And that part knows that I'm loyal not out of faith, but from reason."

DeCade grinned and clapped him on the shoulder. Dirk picked himself up off the ground and looked up at the giant, whose face had turned grim. "The others will do as I say, blindly, unthinking. But you will question me if I may be wrong."

Dirk nodded. "Oh yes. You can bet on that. I know a little about the Lords that they don't, you see."

DeCade nodded. "Yes. You have studied these Lords from the sky since I died, have you not?" His brows drew down. "Question me indeed, if you think I am wrong—but do not do it at the wrong time."

Dirk stared up into the burning eyes, and felt a chill down his back.

The Lords and their Gentlemen rode up to Albemarle, their women and children in their center. As they came near the town, they watched the roadsides in fear and suspicion; they trotted their horses, ready to break into a gallop at the first cry of alarm. They clumped together in the center of the highway; the shoulders had become very treacherous.

But they began to mutter to one another as they rode out of the forest; they had ridden through two miles ideal for ambush, and no deadly hail of arrows had come. Only an occasional man disappeared from their fringe. And that made them even more fearful and uncertain; why would the churls let them ride unmolested? The more contemptuous among them put it down to cowardice—the churls would not attack them now, when they were awake, clad in armor, mounted, ready for battle. Others suggested the peasants had sickened of battle already and gone home to their cottages. Only a few of the older, grimmer hearts were seized with foreboding; they knew some excellent military head had planned the assaults on the castles, and if that tactician were letting them gather together all in one place, what did he plan? But there was nothing else to do; if they scattered to strong places, the churls would cut them down one by one.

So they rode to Albemarle.

But these realists were few. Most spirits began to rise as they rode out of the forest, across the river and up the road that wound up the hill to high Albemarle. As they climbed, they began to sing; some began to joke and laugh. This slackened as they rode through the King's Town, eyeing the shuttered houses and shops warily. Then one man began to sing a battle song; others joined in, and, as they rode through the high gate beneath the grim portcullis, they began to believe they might yet put down this rebellion.

So they came into Albemarle in bands of hundreds, the tattered remnants of thousands; but they came into Albemarle with laughter and song.

But there was song in the forests, too, where renegade Soldiers and freed churls, outlaws and Guildsmen sat around their fires, chanting the Lay of DeCade.

CHAPTER 13

The churls had slept for six hours and come awake as the sun was going down. Most of them brought out biscuits and cheese from their wallets and made a supper. A small army of old men moved among them, distributing food from nearby estates, to those who hadn't brought any; but they were bitter about being too old to contribute more than food. As they went, they reminded the churls to eat lightly; there was hard work coming.

Hugh, Lapin, and Madelon came pacing up to DeCade, where he sat alone on his log. Dirk looked up, saw, and hurried to join them.

"There are five thousand Lords and their men come into Albemarle," Lapin was saying as he came up. "There were a thousand before; now there are six."

DeCade nodded. "What of their churls?"

"They went out when the Bell was rungen," Hugh reported, "though they longed to stay and turn upon their Lords."

DeCade shook his head firmly. "No. We must have a baited trap for our rats."

Hugh shrugged. "Most of them are here among us. We have eleven thousand churls within this wood and spread throughout the fields around and about."

"Eleven thousand to six?" Dirk frowned. "Not good odds when they've got laser cannon."

DeCade shook his head. "Their cannon cannot shoot straight down, and we shall be beneath their walls before they realize we have come. Indeed, their cannon should be ours before they sound the alarm."

Dirk scowled. "Don't have much faith in their sentries, do you?"

"Not greatly, but I have great faith in my outlaws." DeCade turned to Hugh. "Did you discover how their cannon are mounted?"

"Aye, we have many of the King's Soldiers here, now." Hugh sounded a little nervous as he said it; old habits die hard. "They will not turn about."

DeCade grimaced with exasperation. "Then we can only capture them; we cannot use them to keep the courtyard clear."

Lapin shrugged. "We will do well enough, Grandmaster. Once our outlaws have scaled the walls and taken out the sentries, they may shoot down upon the courtyard with their new lasers."

"And the Lords may fire down on them from the central keep," DeCade said dourly. "Still, it will be some cover, and it may give the churls time to charge the gate."

"We will have it open for them," Hugh promised. He grinned. "There will be great fighting in the King's grand hall."

"And in the courtyard," DeCade pointed out. "Once our own men are there, we cannot fire upon it."

"Neither shall the Lords," Lapin said grimly. "Our firebeams shall keep them from their Tower windows—never fear."

DeCade nodded sardonically. "So they shall come out to the courtyard, to give us welcome." He turned to Dirk. "That is when *your* towers must drop down, to overawe them."

Dirk shook his head. "Won't work. They'll know we wouldn't fire on our own."

"But we shall," Lapin said harshly.

Dirk stared at her.

The huge woman shrugged impatiently. "If we die, we die. Death in battle, or death from a lordling's whim—what difference?"

"That is a source of strength," DeCade agreed. "Are all our people divided up by bands, and captains and lieutenants appointed?"

Hugh nodded and Madelon said, "We have made a chart of the castle from the servants' memories. Each troop is appointed a hall, and each band a chamber."

Dirk listened numbly, trying to decide whether it was fanaticism—or logic.

DeCade nodded. "Then all is ready—save one thing."

Dirk came out of his daze. "I can't imagine what."

"The King." DeCade's eyes burned.

Dirk stared at him.

"We must take the King." DeCade stood up, pacing. "This is the keystone of the Wizard's plan. Even if we slew every Lord but let the King live, he could escape, and forces gather round him."

Dirk thought of some of the interplanetary freebooters and soldiers-of-fortune, and realized the Wizard's wisdom. If the King escaped and managed to get word off-planet, a whole mercenary army would come blasting in to win back his kingdom for him—and just incidentally, for themselves.

"But if we take him," DeCade went on, "and show him, bound, to his Lords, they may lose heart and surrender."

Dirk scratched behind his ear. "I wouldn't put too much faith in that. They strike me as a pretty independent lot. Matter of fact, I don't think there's a one of them who wouldn't cheerfully watch the King hang, if it'd save him a few pennies."

DeCade shrugged. "In that case, we can kill him and be done with it. Still, 'tis worth the try."

Dirk wondered if he was the only man there who didn't have callouses on his conscience. "Well, it sounds good," he said dubiously. "But aren't you going to have to cut through all the Lords anyway, to get to him?"

DeCade cupped his hands over the tip of his staff and propped his chin on them. "I shall tell you a tale."

"Oh goody!" Dirk sat down and propped *his* chin on a fist. "I'm just in the mood for a bedtime story." Lapin scowled at him, but he ignored her.

"Many years ago," DeCade intoned, "when first this land was peopled, our noble King's first forefather set ten thousand churls to building his castle. A hundred of them slept and ate apart, the while they built his bedchamber; and, when it was done—he killed them."

Dirk stared back at him for a moment. Then: "Nice guy. . . . You'd almost think he had something to hide."

"Aye," DeCade agreed. "But alas, poor King! One churl, before he died, had managed to tell a churl outside the hundred, who told a churl who told a churl . . . and thus the word came to his son."

"You don't say."

"I do. And, before he died, the son told *his* son, who told his son, who told his son . . ."

Dirk held up a hand. "Let me guess. There was still one of them around the first time you tried this project."

DeCade nodded, his eyes glowing.

Madelon, Lapin, and Hugh stared. Then they began to smile.

Dirk noted it with foreboding; whenever they

got happy, he got worried. "Let me guess again. The secret was a tunnel."

DeCade nodded. "A tunnel leading to a passage, which leads to a door that opens on the King's private chamber."

"And he told you where to find it."

"Nay; he showed it to me." DeCade's eyes unfocused as he looked off into a distance centuries long. "One dark night, when we'd come close to Albemarle, he and I crept out, behind the King's own lines, and found . . ." He shook the mood off. "No matter. It is there, and I can lead you to it."

"If it's still clear," Dirk said dubiously.

DeCade shrugged. "If not, I'll clear it."

He did have one thing in common with Gar, Dirk decided. He was so damn sure of everything.

The outlaws moved out about an hour after sunset. The churls stayed longer, sharpening their weapons, talking to one another in low, hushed voices, and generally working up a good case of nerves. Then, finally, they began to move out, by squads. Their faces were grim and their eyes were hard. Soon there was no one left in the clearing but DeCade, Dirk, and the twenty most skilled outlaws with staves in their hands, knives and laser pistols in their belts, and mayhem in their hearts. DeCade looked them over, then nodded curtly. "Put out the fire."

The youngest outlaw stooped to throw dirt on the campfire. Its light dimmed and was gone. The troop stood silent in the soft light of the stars.

Without looking at them, DeCade turned and strode away. Dirk leaped to catch up with him.

DeCade led them through the forest to a wooded gully that once must have housed a small river. But it had come down in the world woefully; a mere brooklet chinked and chattered its way over rocks at the bottom. DeCade turned to follow it downstream. Dirk turned with him, suppressing the impulse to look back over his shoulder. He knew what he would see—a score of outlaws following them in lockstep.

He looked up at DeCade. "Has it occurred to you that the King might have an unpleasant surprise waiting for us in that chamber?"

"There will be many surprises this night," DeCade said dourly. "Have no fear; I have one of my own for each of theirs."

Dirk pursed his lips. "Care to let me in on the secret?"

DeCade shook his head. "You would understand mine no more easily than I understand yours, Outworlder."

Dirk thought that one over. Considering that DeCade had full access to Gar's memories. . . . However, it was a moderately polite way of saying no. Even so . . . "Surely our secrets cannot be so alien, one to another, DeCade. We are, after all, of one blood."

"Yes, but both of us are alienated from that blood, Dirk Dulain—you in one direction, I in another. The sum and total is too wide a gap for talk."

Dirk frowned, telling himself he had no reason

to feel rejected. "Don't tell me that, DeCade. Because, if it were true, I could never find a home."

"Only by forcing yourself to fit into one," DeCade agreed. "Which would you rather have, Dulain—the contentment and acceptance of a home, with the gnawing certainty that you are not really like yourself as long as you are in it, that you live a lie and are not really like the people about you? Or to be able to live without pretense, being as you really are, but with the loneliness of the stranger forever hollowing your bowels?"

Dirk tried to swallow that one, but it stuck in his throat. He swiveled his head forward and strode down the gully in silence. DeCade was companionably silent, too, for a time; then, he stopped abruptly and pointed to a shadow in the wall of the gorge. "There it lies."

Dirk came out of his brown study and looked, but all he saw was brush and grass. "Where?"

But DeCade was already climbing the slope, and Dirk had to hurry to keep up with him.

Finally DeCade stopped and lashed out at the grass with the tip of his staff, ripping out greenery and uncovering a heap of humus. He wielded the staff like a great broom, and peat and mulch went flying, till Dirk saw a round cave-mouth, just large enough for a man of normal height. DeCade turned, gesturing to the outlaws; a laser pistol sizzled, its ruby beam slicing the darkness to kindle a pine knot. Torchlight flared and the laser beam winked out. DeCade nodded, turned, and stepped into the tunnel, stooping. Dirk nodded to the outlaws and followed. The light came behind him, wavering on the wall.

"Has it occurred to you," he said carefully to DeCade, "that there might be booby traps in here?"

DeCade came to a halt and stared down at him. "What manner of traps?"

"Well," Dirk said slowly, "from the tale you tell me, the first King built this place; and that means he was an, ah, immigrant, from Terra. He'd have been very up-to-date on the latest burglar-proofing technology, and paranoid enough to use it."

"And just what kinds of machines are these?"

Dirk shrugged. "Oh, I expect you know them as well as I do—or part of you, at least. Hidden lasers, sonic beams to jelly your brains, that sort of thing."

DeCade's mouth was tight with amusement. "And how are these pleasant toys triggered?"

"Oh, the usual—pressure-sensitive plates in the floor, ultra-violet electric eyes, sonar, infrared detectors, brainwave analyzers ... like that. So if you can manage to weigh nothing, keep from walking through any light beams you can't see, not reflect any sound waves, stop thinking, and cool your body down to eighty-five degrees, you won't have a thing to worry about."

"None at all," DeCade agreed. "Thank you for the timely warning; I'll bear it in mind." And he turned away to start up the tunnel again.

Dirk stared at him.

Then he jumped to catch up with him. "After all

that, you're just going to march ahead? What are you, a walking death-wish?"

"A nice hypothesis, now that you mention it. Still, I don't plan to die till the Lords are dead." DeCade gestured ahead. "Look there."

Dirk looked ahead, frowning, trying to pierce the darkness beyond the circle of torchlight. Then he saw it—a shimmer, filling the tunnel from wall to wall and floor to ceiling, like a heat haze, although the tunnel was dank and cold. He glanced at DeCade's face, saw the tension, the telltale look of pain—but very slight, now; he was adapting to it—and a chill went down Dirk's spine. Apparently Gar had some abilities Dirk hadn't known about. "What is it—a force field?"

DeCade smiled through the headache. "You shall see quickly enough. These may be an outworlder's powers, but I think they are beyond most outworlders' ken. He has lost none of himself, this one—and I think he has been lonely. Very."

" 'Think?' " Dirk frowned. "Don't you know?"

DeCade shook his head. "His most important memories he keeps locked away from me, in a small, dark, hard shell at his core. He is wise. He knows he is alien; he will not try to be otherwise."

"So he loses none of himself?" Dirk shook his head. "That can't be the only choice a man has—to lose part of himself, or to be lonely."

DeCade shrugged. "Many men adjust their behavior to those around them and keep their true selves locked away safely, in a small, dark part of their souls. They feel that part in them and cherish it; thus they know who they are and lose nothing of themselves while having all benefits of company—but I think such men always yearn for just one soul who is like them. They die with that yearning. Still, most men seem to have no difficulty at all; they are enough like their fellows so that they need not think about it. You and I, though, who are of our people, but not like to them . . ." He shrugged. "We may try to become as much like our fellows as we can, to completely change ourselves so that we are like them."

Dirk shook his head. "That doesn't work. You can't change who you are; all you can do is a good job of acting, good enough to fool your fellows and maybe even fool yourself—but that's all you'd be doing. Fooling. And sooner or later, what you really are would roar out to loom up over you, demanding retribution."

"Yes." DeCade said promptly. "That is the trouble with the third way, is it not?"

Dirk thought that one over as they paced ahead through the tunnel. Then he said slowly, "I think I know another way; to search and keep searching, till you find people who are like you."

DeCade smiled politely. "True, that is *possible* . . ."

Dirk didn't like the emphasis.

"But why do you speak of this, friend Dulain?" DeCade rumbled. "Are you not like other skymen?"

"Yes, of course." Dirk frowned. "But that's begging the question. It's saying that you can stop being a wanderer by becoming a part of a group of wanderers."

"Yes." DeCade nodded, with full conviction. "And I think your question has been answered, Dirk Dulain; it—" Suddenly he froze, staring ahead of him.

Dirk came to a halt, frowning up at him; then he turned to look forward. . . .

Ruby light spat out from both walls, gouging holes in the stone three feet in front of them.

Dirk could feel his eyes trying to bulge out of their sockets.

The beams cut off, leaving no light but the torch. Behind Dirk, the outlaws muttered fearfully.

"Triggered by the force-field we passed through."

DeCade's voice cut through the mutters. "It is no matter. They told me it was coming. Follow." And he stepped forward again.

Dirk frowned up at him. Then, hesitantly, he stepped forward himself. He took the second step a little more surely; with the third step, he felt a gush of fervent faith in DeCade that threatened to overwhelm him. He suppressed it quickly—almost in panic—as he caught up with DeCade. He looked up at the giant, frowning. "Who told you it was coming?"

"The men who built this place." DeCade licked his lips and swallowed; sweat sheened his forehead. "There was suffering between these walls, Dirk Dulain."

Of course, Dirk thought, chagrined. If the workmen who put the lasers in had been men of any conscience, they would have been in agony over what the devices they were installing could do to human beings—and, they must have realized, human beings of their own kind; who else would want to sneak into the King's castle through the back door? Echoes of that guilt would still linger near each installation—for a psychometrist.

Then the other implication hit him. Dirk stared up at DeCade, appalled.

The giant nodded. "Yes, Dirk Dulain. When they killed them, they buried the workmen in the walls."

"Odd gods, man! You must be in agony!"

"It . . . is not pleasant," DeCade admitted.

Dirk peered up at him in the torchlight, looking closely. "Are you sure you're—"

"I am," DeCade said curtly. "I can bear it easily, Dulain; there were only a hundred of them." And he marched ahead.

Dirk followed slowly, mentally revising his estimate of the giant's strength upward; and it had been high to begin with. Or was it Gar's strength he was estimating?

DeCade jerked to a halt again. In a low, soothing voice, he called out, "Steady. It comes now, once again." He scowled; an uneasy murmur rose behind him. DeCade ignored it, glowering straight ahead. Dirk wondered what he was doing—putting greater weight on the floor with a force-field, pushing out heat in front of himself, stopping a stream of photons? Whichever one it was, Gar must have also been a telekineticist; by speeding up the motion of the molecules, he could raise the temperature of the air. By slowing them down, he could free energy to bind into a force field—and if he could do that, he was some kind of psi Dirk had never even heard about. Dirk found himself wondering if there had been anything psionic Gar *hadn't* been able to do.

A thundering crash, and a huge portcullis slammed down to bite into the rock of the tunnel floor.

Dirk started back, scared half out of his skin.

The tunnel was totally silent.

Then a low, frantic muttering began.

DeCade's voice cut through it like a buzz saw. "It is done; they have shot their bolt. Now let us tear this iron from our path." He nodded to Dirk. "Your laser."

Dirk pulled out his pistol and held down the firing stud. The ruby beam sizzled out to the top corner of the portcullis and began to shear through the iron. Behind him, three outlaws unlimbered their own pistols, gaining confidence now that they had something to do. Four ruby beams slashed out, moving slowly, one along each side.

Dirk couldn't help a moment of admiration for the first King. Just in case time deteriorated his electronic defense, he'd had a primitive mechanical one as a fail-safe. Primitive, yes, but effective— unless you happened to have an all-purpose psi along.

Each pair of laser beams met at a corner and winked out. DeCade stood waiting a few moments, watching the glowing metal; then he raised his staff with both hands clasped at the top, swung it high above his head like a battering ram, and shot it forward. The tip hit the iron grille a little above center. The last few strands of iron snapped, and the huge gate slammed back and down with a crash.

DeCade stood staring at it a moment. Then, slowly, he said, "The way is clear, good lads. Follow." And he stepped onto the grille, carefully avoiding the hot edges, and strode ahead. Dirk followed. So did the outlaws.

As the torchbearer cleared the far edge of the portcullis, the light fell on a steep, narrow flight of stairs, thick with dust. DeCade grinned down at Dirk. "Only a long climb now, friend Dulain, and we will have come to the place we seek." Then he frowned, his head snapped up, as though he had heard something.

Dirk had felt it, too—that sudden inner certainty that *now* was the time.

"We are laggard," DeCade said grimly. "They are storming the walls. Come."

He turned and strode away up the stairs.

The young Lord on sentry duty at the northeast point of the wall leaned on the battlement, staring down at the wide talus slope below him, newly sprinkled with lime, white even in the starlight. He smiled at the sight, nodding with satisfaction; not a single churl could creep across that expanse of whiteness without being as clear as a hot woman's hunger. The rabble had pushed their rightful lords back into Albemarle, but now the pushing was done; the Lords were here in the King's castle, and here they would stay while Core and the King summoned an army from across the galaxy—there were always mercenaries for hire, and any aristocracy was a good credit risk. A fleet of ships would be on its way before morning; and the Lords could stay, safe and snug, in this castle, until the great ships came thundering down. There was plenty of food, and Albemarle had never been taken.

The young Lord failed to remember that Albemarle had never been attacked.

Below him, in the fringe of forest across the white talus slope, churls cherished new laser pistols given to them by sky-men. Directly below the young Lord, a sky-man lay prone, cradling a sniper's laser rifle to his shoulder, centering infrared scope sights on the sentry. Next to him knelt an outlaw, his hand on the sky-man's shoulder, waiting.

On the wall above, eight sentries watched, hawk-eyed and nervous, alert for the slightest sign of attack, wishing their watches were over.

Below each of them lay a sky-man with a rifle, and a churl with his hand on the sky-man's shoulder—almost immobile, scarcely breathing—waiting.

Then somehow, each churl felt it within him—*now* was the time.

Eight hands tightened on shoulders.

Eight beams of ruby light lanced out at the same moment; eight sentries fell, with holes burned in their chests. One screamed and another managed a rattling bark; then all was still. Each lordling lay next to the huge laser cannon that had been his charge.

On the white talus slope, eight groups of out laws appeared, running toward the wall with long ladders, grappling hooks, and cables. The butts of the ladders grounded just outside the moat; their tops swung up, over, and thudded home high on the castle walls. Outlaws scrambled up the ladders. They stopped at the topmost rungs, slipped the grappling hooks from their shoulders, swung them seven times about their heads, and let fly. Eight irons arced up through the night, over the wall and down, to clatter on stone. Below, on the ground, other churls caught the trailing ropes and pulled. The grappling irons clattered along the stone and caught in crevices. More churls threw their weight on the ropes, and steel points bit deep into stone.

Above on the ladder, the climbers caught the ropes again, pulled on them, rested their weight on them, then swung out, and set their feet against the walls, and started walking upward. A few minutes later, they hauled themselves over the top and onto the battlements. They pulled themselves to their feet, pulling out hammers and ringbolts, and turned to drive the ringbolts deep into the granite. Then they loosened the grappling irons and pulled up the ropes. At their ends came rope ladders. They made the ladders fast to the ringbolts, then leaned over the outer wall, waving down. A few minutes later, sky-men clambered up and over the walls, dropped to their knees next to the laser cannons, pulled out small tool kits, and got busy taking out a few vital parts. The climbers hadn't waited; they were already down in the courtyard, running, converging on the main gate. As they ran, they unlimbered truncheons and drew laser pistols.

The Lord of the Watch sat at a table with three other Lords, playing cards by the light of an oil lamp. Its light flickered on the great windlass that operated the drawbridge, but didn't quite penetrate to the door and corners. Three outlaws eased silently through the door.

One of the Lords threw down his cards in disgust and leaned back in his chair, looking up. His eyes widened and his mouth opened to shout.

The outlaws sprang, and five more leaped in behind them.

One Lord went down as a club caught him behind the ear. The other three stared, then leaped to their feet, shouting and yanking at their swords. One went down with a bad dent in his skull; a truncheon stabbed into another's solar plexus. The last screamed as a club broke his wrist; then another caught him at the base of the skull, and his scream cut off, his eyes rolling up as his knees collapsed and he folded to the floor.

The outlaws stood panting a moment, staring down at their erstwhile masters, not quite believing. Then four of them whipped ropes and gags from their belts and knelt to get busy wrapping the Lords for storage. The other four turned to the great windlass.

Outside, an army of churls streamed up across the white talus slope with Hugh at their head. The great drawbridge groaned, then swung slowly down with a rattling of chains. It thudded home on the bank, and the portcullis creaked up as a vanguard of a thousand churls came charging across the bridge, their eyes burning with silent triumph. They burst into the courtyard. Behind them, thousands more swelled up out of the woods in an orderly, quick-moving column.

The brazen bellow of a gong split the night, rolling out from the great central keep.

Hugh cursed under his breath; some lordling had looked out a window, and seen what was happening in the courtyard, and raised the alarm. It wouldn't be quite a clean sweep, after all.

But close enough ...

He charged the great door of the keep, leveling his laser to burn out the lock; but the door boomed open, and a double column of Lords charged out, formed into a skirmish line, and opened fire as other Lords came running out onto the battlements from upper doors. Hugh and his men threw themselves flat and dived for cover behind carts, water troughs, anything, as the sky-men on the battlements opened fire on the Lords up above, and a thousand churls came vaulting up stone steps to join them. Laser beams embroidered the night with bright geometric patterns. Churls and Lords screamed and died, but others leaped to fill their places. The churls pressed forward foot by foot; but a thousand Lords were now spread out by the base of the Keep, and half again that number warred on the battlements. More pressed behind them.

Then a score of churls together blasted ten

Lords out of the line and charged up to three feet of them before other Lords could replace them. The replacements came out firing, but wildly; ten churls survived to burn into the center of the packed mass of Lords, and a hundred followed them. The Lords turned on the invaders, but realized that a laser was as apt to burn a fellow Lord as a churl. They threw their pistols down with curses and whipped out their swords.

The churls met them with long knives.

In a few minutes, a knot of chaos had formed in front of the keep door as Lords paired off with churls in hand-to-hand combat. Other Lords charged in to help their fellows, and hundreds of churls ducked laser fire to plunge in to have a personal chance at a Lord. The whole courtyard became one huge melee, Lords bellowing and howling as they fought silent, flint-eyed churls. And still the Lords poured out from the keep, and still more churls poured in through the gate.

CHAPTER 14

An outlaw threw his weight on a lever and, slowly, the oak door at the top of the stairs groaned open. DeCade leaped forward, ducking and whirling out into an opulent bed-chamber, staff lashing out in case of ambush. But the chamber was empty. He straightened slowly, looking about him, too, curious to see how the top percent of the other half lived. The carpet on the floor felt like a lush lawn beneath his feet. The walls were hung with rich, brightly worked tapestries, and the chairs, dressers, and tables were beautifully carved of a dark, rich wood. A huge canopied bed stood in the center of the room, hung with burgundy velvet curtains—drawn tightly, now.

DeCade stepped toward it, motioning them to

follow. He eased up to the side of the bed, Dirk beside him. Half of the outlaws oozed over to the curtains on the far side.

DeCade reached out a huge hand and yanked the curtains open.

A fat, bearded young man started up out of a sound sleep, staring about him wildly. He took one look at DeCade, gave a shriek of terror, and burrowed back into the bedclothes, plastering himself against the headboard, trembling and staring at them with wide, dull eyes. His nightshirt was silk, heavily embroidered—and stained with food. There was a golden coronet on his head.

DeCade's mouth drew up in contempt. "Is *this* a King?"

The hair was long, black, and straggling; the beard was sparse and scrubby. The creature pressed back against the headboard, mewling in terror, clawing at the bedclothes.

DeCade doffed his cap in sarcastic respect. "Well met, your Majesty . . . Have you nothing to say?"

"You know he doesn't," Dirk said gently. "Look at his eyes."

The eyes were huge, wide, dull—and empty. Spittle glistened on the thick lips and dripped down into the beard.

DeCade nodded, with heavy irony. "Yes, I know. The churls are not alone in inbreeding."

"He is always spoken of but never seen," Dirk said slowly.

"Small wonder. Would *you* display an idiot for your King?"

Dirk shook his head. "But who's been governing the kingdom?"

"I have."

Dirk whipped around, his laser drawn. DeCade turned more slowly, with a sardonic smile.

A tapestry swung aside, and Lord Core stepped out into the room, laser in his hand. He bowed his head in mock greeting, a vindictive smile on his lips. "Welcome, Lords of the Torn Smocks. It seems I have anticipated you."

DeCade seemed almost amused. "You have; but then, it took no great deal of thought to know we would seek the King first."

Core frowned, nettled. "Nor did it take any great thinking to realize who led these rebels. But if you were able to guess I would be here to meet you, you were quite foolish to walk into my arms."

"Indeed?" DeCade raised his eyebrows politely, glancing at the outlaws behind him. "May I inquire as to who has walked into whose trap?"

Core smiled and gestured. All around the room, tapestries parted, and fifty armed Lords stepped through, swords in one hand, pistols in the other.

"*My* trap, I think," Core murmured, with a gloating smile.

DeCade threw back his head, roaring laughter—and his staff whipped up, lashing out at Core as he fell prone to the floor. Dirk fell with him, almost before he realized it, and fired his laser as he fell. A Lord screamed, and went down—and so did twenty others, as a ruby beam lanced upward from every fallen outlaw. The remaining Lords fired; but DeCade was on his feet again, and so were the outlaws. Two screamed and went down with burned feet; the others fired again, while the Lords were still burning the carpet—and screaming, as the outlaws' shots burned home.

Then DeCade's staff sent Core's pistol spinning, but the Lord chopped left-handed with his sword. DeCade parried with his staff and stepped in to close quarters, as the outlaws leaped in to grapple with the remaining Lords, man to man.

Dirk jabbed his man under the breastbone with his knife, yanked it out as the Lord fell with a shriek, and turned to cut his way through to De-Cade's side. He had a certain respect for Core. . . .

DeCade chopped at the Lord's head with his staff; Core blocked the blow with his sword, and DeCade whipped the butt of his staff toward Core's temple. The Lord ducked and swung his sword up in a vicious stab at DeCade's belly. De-Cade leaned to the side, and the tip of the sword flashed by to tangle in his cloak. The butt of the staff leaped forward at Core's head again. Again, Core ducked, but the staff dipped down with him and caught him under the chin. He slammed back against the wall, dazed. A huge hand caught him on the rebound, caught him by the throat, and squeezed. Core choked, his eyes cleared, and he whipped a dagger from a sheath at the small of his back, stabbed at DeCade's side. DeCade twisted, but the knife slashed his chest open. Snarling with pain, he caught the Lord's knife hand, twisting it sharply. Core screamed as bone cracked, and the knife clattered to the floor. DeCade spat with contempt and flung Core into the four-poster bed. The idiot screamed and clawed at Core, trying to get away from him. Core slapped him across the mouth with a snarl; the King fell back, dazed, and Core rolled from the bed, a new laser appearing from his boot, centered on DeCade.

The giant stepped back, alert and watchful. Core smiled, gloating, and stepped toward him.

Dirk's dagger drove into his side.

Core screamed and whirled about, his pistol spraying fire, but Dirk had dropped to one knee. He caught the Lord's wrist as it went by overhead, and twisted; the pistol dropped to the floor, and Core screamed again. Dirk yanked out the dagger as he leaped to his feet, stabbed home again, into Core's chest, then again as the Lord fell, and again, and again. "For my mother, who died from the lack of your medicine. . . . For my father, who died from your scourge. . . . For my sister, who fled from your lust. . . . For the year that I spent hiding from your hounds, hiding and starving. . . . For the—"

A hand caught his wrist on the upswing. Dirk whipped about, snarling . . . and stared up into DeCade's impassive face.

"You butcher dead meat," said the giant.

Dirk stared up at him, reason slowly returning. He turned to look down at Core.

The Lord was a fountain of blood, a dozen red mouths pumping life from his chest. Dirk raised his eyes; Core's eyes were dull, glazed, his mouth twisted in a last agony of humiliation.

"He *is* dead," Dirk muttered, scarcely able to believe it.

Slowly he rose, eyes still on the corpse. "He's always been there, as long as I can remember—my nemesis, looming up, deadly, at the center of creation, his shadow darkening my world, preventing me from doing anything good. . . ."

"So they all have been, to all of us," DeCade rumbled. "Believe it, Dulain, and know peace in the depths of your heart: he is dead."

And finally, Dirk began to believe it.

At last he raised his eyes, realizing that the chamber was quiet. The outlaws stood, silently watching him—ten of them. The other ten lay dead with the Lords, in the carpet of blood. Dirk looked at the living, at their set, brooding faces, and realized each man saw himself in Dirk, at that moment.

Tiny in the stillness, there was whimpering.

CHAPTER 15

Dirk turned slowly, frowning. The idiot King was huddled into a ball at the head of the bed, his beard filled with spittle, his lips flecked with foam. His eyes were blank with terror. Disgust welled up in Dirk—and the beginning of a vast guilt.

"There is no time for pity," DeCade rumbled. "They fight in the courtyard below. Quickly! Take this poor hunk of flesh; bind his arms and bring him with us."

The idiot huddled himself tighter against the headboard, hands in his mouth, mewling.

Dirk frowned. "Why? Can't we leave the poor thing alone?"

DeCade shook his head. "Idiot he may be, but he is nonetheless King. Do you not know what kings are, Outworlder? They are symbols, most powerful ones. Show a symbol in chains, and the men who fight for it fight as though they, too, were weighed down by chains."

Dirk closed his eyes, nodding, and three outlaws laid hands on their King, to bind his arms and pull him to his feet. They handled him as gently as they could, Dirk noticed; he wondered whether it was from the dimmed aura of royalty that still clung to him, or from sympathy.

Then they were rushing down the hallway to keep up with DeCade's long strides, half-carrying the poor idiot. As Dirk caught up with him, De-Cade said over his shoulder, "Summon your ships. Tell them to land just outside the castle walls and fire a shot over the battlements."

Dirk stared up at him in surprise. Then he shrugged and took off his rope belt. "It's your party." He contacted the ship and relayed the message. All the Captain said was, "Copied, and in execution. End contact."

They strode on through hallways eerily deserted. "Did they leave none to guard their keep?" De-Cade growled, glancing suspiciously from side to side.

"I don't think they were planning on an inside job," Dirk said dourly. "You must admit that the party you ordered for the front yard doesn't exactly look like a diversion."

Then they burst out onto a balcony, and Dirk stared down at the "party," appalled, as the roar of battle struck him. The courtyard was one huge, clamoring, churning mass. It was steel and wooden clubs—nothing more—for the churls were so thoroughly intermingled with Lords that no one dared fire a laser, for fear of hitting a friend. Steel rang and clattered below; steel hewed heads and drank blood. Steel would decide the night.

And the Lords had been trained to the sword from their cradles. The courtyard was clogged with dead bodies, among whom the Lords were not fairly represented.

But still the churls pressed in through the gate, every man eager for his chance at his persecutors. It was steel against masses of flesh, swords against numbers; and Dirk saw clearly that the numbers would weigh down the swords and grind them into the earth—but only at an unbelievable cost. The churls would win the land they tilled, but they would pay with seas of blood.

Beside him, DeCade called, "They must be silenced long enough to hear my voice. *Where are your ships?*"

Dirk searched the skies, craning his neck. Then he saw it—a star that moved. "There!" He grasped DeCade's head, to sight along his pointing arm. "One mass diversion coming up—or down, as the case may be."

The star separated into two; both grew, swelling into planets, then moons; and, faintly over the roar of battle, Dirk began to hear a mutter. It grew to a bellow as the two moons swelled up and stretched out into tall, pointed flareships, dropping down at them on cushions of flame. Thunder shook the whole castle as two huge, bright towers fell out of the sky, screaming and howling. Then at last, ev-

ery man in the courtyard froze, staring up in terror
at the huge fiery mouths that spewed down toward
them. Dirk saw men cower, saw lips stretched
wide in shrieks. But all he could hear was the
thunder that filled the world.

At the last moment, the two towers seemed to
veer to the sides as they shot down outside the castle walls, tall, bright turrets stretching up above the
top of the keep. Still the thunder bellowed. Then
the engines cut out, and silence struck the courtyard like a physical blow.

Then a double thunderclap split the night as two
huge white balls of flame exploded above the
courtyard from the ship's guns. A vast, raw scream
of fear raked up from the packed mass of men, and
a cleared circle appeared magically in the center of
the court as Lords and churls alike jammed back
frantically toward the walls, clambering over their
fellows to get away from the juggernaut that must
surely fall on them.

Dirk took a long, deep breath. It was definitely
a most glorious way of stopping a battle.

Then he realized that it wasn't. The Lords knew
what spaceships were; they would come out of it
quickly, and turn to slaughter dazed churls.

Just then, DeCade's voice roared in his ear, filling the courtyard: *"Behold your King!"*

Every head in the courtyard swung about, staring. DeCade gestured, and two outlaws swung the
idiot King high for all eyes to see. He screamed
and struggled, kicking wildly, trying to break free,
then went limp, sobbing in terror. Looking down,

Dirk saw all the Lord's faces loosen, saw the certainty of doom settle over them.

With one ragged voice, the churls cheered; and Dirk saw the Lords' faces hardening again, in despair.

Thunder split the night again; a searing white fireball exploded, chopping a watchtower off the battlements.

Silence held the night again; and the look of doom came back to the Lords' faces, as they realized how high above them the gun turrets stood, how easily they could fire down on them.

Then one of the tall towers spoke, in a booming, gargantuan voice. *"At your pleasure, Grandmaster DeCade! What would you have us do?"*

DeCade glared down at the packed Lords, waiting, and Dirk saw understanding begin in their eyes. DeCade saw it, too. Only then did he speak, in a voice that carried to every inch of the yard: "If these Lords do not do as I command—*burn out this courtyard!*"

The churl's eyes stretched wide in disbelief, but the Lords looked on DeCade's set, granite face and knew he was as good as his threat.

After a long, deathly pause, the great ship spoke again, in a voice weary with resignation: *"As you command, Grandmaster DeCade."*

And now, at last, Dirk saw naked fear on the Lords' faces.

Almost quietly, DeCade commanded, "Milords—throw down your swords, and step to the center of the yard, with your hands on your heads."

An awed mutter passed through the churls, growing, gaining glee.

DeCade chopped it off. "If any churl touches a Lord who has laid down his sword, *I* will kill him!"

The churls were silent, shrinking back in superstitious terror.

DeCade surveyed them, and nodded. "At your pleasure, milords—*now!*"

Silence held the courtyard a moment longer. Dirk felt as though he were standing on the edge of a razor blade.

Then a sword rang on the cobbles, and a Lord stepped into the center of the courtyard, his hands on his head. There was a moment of waiting. Then another sword clattered down, then another and another, till the air was filled with the clatter of steel, and the Lords filed into the center of the yard, their hands clasped on their heads, sick despair on their faces. The churls pressed back, leaving room for them, eyeing the stony figure of DeCade nervously, till the center of the yard was packed with an unmoving mass of Lords, ringed in by bright steel.

A tall, broad-shouldered Tradesman elbowed his way through to stand under the balcony. Hugh. "They are all there, DeCade. No Lord remains living outside this circle."

DeCade nodded slowly. "Take them into the great hall, and set a strong guard upon them— beginning with these." He nodded to the ten outlaws behind him, then turned to the two who held the King. "Take him in with his fellows—and make certain none harm him."

The outlaws nodded, almost genuflecting, their faces filled with awe, and turned away to find their way back through the castle to the great hall.

Below, Hugh was mustering his most trusted men with harsh, barking shouts. They formed two files, clearing a path between the packed Lords and the door of the keep. Then, one by one, the Lords began the long march down that gamut of churls to the keep, their backs prickling with the expectation of a sudden laser shot—but not a man touched them.

Peaceably, and in good order, the defeated Lords filed back into the King's castle.

Then, finally, DeCade's whole body seemed to loosen. He bowed his head, gave a long hissing sigh, and collapsed.

Dirk dropped to one knee beside the fallen giant, panic clawing at his throat. DeCade lay slumped against the wall, mouth slack, eyes closed. Dirk slapped his face lightly, quickly. "Come out of it, man! It's all over; you won! Come on, wake up!"

DeCade's eyes opened, staring up at Dirk—and right on through him. Suddenly his whole body stiffened, rigid as a board, muscle straining against muscle, as DeCade swung his staff high in both hands and brought it crashing down across his knee.

The broken halves of the staff fell clattering to the paving stones. The huge body relaxed, and the giant leaned forward, resting his head in his hands.

Dirk hovered over him, almost frantic, not knowing what to do. Finally he grasped the man's shoulder, and shook him. "What's the matter? What happened? Are you okay now? Wake up—you won!"

Slowly, then, the huge head rolled to the side, looking up at him with a queer, sad smile. "Yes, I won—but I've lost, too."

Dirk looked into his eyes and felt a ghostly wind pass through him, chilling him to the marrow.

The arrogance was substantially lessened, and the eyes were no longer compelling. And the voice wasn't as deep and harsh any more.

Dirk nodded slowly. "Welcome back, Gar."

CHAPTER 16

The moon had risen, picking out the glints of metal and jewels in the clothing of the lordly prisoners who stood huddled together in the center of the courtyard again. High above them, Lapin sat on a jury-rigged scaffold, hands flat on her knees. Hugh and the Guildmaster stood to one side of her. Now and again, they glanced furtively at the shadows of the northwest corner, where Gar sat hunched over, staring at the broken fragments of the staff.

Dirk stood apart from both, with Captain Domigny and his officers. From time to time, he glanced at Madelon where she sat at the foot of the scaffold with Father Fletcher and several other men and women whom Dirk had never seen. He assumed they were other junior "officers" and provincial captains.

"We cannot kill so many out of hand," Lapin said with a flat finality that left nothing open to debate. "What, then, shall we do with them?"

The Guildmaster growled, "There are some who do deserve death, Lapin—the slowest and most painful death we can devise."

"Must we try them one by one?" Hugh demanded. "It will take a year; and, like as not, some with slick tongues will escape unscathed when they truly deserve some great punishment."

Captain Domigny stepped forward. "If I may speak here—"

"You may not," the Guildmaster said curtly.

The Captain stared, speechless. Then he scowled and started to speak again.

Lapin turned her head slowly toward him. "Do not misunderstand, sky-man—we are grateful for all you have done. Indeed, we could have done nothing without you, and well we know it. But you have not suffered as we have suffered; most of your lives you have been free, and away from this sink of misery. You have not tried to feed a family beneath a Lord's heavy hand; you have not seen your wife or your daughter taken for a lordling's lust, nor your son taken to the arena. You can not know how these things stand here, nor how the people feel—not truly."

"I think I might have a halfway decent idea." Dirk's voice crackled through the courtyard. "Just in the last week, I've come a hairsbreadth from death a dozen times. I've been in the arena. I've run and hidden like an outlaw. And this isn't the first time. I've served seven missions on this planet, and I've shaved death every time. We all have. And there's a little matter of the rest of my life—all our lives." He gestured to his companions. "We've spent our lives for one thing only; to keep the line between Melange and the rest of the universe in churl hands so that, when this day came, the Wizard's tall towers *could* come dropping down from the skies. Nice, safe, easy job—crammed cheek by jowl with twenty other men in a fragile shell of a ship, floating in emptiness, where any one of a hundred tiny things could go wrong and kill us. Our dangers have been as great as yours, our trials as painful. Few of us have married—why do you think we always brought up new recruits? We knew a wife and children would divide our loyalty, and we couldn't risk that—we devoted our lives completely and solely to someday—*someday*—winning your freedom! We condemned ourselves to lonely lives full of back-breaking work, for one purpose, and one purpose only—your freedom!"

"I know you have been tried, perhaps as sorely as we," Lapin said judiciously, "but they were different trials, different pains—and, withal, you all were free."

Dirk's lips pressed into a thin, straight line. "Free! Never a one of us was free! We've been slaves to you, all of you, all our lives—and the lives of the men who came before us—for *five hundred years*! Working for this day—the day when the churls would be free and we could come back to our home!

"And now you tell us our home is not here for us to come back to!"

"We do." He could hear the pain in Lapin's voice; nevertheless, she spoke the words. "For the fact remains, you have become apart from us, Dirk Dulain, you and all the sky-men. You are no longer really of us, here. The things you want are no longer the things we want."

Beside her, Hugh nodded. "We do not deny you home—you may settle among us; we will give you lands, and any aid that we can, and shares of the lordlings' loot to start merchant shops and work-shops—we know, at least, that we need that, and that none but you can begin them. We will build you schools where you may teach; we will give you honor and respect—"

"But you will not give us a voice in your government," Domigny said grimly.

Hugh met his eyes and nodded. "We will not."

But Domigny wasn't looking at him. He had stepped apart, arms folded, staring at Lapin.

She returned his stare, unwavering.

Dirk stepped up to him, hissing in his ear, "They can't do this, Captain! All our work, all our waiting—"

"They *can* do it," Domigny ground out. "They are the rightful government."

"But we've got ships, we've got cannon! Give the word, and we'll—"

"We will not kill our own," Domigny said heavily, still watching Lapin.

"Yes, and she knows it, too; she's taking advantage of our goodness! There's no justice to it, Captain—not after all our years, all our work, just for them!"

Then Domigny turned, with a sardonic smile. "What did you expect, Dulain? Gratitude?"

Dirk could only stare at him.

"And what of me?" demanded a rumbling voice from the shadows.

All eyes swung to the northwest corner.

Gar stood, the broken halves of the staff in his hands, glaring at Lapin.

He strode forward to the foot of the scaffold. "Me, what of me? Shall I also have no voice here among you?"

"You are DeCade," Madelon breathed, eyes shining and worshipful, and Lapin echoed her: "You are DeCade. Your voice shall always be heard." She rose with the majesty of a mountain, stepping to the side. "Come, take the seat of judgment here among us; it is yours, as is the final voice in any decision of our affairs, if you wish it. You are DeCade."

"I am not," Gar said harshly.

Total silence hit the courtyard. Every eye fastened on the giant.

Slowly, he raised the broken halves of the staff. "DeCade lived in this. It is broken; he is gone. I am only myself again, the man you knew as Gar."

Lapin's eyes widened, and Madelon's were huge and glistening with tragedy. But as Dirk watched, she managed a tremulous smile through her tears, gazing up at Gar with warmth and trust.

"There is more," Gar said grimly, with a bitter smile. "I have said it; you have known it: I am an outworlder. Now—have I a voice in your councils?"

"You have not," Lapin said, as though the words were dragged out of her.

Gar nodded, as though pleased with the bitter answer. "No voice for the bearer? No voice for the man who gave you victory by bearing DeCade within him?"

"Cease to torment us!" Lapin cried. "You know that you merit it, but you know we cannot give it!"

Gar nodded slowly, drawing himself up, mouth a grim, satisfied line. "Yes, I know it, and now I will free you. Know that my name is d'Armand, and that I am the son of a cadet branch of a noble house!"

The churls froze, staring at him. Then a slow, anguished hiss escaped from the Lords. Their guards looked up, bracing their weapons; but the burning in the Lords' eyes faded back to a dull glow, and the guards relaxed.

Lapin still stared down at the giant. Finally, she demanded, "Where is DeCade?"

"His task was done, his thirst slaked; for a moment, he was weak, his purpose gone. In that moment, I rose up, burst out of the lock he had on me, and broke his staff. He has gone, faded—back to his centuries of sleep." Gar held up the broken halves of the staff. "I have my own life again; I am master of my own body again."

He stood in the midst of a sea of burning eyes. A low, ugly mutter began around him and grew, swelling to fill the courtyard. But Lapin held up a hand, still staring down stonily at Gar; and the mutter slackened, faded, and died. Into the stillness, the huge woman spoke. "If DeCade is gone, he is gone. Was it needful to break his staff?"

"It was; for if I had not, I would be a prisoner within myself still. It was needful; for if any man lesser than I sought to take up this staff, DeCade would have killed him."

Hugh and the Guildmaster glared down at him. Gar stared back, unmoved.

So did Lapin. Slowly, she held out her hand. "Then give us the parts of his staff."

Dirk stiffened, electrified by a vision of churl after churl trying to mend the staff and being fried by a lifetime of memories of a very passionate man.

Hugh echoed Lapin. "Give us the staff!" And his guerrilla outlaws stepped forward, toward Gar.

The big man whirled, setting his back against a balk of timber, holding up the two staff-ends like mated clubs.

The outlaws hesitated, eyeing the clubs in awed fascination.

The courtyard held silence while they stared at one another, at an impasse.

Then Gar smiled sourly. He stepped forward and knelt, laying the two halves of the staff on the ground, rose, and stepped back. "Let him who wishes take them up!"

The courtyard was still. Every man stared at the staff-ends with avarice, and fear. Even Hugh, looking down, took a half-step forward, then hesitated.

The moment held taut; then, slowly, Dirk could feel the tension begin to bleed away.

Gar straightened, relaxing a little, nodding with a sour smile. "I had thought not." He turned back to the scaffold, raising his eyes to Lapin. "I am an outworlder, like these to whom you have just denied voice—but I have borne your hero within me; he was no light load, and without him, you would all still be bondsmen. You would have no freedom without me, but you have denied me a voice. Now I ask: am I welcome among you?"

Madelon started up, eyes full of tears, her lips parted; but she hesitated, then sank back down in misery.

"No," Lapin pronounced, and the pain was harsh in her voice. "We owe greatly to you, but we cannot have you among us, for you are Lords' blood."

"So I had thought," Gar said grimly. He turned to look out at the assembled churls. "I have come among you. I have fought and bled for you, and you have cast me out. But I have accomplished my purpose, and now I will go." In one quick motion, he knelt, caught up the broken staff, and stood straight again. "And I will take this staff with me, for it is a thing of greater power than any of you know."

A frenzied mutter started up, but Gar barked out into it, "He who thinks he can stop me, let him try!"

On the scaffold above, Hugh leveled a laser pistol; but Lapin struck his hand down. "Fool! You might hit the staff!"

Good point, Dirk thought. If a laser beam caught that circuitry, who knew what would happen? It would be instructive to find out; but personally, Dirk had no wish to determine it empirically.

The churls had all seen Lapin's action and seemed to be equally fearful; lasers were half-raised, then lowered again.

Gar surveyed them, and nodded once, with a sardonic smile. Then, slowly, he began to stalk across the great courtyard. He approached the skirmish line of outlaws; they tensed, swords coming up.

Gar kept coming, clubs raised, ready for the fight, eyes glowing.

The churls stood steadfast, but their eyes were sick.

Gar was ten feet from them.

Five feet.

At the last moment, Hugh signed to the outlaws. They gradually lowered their swords, and stepped aside to leave a channel for Gar to pass through, with surly growls, but they looked relieved.

So did Hugh.

A long, hissing sigh passed through the courtyard.

Gar stalked on toward the main gate, smiling grimly. He came to the front rank of the crowd; at the last second, men pressed back from him, and a passageway opened for him through the throng, opening only a few feet ahead of him as he strode on; but in a minute, it was a long avenue, stretched out to the gate.

Gar stalked down that avenue, passed beneath the portcullis, out across the drawbridge, and was gone.

Madelon stared after him, eyes huge, huddled in on herself, forlorn.

Dirk saw, and the bile rose in his throat.

He rounded on Captain Domigny, demanding, "Will you do as he has done, Captain? Or will you stay here, to slave for the people you've freed, and be a second-class citizen?"

Captain Domigny turned slowly, looking Dirk full in the eye. "I'll stay."

Dirk's mouth hooked down in contempt. "Is this what we've waited for, then? Why we've worked our whole lives, what we've given up house and home for—to be highly trained serfs? 'Oh, surely, sir, we'll set up industries for you! Certainly, madame, we'll organize your commerce. Thank you, thank you kindly, for giving us the chance! Schools? Oh, delighted! We'll start them right away—no problem at all. All the things you can't do for yourself, we'll be oh-so-glad to do for you. Just give us a pat on the head now and then, and maybe a bone, and we're happy!' Is this why we gave up our *lives*?"

Domigny reddened. "I've worked my whole life for the good of my people, Dulain—and I'll keep doing it!"

Dirk stared at him.

Domigny turned his head from side to side. "No, Dirk Dulain. Do as you will; but for myself, I did not do what I did for gratitude or adulation—or for power! I did it because I believed it right—and whatever the consequences of that action, I accept them!" He turned to Lapin and called out, "I will stay here among you, Lapin, and gladly! The wealth and position you offer I accept, and will not seek voice in your affairs."

"What will you do, then, among us?" she demanded.

"What you will. If you want schools, industry, commerce, I will build them for you—or whatever else the people want done. I will work for the good of the churls of this planet!"

A huge cheer exploded all about him, filling the courtyard. Dazed, the officers looked at one another; then they looked at their captain and began to grin.

Dirk turned away, sickened. He looked up at Lapin and Hugh, both smiling, satisfied; then his eyes dropped down to Madelon. She looked up, meeting his gaze with a long, pleading look. He turned his face away and looked at the Captain again. Then, as the cheers began to fade, he turned on his heel and stalked toward the gate.

The courtyard fell silent about him. Then he heard the quick patter of heels. He looked back as Madelon caught his sleeve, looking up at him breathlessly. "You will not go now! Stay here among us!"

Dirk looked down at her, his mouth twisting. "Why? Why should I?"

She looked up at him, her face grave. "Do I mean nothing to you?"

He looked into her eyes for a long, wordless moment. Then he leaned his weight on one hip, cocking his head to the side. "How is this? A moment ago, I saw your face filled with the tragedy of Gar's leaving."

"True," she said gravely, "but when he said that the spirit of DeCade had left him, I began to remember what had happened, and to wonder why it had come about as it did—and it was you, all of it. It was you who paved the way for the churls in the arena to call him leader, you who prepared him to receive DeCade and guided the staff to his hand, you who guided him when his plans seemed to fall apart, you who guided his arm and called down the tall towers; and I think it is you, Dirk Dulain—you more than any other—who has brought us our freedom, as surely as though the Wizard's spirit moved in you!"

"It is not true," Dirk denied, "none of it. I was moved about like a chess piece on a board. How can you see it that way? Is it because, now that the giant has left, you must find reasons for turning to another?"

Madelon winced but retorted, "I say what I see. Like any man, you are too blind to see yourself truly!"

Dirk nodded, heavy with irony. "So now you want me."

"Yes, I want you!" she hissed fiercely. "Can you blame me?"

"Yes," he answered, "for if DeCade came alive again, you would turn from me in an instant."

He saw the sick, stricken acknowledgment of what he had said in her eyes and was instantly filled with remorse. He touched her face gently, spoke softly. "Forgive me—I've spoken too harshly. But you must see that I cannot accept being second choice."

He held her eyes a moment longer, then turned and walked away.

The ranks of the churls parted for him, as they had for Gar, and the courtyard was silent as he marched down that long avenue, looking neither to the right nor the left. Memory hemmed him in on both sides, likeness of kind clung to him, but he strode through it as though it was a room full of cobwebs. Every face turned to him in silent respect; every eye followed him as he passed under the portcullis and was gone from their sight.

He strode across the drawbridge and out onto the barren hillside.

There he stopped and took a slow, deep breath. He let his shoulders slump and bowed his head, feeling the adrenaline ebb from his system.

There, far below him, lay the town, its lights warm and few amidst the darkness.

He took a deep, shuddering breath, composing himself. There was no time to let go now; there was a man he had to catch, and Dirk had a strangely certain idea of where that man would be.

He turned away to find a horse.

He stepped under the stone archway and into the great cavern, his footsteps totally silent. It was the dark, chill hour before dawn; a few shafts of crystalline moonlight streaked down from the crevices high in the walls, bathing the great skeleton in frozen light.

A shadow bent over it—a tall, black-cloaked figure, gazing down at the silvered, almost-living skeleton. He stood that way a long time, unmoving, meditating; and Dirk knew enough not to make the slightest sound.

Then at last, the tall, black figure moved. Slowly, he drew two oaken sticks from beneath his cloak and laid them, gently, one on each side of the great skeleton. Then he stood back, head bowed; and Dirk saw the glint of light and shadow on the eagle face, silvered on the brow and nose, hollowed at the eyes and cheeks.

Gar sighed, lifting his head and squaring his shoulders, turned toward the archway—and saw Dirk.

Dirk braced himself.

Gar gazed at him, his face grave.

Then he stepped forward, grasping Dirk's shoulder, and murmured, "Let us go out from this place; for I knew this man, and he is dead."

Dirk turned with him; together, they passed under the archway and into the spiral.

As they came out into the lower cave, Dirk murmured, "That was not an easy thing to do."

Gar nodded. "His staff is a thing of awesome strength, Dulain—it would magnify every power I have a hundredfold. With it, I would be the mightiest psi in the galaxy."

"Then why did you put it down?"

"Because it is not mine," Gar said without hesitation. "It is DeCade's; and while he is dead, it belongs to his people." He lifted his head, gazing thoughtfully at the pale dawnlight in the cave mouth ahead. "Then, too, I think it would be an addictive thing. Holding power like that, I would use it and use it again till I could not bear *not* to use it. If it cried for blood, it would have it."

They came out at the base of the hill, and Gar threw his shoulders back with a sigh, looking up at the moon, drifting palely in the sky of false dawn.

Dirk watched him, brooding. "Is that why you broke the staff?"

"No, not quite." Gar frowned. "But like it. DeCade was a great man, but he was like his staff—he could never stop fighting. Even as it is, I have all his memories, the print of his personality—and I think I'll always have to be on my guard for the rest of my days, to be sure that personality doesn't overwhelm me. But with his staff whole, I wouldn't've had a chance—it pumped power into him; it made him a superman." He turned his head slowly, looking down at Dirk. "It was a great temptation to leave his staff whole, Dirk Dulain—but it would have destroyed me."

Suddenly, he squeezed his eyes shut, pressing his middle finger and thumb against his temples. "And, oh, I hope to tell you, may I never have to live through something like that again! It was—horrible, at first; another man's mind inside my own, thought-tendrils reaching out, grappling. We fought on a figurative plain, beneath a symbolic sky, in the country of the mind; and we came close to killing each other. But at last we made peace and became friends of a sort; though there was always the tension, always the wariness—for we both wanted life, in the body. It was a constant threat—another fight for survival—there, in the midst of my own mind, my own flesh and body."

"But it didn't come," Dirk murmured.

Gar shook his head. "No. We were allies; we worked together for a dream we both burned for. And now—he is gone, no vital power, no soul left, only a set of memories. He died of his own accord, almost; when he'd had his revenge, the power drained out, and he went back where he'd come from—but he couldn't have lain easy if that staff had remained whole. Of course I laid him to rest—no man wishes to be a ghost."

"No," Dirk said slowly, "including me."

"Ah." Gar nodded; that seemed to explain a lot to him.

He lifted an arm, pointing to the top of the hill. "Come, let us climb. I cannot think of a better place to survey this world, than the top of De-Cade's tomb."

They turned their faces up and began to climb.

Gar turned to Dirk, his eyes probing keenly. "She had that deep a hold on you, then?"

"Yes," Dirk said sourly, "and you had that deep a hold on her."

"I? Or DeCade?"

Dirk shrugged. "Either. It didn't really seem to matter. Any way you looked at it, I came in last."

Gar strode upward in silence. Then he said, "That's a pretty weak reason for leaving a planet."

Dirk shrugged irritably. "Her, or the rest of them—it came out the same. Half-liking is a pretty poor sequel to loyalty."

Gar shook his head. "That still rings hollow."

Dirk stopped, scowling. "What are you getting at? The Wizard? The unseen hand that's moved me, every step?"

"No, of course not." But Gar was suddenly a little too casual about it.

Dirk frowned, puzzled; then he smiled, amused. "Oh, don't worry, I figured that one out long ago. You were the source of the rumors, weren't you? You started the discontent running through the land —the feeling that *it* was about to happen—and the word of the Wizard being seen, here and there."

Gar nodded. "Just the usual whispering campaign—and a little projective telepathy, of course."

Dirk raised his eyebrows. "Oh, you list that among your talents, too?"

"I am nothing if not versatile."

"Yes, very." Dirk frowned. "When Lord Core's men found Madelon and me dead, and took you away—how'd you manage that, faking our deaths? I don't know of any psi power than can swing that one."

Gar flashed him a grin and turned away.

Dirk waited for the answer.

He was still waiting when they came to the hilltop.

Gar planted his feet firmly and heaved a sigh, looking out over the countryside, slumbering in the false dawn. "Peaceful, isn't it?"

"Yes," Dirk agreed. "Now."

"And yourself?" Gar raised an eyebrow.

Dirk looked back at him, his face carefully neutral. Then he nodded. "Not bad, now that you mention it. Surprisingly."

Gar shrugged. "You've got it mostly threshed out now. She doesn't really mean that much, does she?"

"No," Dirk said after a few minutes, "she doesn't. The people do—but not right now. Not yet."

Gar nodded. "They're done with their need for you—and you don't need them yet. Not really."

"No," Dirk said slowly. "I'm young. I don't need it. There'll be time for a home."

"Oh?" Gar cocked an eyebrow at him. "What were you planning to do in the meantime?"

"Clear out," Dirk said, with a sour smile. "Epsilon Eridani, for starters—that's the nearest main port. Trouble is, I'd rather not travel with my own crew, things being as they are; they don't seem to be in any great rush to lift off. Can you stand a hitchhiker?"

Gar laughed and clapped him on the shoulder. "Glad to have you, Dulain. We can spend the trip trying to figure out what happened back here."

Dirk found himself grinning, in spite of himself. "Hey . . . I thought we were supposed to be rivals."

Gar shook his head. "Friends, Dulain—right from the start. But I couldn't tell you that then, could I?" He rolled up his sleeve to the armband and put his finger on the stud to call his ship.

"No, I suppose not," Dirk said, amused. "Tell me—when did you realize you'd *become* the Wizard?"

But Gar only gave him a grin as he pressed the stud.

The golden ship fell down from the sky.